Select Epigrams from the Greek Anthology

John William Mackail

Copyright © 2017 Okitoks Press

All rights reserved.

ISBN: 1547246243

ISBN-13: 978-1547246243

Table of Contents

PREFACE 3
INTRODUCTION 3
ANTHOLOGY 56
    CHAPTER I 56
    CHAPTER II 64
    CHAPTER III 69
    CHAPTER IV 74
    CHAPTER V 79
    CHAPTER VI 81
    CHAPTER VII 84
    CHAPTER VIII 86
    CHAPTER IX 88
    CHAPTER X 91
    CHAPTER XI 95
    CHAPTER XII 101
    BIOGRAPHICAL INDEX OF EPIGRAMMATISTS 105

PREFACE

The purpose of this book is to present a complete collection, subject to certain definitions and exceptions which will be mentioned later, of all the best extant Greek Epigrams. Although many epigrams not given here have in different ways a special interest of their own, none, it is hoped, have been excluded which are of the first excellence in any style. But, while it would be easy to agree on three-fourths of the matter to be included in such a scope, perhaps hardly any two persons would be in exact accordance with regard to the rest; with many pieces which lie on the border line of excellence, the decision must be made on a balance of very slight considerations, and becomes in the end one rather of personal taste than of any fixed principle.

For the Greek Anthology proper, use has chiefly been made of the two great works of Jacobs, which have not yet been superseded by any more definitive edition: /Anthologia Graeca sive Poetarum Graecorum lusus ex recensione Brunckii; indices et commentarium adiecit Friedericus Iacobs/ (Leipzig, 1794-1814: four volumes of text and nine of indices, prolegomena, commentary, and appendices), and /Anthologia Graeca ad fidem codicis olim Palatini nunc Parisini ex apographo Gothano edita; curavit epigrammata in Codice Palatino desiderata et annotationem criticam adiecit Fridericus Jacobs/ (Leipzig, 1813-1817: two volumes of text and two of critical notes). An appendix to the latter contains Paulssen's fresh collation of the Palatine MS. The small Tauchnitz text is a very careless and inaccurate reprint of this edition. The most convenient edition of the Anthology for ordinary reference is that of F. Dübner in Didot's /Bibliothèque Grecque/ (Paris, 1864), in two volumes, with a revised text, a Latin translation, and additional notes by various hands. The epigrams recovered from inscriptions have been collected and edited by G. Kaibel in his /Epigrammata Graeca ex labidibus conlecta/ (Berlin, 1878). As this book was going through the press, a third volume of the Didot Anthology has appeared, edited by M. Ed. Cougny, under the title of /Appendix nova epigrammatum veterum ex libris at marmoribus ductorum/, containing what purports to be a complete collection, now made for the first time, of all extant epigrams not in the Anthology.

In the notes, I have not thought it necessary to acknowledge, except here once for all, my continual obligations to that superb monument of scholarship, the commentary of Jacobs; but where a note or a reading is borrowed from a later critic, his name is mentioned. All important deviations from the received text of the Anthology are noted, and referred to their author in each case; but, as this is not a critical edition, the received text, when retained, is as a rule printed without comment where it differs from that of the MSS. or other originals.

The references in the notes to Bergk's /Lyrici Graeci/ give the pages of the fourth edition. Epigrams from the Anthology are quoted by the sections of the Palatine collection (/Anth. Pal./) and the appendices to it (sections xiii-xv). After these appendices follows in modern editions a collection (/App. Plan./) of all the epigrams in the Planudean Anthology which are not found in the Palatine MS.

I have to thank Mr. P. E. Matheson, Fellow of New College, for his kindness in looking over the proofsheets of this book.

INTRODUCTION

I

The Greek word "epigram" in its original meaning is precisely equivalent to the Latin word "inscription"; and it probably came into use in this sense at a very early period of Greek history, anterior even to the invention of prose. Inscriptions at that time, if they went beyond a mere name or set of names, or perhaps the bare statement of a single fact, were necessarily in verse, then the single vehicle of organised expression. Even after prose was in use, an obvious propriety remained in the metrical form as being at once more striking and more easily retained in the memory; while in the case of epitaphs and dedications—for the earlier epigram falls almost entirely under these two heads— religious feeling and a sense of what was due to ancient custom aided the continuance of the old tradition. Herodotus in the course of his History quotes epigrams of both kinds; and with him the word {epigramma} is just on the point of acquiring its literary sense, though this is not yet fixed definitely. In his account of the three ancient tripods dedicated in the temple of Apollo at Thebes,[1] he says of one of them, {o men de eis ton tripodon epigramma ekhei}, and then quotes the single hexameter line engraved upon it. Of the other two he says simply, "they say in hexameter," {legei en exametro tono}. Again, where he describes the funeral monuments at Thermopylae,[2] he uses the words {gramma} and {epigramma} almost in the sense of sepulchral epigrams; {epigegrammai grammata legonta tade}, and a little further on, {epixosmesantes epigrammasi xai stelesi}, "epitaphs and monuments". Among these epitaphs is the celebrated couplet of Simonides[3] which has found a place in all subsequent Anthologies.

In the Anthology itself the word does not however in fact occur till a late period. The proem of Meleager to his collection uses the words {soide}, {umnos}, {melisma}, {elegos}, all vaguely, but has no term which corresponds in any degree to our epigram. That of Philippus has one word which describes the epigram by a single quality; he calls his work an {oligostikhia} or collection of poems not exceeding a few lines in length. In an epitaph by Diodorus, a poet of the Augustan age, occurs the phrase {gramma legei},[4] in imitation of the phrase of Herodotus just quoted. This is, no doubt, an intentional archaism; but the word {epigramma} itself does not occur in the collection until the Roman period. Two epigrams on the epigram,[5] one Roman, the other Roman or Byzantine, are preserved, both dealing with the question of the proper length. The former, by Parmenio, merely says that an epigram of many lines is bad—{phemi polustikhien epigrammatos ou xata Mousas einai}. The other is more definite, but unfortunately ambiguous in expression. It runs thus:

{Pagxalon eot epigramma to distikhon en de parelthes tous treis rapsodeis xoux epigramma legeis}

The meaning of the first part is plain; an epigram may be complete within the limits of a single couplet. But do "the three" mean three lines or three couplets? "Exceeding three" would, in the one case, mean an epigram of four lines, in the other of eight. As there cannot properly be an epigram of three lines, it would seem rather to mean the latter. Even so the statement is an exaggeration; many of the best epigrams are in six and eight lines. But it is true that the epigram may "have its nature", in the phrase of Aristotle,[6] in a single couplet; and we shall generally find that in those of eight lines, as always without exception in those of more than eight, there is either some repetition of idea not necessary to the full expression of the thought, or some redundance of epithet or detail too florid for the best taste, or, as in most of the Byzantine epigrams, a natural verbosity which affects the style throughout and weakens the force and directness of the epigram.

The notorious difficulty of giving any satisfactory definition of poetry is almost equalled by the difficulty of defining with precision any one of its kinds; and the epigram in Greek, while it always remained conditioned by being in its essence and origin an inscriptional poem, took in the later periods so wide a range of subject and treatment that it can perhaps only be limited by certain abstract conventions of length and metre. Sometimes it becomes in all but metrical form a lyric; sometimes it hardly rises beyond the versified statement of a fact or an idea; sometimes it is barely distinguishable from a snatch of pastoral. The shorter pieces of the elegiac poets might very often well be classed as epigrams but for the uncertainty, due to the form in which their text has come down to us, whether they are not in all cases, as they undoubtedly are in some, portions of longer poems. Many couplets and quatrains of Theognis fall under this head; and an excellent instance on a larger scale is the fragment of fourteen lines by Simonides of Amorgos,[7] which is the exact type on which many of the later epigrams of life are moulded. In such cases /respice auctoris animum/ is a safe rule; what was not written as an epigram is not an epigram. Yet it has seemed worth while to illustrate this rule by its exceptions; and there will be found in this collection fragments of Mimnermus and Theognis[8] which in everything but the actual circumstance of their origin satisfy any requirement which can be made. In the Palatine Anthology itself, indeed, there are a few instances[9] where this very thing is done. As a rule, however, these short passages belong to the class of {gromai} or moral sentences, which, even when expressed in elegiac verse, is sufficiently distinct from the true epigram. One instance will suffice. In the Anthology there occurs this couplet:[10]

{Pan to peritton axaipon epei logos esti palaios os xai tou melitos to pleon esti khole}

This is a sentence merely; an abstract moral idea, with an illustration attached to it. Compare with it another couplet[11] in the Anthology:

{Aion panta pserei dolikhos khronos oioen ameibein ounoma xai morpsen xai psuain ede tukhen}

Here too there is a moral idea; but in the expression, abstract as it is, there is just that high note, that imaginative touch, which gives it at once the gravity of an inscription and the quality of a poem.

Again, many of the so-called epideictic epigrams are little more than stories told shortly in elegiac verse, much like the stories in Ovid's Fasti. Here the inscriptional quality is the surest test. It is this quality, perhaps in many instances due to the verses having been actually written for paintings or sculptures, that just makes an epigram of the sea-story told by Antipater of Thessalonica, and of the legend of Eunomus the harp-player[12]; while other stories, such as those told of Pittacus, of Euctemon, of Serapis and the murderer,[13] both tend to exceed the reasonable limit of length, and have in no degree either the lapidary precision of the half lyrical passion which would be necessary to make them more than tales in verse. Once more, the fragments of idyllic poetry which by chance have come down to us incorporated in the Anthology,[14] beautiful as they are, are in no sense epigrams any more than the lyrics ascribed to Anacreon which form an appendix to the Palatine collection, or the quotations from the dramatists, Euripides, Menander, or Diphilus,[15] which have also at one time or another become incorporated with it.

In brief then, the epigram in its first intention may be described as a very short poem summing up as though in a memorial inscription what it is desired to make permanently memorable in any action or situation. It must have the compression and conciseness of a real inscription, and in proportion to the smallness of its bulk must be highly finished, evenly balanced, simple, and lucid. In literature it holds something of the same place as is held in art by an engraved gem. But if the definition of the epigram is only fixed thus, it is difficult to exclude almost any very short poem that conforms externally to this standard; while on the other hand the chance of language has restricted the word in its modern use to a sense which it never bore in Greek at all, defined in the line of Boileau, /un bon mot de deux rimes orné/. This sense was made current more especially by the epigrams of Martial, which as a rule lead up to a pointed end, sometimes a witticism, sometimes a verbal fancy, and are quite apart from the higher imaginative qualities. From looking too exclusively at the Latin epigrammatists, who all belonged to a debased period in literature, some persons have been led to speak of the Latin as distinct from the Greek sense of the word "epigram". But in the Greek Anthology the epigrams of contemporary writers have the same quality. The fault was that of the age, not of the language. No good epigram sacrifices its finer poetical qualities to the desire of making a point; and none of the best depend on having a point at all. ——————

[1] Hdt. v. 59.
[2] Hdt. vii. 228.
[3] III. 4 in this collection.
[4] Anth. Pal. vi. 348.
[5] Ibid. ix. 342, 369.
[6] Poet. 1449 a. 14.
[7] Simon. fr. 85 Bergk.
[8] Infra, XII. 6, 17, 37.
[9] App. Plan. 16.
[10] Anth. Pal. ix. 50, 118, x. 113.
[11] Anth. Pal. ix. 51.
[12] Infra, IX. 14, II. 14.
[13] Anth. Pal. vii. 89, ix. 367, 378.
[14] Anth. Pal. ix. 136, 362, 363.
[15] Ibid. x. 107, xi. 438, 439.

II

While the epigram is thus somewhat incapable of strict formal definition, for all practical purposes it may be confined in Greek poetry to pieces written in a single metre, the elegiac couplet, the metre appropriated to inscriptions from the earliest recorded period.[1] Traditionally ascribed to the invention of Archilochus or Callinus, this form of verse, like the epic hexameter itself, first meets us full grown.[2] The date of Archilochus of Paros may be fixed pretty nearly at 700 B.C. That of Callinus of Ephesus is perhaps earlier. It may be assumed with probability that elegy was an invention of the same early civilisation among the Greek colonists of the eastern coast of the Aegean in which the Homeric poems flowered out into their splendid perfection. From the first the elegiac metre was instinctively recognised as one of the best suited for inscriptional poems. Originally indeed it had a much wider area, as it afterwards had again with the Alexandrian poets; it seems to have been the common metre for every kind of poetry which was neither purely lyrical on the one hand, nor on the other included in the definite scope of the heroic hexameter. The name {elegos}, "wailing", is probably as late as Simonides, when from the frequency of its use for funeral inscriptions the metre had acquired a mournful connotation, and become the /tristis elegeïa/ of the Latin poets. But the war- chants of Callinus and Tyrtaeus, and the political poems of the latter, are at least fifty years earlier in date than the elegies of Mimnermus, the first of which we have certain knowledge: and in Theognis, a hundred years later than Mimnermus, elegiac verse becomes a vehicle for the utmost diversity of subject, and a vehicle so facile and flexible that it never seems unsuitable or inadequate. For at least eighteen hundred years it remained a living metre, through all that time never undergoing any serious modification.[3] Almost up to the end of the Greek Empire of the East it continued to be written, in imitation it is true of the old poets, but still with the freedom of a language in common and uninterrupted use. As in the heroic hexameter the Asiatic colonies of Greece invented the most fluent, stately, and harmonious metre for continuous narrative poetry which has yet been invented by man, so in the elegiac couplet they solved the problem, hardly a less difficult one, of a metre which would refuse nothing, which could rise to the occasion and sink with it, and be equally suited to the epitaph of a hero or the verses accompanying a birthday present, a light jest or a great moral idea, the sigh of a lover or the lament over a perished Empire.[4]

The Palatine Anthology as it has come down to us includes a small proportion, less than one in ten, of poems in other metres than the elegiac. Some do not properly belong to the collection, as for instance the three lines of iambics heading the Erotic section and the two hendecasyllabics at the end of it, or the two hexameters at the beginning of the Dedicatory section. These are hardly so much insertions as accretions. Apart from them there are only four non-elegiac pieces among the three hundred and eight amatory epigrams. The three hundred and fifty-eight dedicatory epigrams include sixteen in hexameter and iambic, and one in hendecasyllabic; and among the seven hundred and fifty sepulchral epigrams are forty-two in hexameter, iambic, and other mixed metres. The Epideictic section, as one would expect from the more miscellaneous nature of its contents, has a larger proportion of non-elegiac pieces. Of the eight hundred and twenty-seven epigrams no less than a hundred and twenty-nine are in hexameter (they include a large number of single lines), twenty-seven in iambic, and six others in various unusual metres, besides one (No. 703) which comes in strangely enough: it is in prose: and is the inscription in commendation of the water of the Thracian river Tearos, engraved on a pillar by Darius, transcribed from Herodotus, iv. 91. The odd thing is that the collector of the Anthology appears to have thought it was in verse. The Hortatory section includes a score of hexameter and iambic fragments, some of them proverbial lines, others extracts from the tragedians. The Convivial section has five-and-twenty in hexameter, iambic, and hemiambic, out of four hundred and forty-two. The Musa Stratonis, in which the hand of the Byzantine editor has had a less free play, is entirely in elegiac. But the short appendix next following it in the Palatine MS. consists entirely of epigrams in various metres, chiefly composite. Of the two thousand eight hundred and thirteen epigrams which constitute the Palatine Anthology proper, (sections V., VI., VII., IX., X., and XI.), there are in all a hundred and seventy-five in hexameter, seventy-seven in iambic, and twenty-two in various other metres. In practise, when one comes to make a selection, the exclusion of all non-elegiac pieces leads to no difficulty.

Nothing illustrates more vividly the essential unity and continuous life of Greek literature than this line of poetry, reaching from the period of the earliest certain historical records down to a time when modern poetry in the West of Europe had already established itself; nothing could supply a better and simpler corrective to the fallacy, still too common, that Greek history ends with the conquests of Alexander. It is on some such golden bridge that we must cross the profound gulf which separates, to the popular view, the sunset of the Western Empire of Rome from the dawn of the Italian republics and the kingdoms of France and England. That gulf to most persons seems impassable, and it is another world which lies across it. But here one sees how that distant and strange world stretches out its hands to touch our own. The great burst of epigrammatic poetry under Justinian took place when the Consulate of Rome, after more than a thousand years' currency, at last ceased to mark the Western year. While Constantinus Cephalas was compiling his Anthology, adding to the treasures of past times much recent and even contemporary work, Athelstan of England inflicted the great defeat on the Danes at Brunanburh, the song of which is one of the noblest records of our own early literature; and before Planudes made the last additions the Divine Comedy was written, and our English poetry had broken out into the full sweetness of its flower:

  Bytuene Mershe ant Averil
  When spray beginneth to springe,
  The lutel foul hath hire wyl
  On hyre lud to synge.[5]

It is startling to think that so far as the date goes this might have been included in the Planudean Anthology.

Yet this must not be pressed too far. Greek literature at the later Byzantine Court, like the polity and religion of the Empire, was a matter of rigid formalism; and so an epigram by Cometas Chartularius differs no more in style and spirit from an epigram by Agathias than two mosaics of the same dates. The later is a copy of the earlier, executed in a somewhat inferior manner. Even in the revival of poetry under Justinian it is difficult to be sure how far the poetry was in any real sense original, and how far it is parallel to the Latin verses of Renaissance scholars. The vocabulary of these poets is practically the same as that of Callimachus; but the vocabulary of Callimachus too is practically the same as that of Simonides. ———

[1] The first inscriptions of all were probably in hexameter: cf. Hdt. v. 59.

[2] Horace, A. P., ll. 75-8, leaves the origin of elegiac verse in obscurity. When he says it was first used for laments, he probably follows the Alexandrian derivation of the word {elegos} from {e legein}. The /voti sententia compos/ to which he says it became extended is interpreted by the commentators as meaning amatory poetry. If this was Horace's meaning he chose a most singular way of expressing it.

[3] Mr. F. D. Allen's treatise /On Greek Versification in Inscriptions/ (Boston, 1888) gives an account of the slight changes in structure (caesura, etc.) between earlier and later periods.

[4] Cf. infra, III. 2, VII., 4, X. 45, XII. 18, I. 30, IX. 23.

[5] From the Leominster MS. circ. A.D. 1307 (Percy Society, 1842).

III

The material out of which this selection has been made is principally that immense mass of epigrams known as the Greek Anthology. An account of this celebrated collection and the way in which it was formed will be given presently; here it will be sufficient to say that, in addition to about four hundred Christian epigrams of the Byzantine period, it contains some three thousand seven hundred epigrams of all dates from 700 B.C. to 1000 or even 1200 A.D., preserved in two Byzantine collections, the one probably of the tenth, the other of the fourteenth century, named respectively the Palatine and Planudean Anthologies. The great mass of the contents of both is the same; but the former contains a large amount of material not found in the latter, and the latter a small amount not found in the former.

For much the greatest number of these epigrams the Anthology is the only source. But many are also found cited by various authors or contained among their other works. It is not necessary to pursue this subject into detail. A few typical instances are the citations of the epitaph by Simonides on the three hundred Spartans who fell at Thermopylae, not only by Herodotus[1] but by Diodorus Siculus and Strabo, the former in a historical, the latter in a geographical, work; of the epigram by Plato on the Eretrian exiles[2] by Philostratus in his Life of Apollonius; of many epigrams purporting to be written by philosophers, or actually written upon them and their works, by Diogenes Laërtius in his Lives of the Philosophers. Plutarch among the vast mass of his historical and ethical writings quotes incidentally a considerable number of epigrams. A very large number are quoted by Athenaeus in that treasury of odds and ends, the Deipnosophistae. A great many too are cited in the lexicon which goes under the name of Suidas, and which, beginning at an unknown date, continued to receive additional entries certainly up to the eleventh century.

These same sources supply us with a considerable gleaning of epigrams which either were omitted by the collectors of the Anthology or have disappeared from our copies. The present selection for example includes epigrams found in an anonymous Life of Aeschylus: in the Onamasticon of Julius Pollux, a grammarian of the early part of the third century, who cites from many lost writings for peculiar words or constructions: and from the works of Athenaeus , Diogenes Laërtius, Plutarch, and Suidas mentioned above. The more famous the author of an epigram was, the more likely does it become that his work should be preserved in more than one way. Thus, of the thirty-one epigrams ascribed to Plato, while all but one are found in the Anthology, only seventeen are found in the Anthology alone. Eleven are quoted by Diogenes Laërtius; and thirteen wholly or partially by Athenaeus, Suidas, Apuleius, Philostratus, Gellius, Macrobius, Olympiodorus, Apostolius, and Thomas Magister. On the other hand the one hundred and thirty-four epigrams of Meleager, representing a peculiar side of Greek poetry in a perfection not elsewhere attainable, exist in the Anthology alone.

Beyond these sources, which may be called literary, there is another class of great importance: the monumental. An epigram purports to be an inscription actually carved or written upon some monument or memorial. Since archaeology became systematically studied, original inscriptions, chiefly on marble, are from time to time brought to light, many of which are in elegiac verse. The admirable work of Kaibel[3] has made it superfluous to traverse the vast folios of the Corpus Inscriptionum in search of what may still be hidden there. It supplies us with several epigrams of real literary value; while the best of those discovered before this century are included in appendices to the great works of Brunck and Jacobs. Most of these monumental inscriptions are naturally sepulchral. They are of all ages and countries within the compass of Graeco-Roman civilisation, from the epitaph, magnificent in its simplicity, sculptured on the grave of Cleoetes the Athenian when Athens was still a small and insignificant town, to the last outpourings of the ancient spirit on the tombs reared, among strange gods and barbarous faces, over Paulina of Ravenna or Vibius Licinianus of Nîmes.[4]

It has already been pointed out by how slight a boundary the epigram is kept distinct from other forms of poetry, and how in extreme cases its essence may remain undefinable. The two fragments of Theognis and one of Mimnermus included here[5] illustrate this. They are examples of a large number like them, which are not, strictly speaking, epigrams; being probably passages from continuous poems, selected, at least in the case of Theognis, for an Anthology of his works.

The epigrams extant in literature which are not in the Anthology are, with a few exceptions, collected in the appendix to the edition of Jacobs, and are reprinted from it in modern texts. They are about four hundred in number, and raise the total number of epigrams in the Anthology to about four thousand five hundred; to these must be added at least a thousand inscriptional epigrams, which increase year by year as new explorations are carried on. It is, of course, but seldom that these last have distinct value as poetry. Those of the best period, indeed, and here the best period is the sixth century B.C., have always a certain accent, even when simplest and most matter of fact, which reminds us of the palace whence they came. Their simplicity is more thrilling than any eloquence. From the exotic and elaborate word-embroidery of the poets of the decadence, we turn with relief and delight to work like this, by a father over his son:

{Sema pater Kleoboulos apepsthimeno Xenopsanto
thexe tod ant aretes ede saopsrosunes}[6]

(This monument to dead Xenophantus his father Cleobulus set up, for his valour and wisdom);

or this, on an unmarried girl:

{Sema PHrasixleias xoure xexlesomai aiei
anti gamou para theon touto lakhous onoma}[7]

(The monument of Phrasicleia; I shall for ever be called maiden, having got this name from the gods instead of marriage.)

So touching in their stately reserve, so piercing in their delicate austerity, these epitaphs are in a sense the perfection of literature, and yet in another sense almost lie outside its limits. For the workmanship here, we feel, is unconscious; and without conscious workmanship there is not art. In Homer, in Sophocles, in all the best Greek work, there is this divine simplicity; but beyond it, or rather beneath it and sustaining it, there is purpose. ⸺

[1] Anth. Pal. vii. 249; Hdt. vii. 228.
[2] Ibid. vii. 256.
[3] Epigrammata Graeca ex lapidibus conlecta. Berlin, 1878.
[4] Infra, III. 35, 47; XI. 48.
[5] Infra, XII. 6, 17, 37.
[6] Corp. Inscr. Att. 477 B.
[7] Ibid. 469.

IV

From the invention of writing onwards, the inscriptions on monuments and dedicated offerings supplied one of the chief materials of historical record. Their testimony was used by the earliest historians to supplement and reinforce the oral traditions which they embodied in their works. Herodotus and Thucydides quote early epigrams as authority for the history of past times;[1] and when in the latter part of the fourth century B.C. history became a serious study throughout Greece, collections of inscribed records, whether in prose or verse, began to be formed as historical material. The earliest collection of which anything is certainly known was a work by Philochorus,[2] a distinguished Athenian antiquary who flourished about 300 B.C., entitled Epigramma Attica. It appears to have been a transcript of all the ancient Attic inscriptions dealing with Athenian history, and would include the verses engraved on the tombs of celebrated citizens, or on objects dedicated in the temples on public occasions. A century later, we hear of a work by Polemo, called Periegetes, or the "Guidebook-maker," entitled {peri ton xata poleis epigrammaton}.[3] This was an attempt to make a similar collection of inscriptions throughout the cities of Greece. Athenaeus also speaks of authors otherwise unknown, Alcetas and Menetor,[4] as having written treatises {peri anathematon}, which would be collections of the same nature confined to dedicatory inscriptions; and, these being as a rule in verse, the books in question were perhaps the earliest collections of monumental poetry. Even less is known with regard to a book "on epigrams" by Neoptolemus of Paris.[5] The history of Anthologies proper begins for us with Meleager of Gadara.

The collection called the Garland of Meleager, which is the basis of the Greek Anthology as we possess it, was formed by him in the early part of the first century B.C. The scholiast on the Palatine MS. says that Meleager flourished in the reign of the last Seleucus ({ekhmasen epi Seleukou tou eskhatou}). This is Seleucus VI. Epiphanes, the last king of the name, who reigned B.C. 95-93; for it is not probable that the reference is to the last Seleucid, Antiochus XIII., who acceded B.C. 69, and was deposed by Pompey when he made Syria a Roman province in B.C. 65. The date thus fixed is confirmed by the fact that the collection included an epigram on the tomb of Antipater of Sidon,[6] who, from the terms in which Cicero alludes to him, must have lived till 110 or even 100 B.C., and that it did not include any of the epigrams of Meleager's townsman Philodemus of Gadara, the friend of L. Calpurnius Piso, consul in B.C. 58.

This Garland or Anthology has only come down to us as forming the basis of later collections. But the prefatory poem which Meleager wrote for it has fortunately been preserved, and gives us valuable information as to the contents of the Garland. This poem,[7] in which he dedicates his work to his friend or patron Diocles, gives the names of forty-seven poets included by him besides many others of recent times whom he does not specifically enumerate. It runs as follows:

"Dear Muse, for whom bringest thou this gardenful of song, or who is he that fashioned the garland of poets? Meleager made it, and wrought out this gift as a remembrance for noble Diocles, inweaving many lilies of Anyte, and many martagons of Moero, and of Sappho little, but all roses, and the narcissus of Melanippides budding into clear hymns, and the fresh shoot of the vine-blossom of Simonides; twining to mingle therewith the spice-scented flowering iris of Nossis, on whose tablets love melted the wax, and with her, margerain from sweet-breathed Rhianus, and the delicious maiden-fleshed crocus of Erinna, and the hyacinth of Alcaeus, vocal among the poets, and the dark-leaved laurel-spray of Samius, and withal the rich ivy-clusters of Leonidas, and the tresses of Mnasalcas' sharp pine; and he plucked the spreading plane of the song of Pamphilus, woven together with the walnut shoots of Pancrates and the fair-foliaged white poplar of Tymnes, and the green mint of Nicias, and the horn-poppy of Euphemus growing on these sands; and with these Damagetas, a dark violet, and the sweet myrtle-berry of Callimachus, ever full of pungent honey, and the rose-campion of Euphorion, and the cyclamen of the Muses, him who had his surname from the Dioscori. And with him he inwove Hegesippus, a riotous grape-cluster, and mowed down the scented rush of Perses; and withal the quince from the branches of Diotimus, and the first pomegranate flowers of Menecrates, and the myrrh-twigs of Nicaenetus, and the terebinth of Phaennus, and the tall wild pear of Simmias, and among them also a few flowers of Parthenis, plucked from the blameless parsley-meadow, and fruitful remnants from the honey-dropping Muses, yellow ears from the corn-blade of Bacchylides; and withal Anacreon, both that sweet song of his and his nectarous elegies, unsown honey-suckle; and withal the thorn-blossom of Archilochus from a tangled brake, little drops from the ocean; and with them the young olive-shoots of Alexander, and the dark-blue cornflower of Polycleitus; and among them he laid amaracus, Polystratus the flower of songs, and the young Phoenician cypress of Antipater, and also set therein spiked Syrian nard, the poet who sang of himself as Hermes' gift; and withal Posidippus and Hedylus together, wild blossoms of the country, and the blowing windflowers of the son of Sicelides; yea, and set therein the golden bough of the ever divine Plato, shining everywhere in excellence, and beside him Aratus the knower of the stars, cutting the first-born spires of that heaven-high palm, and the fair-tressed lotus of Chaeremon mixed with the gilliflower of Phaedimus, and the round ox-eye of Antagoras, and the wine-loving fresh-blown wild thyme of Theodorides, and the bean-blossoms of Phanias, and many newly-scriptured shoots of others; and with them also even from his own Muse some early white violets. But to my friends I give thanks; and the sweet-languaged garland of the Muses is common to all initiate."

In this list three poets are not spoken of directly by name, but, from metrical or other reasons, are alluded to paraphrastically. "He who had his surname from the Dioscori" is Dioscorides; "the poet who sang of himself as Hermes' gifts" is Hermodorus; and "the son of Sicelides" is Asclepiades, referred to under the same name by his great pupil

Theocritus. The names of these forty-eight poets (including Meleager himself) show that the collection embraced epigrams of all periods from the earliest times up to his own day. Six belong to the early period of the lyric poets, ending with the Persian wars; Archilochus, who flourished about 700 B.C., Sappho and Erinna a century afterwards, Simonides and Anacreon about 500 B.C., and a little later, Bacchylides. Five more belong to the fourth century B.C., the period which begins with the destruction of the Athenian empire and ends with the establishment of the Macedonian kingdoms of the Diadochi. Of these, Plato is still within the Athenian period; Hegesippus, Simmias, Anyte, and Phaedimus, all towards the end of the century, mark the beginning of the Alexandrian period. Four have completely disappeared out of the Anthology as we possess it; Melanippides, a celebrated writer of dithyrambic poetry in the latter half of the fifth century B.C., of which a few fragments survive, and Euphemus, Parthenis, and Polycleitus, of whom nothing whatever is known. The remaining thirty- three poets in Meleager's list all belong to the Alexandrian period, and bring the series down continuously to Meleager himself.

One of the epigrams in the Anthology of Strato[8] professes to be the colophon {xoronis} to Meleager's collection; but it is a stupid and clumsy forgery of an obviously later date, probably by Strato himself, or some contemporary, and is not worth quoting. The proem to the Garland is a work of great ingenuity, and contains in single words and phrases many exquisite criticisms. The phrase used of Sappho has become proverbial; hardly less true and pointed are those on Erinna, Callimachus, and Plato. All the flowers are carefully and appropriately chosen with reference to their poets, and the whole is done with the light and sure touch of a critic who is also a poet himself.

A scholiast on the Palatine MS. says that Meleager's Anthology was arranged in alphabetical order {xata stoikheion}. This seems to mean alphabetical order of epigrams, not of authors; and the statement is borne out by some parts of the Palatine and even of the Planudean Anthologies, where, in spite of the rearrangement under subjects, traces of alphabetical arrangement among the older epigrams are still visible. The words of the scholiast imply that there was no further arrangement by subject. It seems most reasonable to suppose that the epigrams of each author were placed together; but of this there is no direct evidence, nor can any such arrangement be certainly inferred from the state of the existing Anthologies.

The Scholiast, in this same passage, speaks of Meleager's collection as an {epigrammaton stephanos}, and obviously it consisted in the main of epigrams according to the ordinary definition. But it is curious that Meleager himself nowhere uses the word; and from some phrases in the proem it is difficult to avoid the inference that he included other kinds of minor poetry as well. Too much stress need not be laid on the words {umnos} and {aoide}, which in one form or another are repeatedly used by him; though it is difficult to suppose that "the hymns of Melanippides", who is known to have been a dithyrambic poet, can mean not hymns but epigrams.[9] But where Anacreon is mentioned, his {melisma} and his elegiac pieces are unmistakably distinguished from each other, and are said to be both included; and this {melisma} must mean lyric poetry of some kind, probably the very hemiambics under the name of Anacreon which are extant as an appendix to the Palatine MS. Meleager's Anthology also pretty certainly included his own Song of Spring,[10] which is a hexameter poem, though but for the form of verse it might just come within a loose definition of an epigram. Whether it included idyllic poems like the Amor Fugitivus of Moschus[11] it is not possible to determine.

Besides his great Anthology, another, of the same class of contents as that subsequently made by Strato, is often ascribed to Meleager, an epigram in Strato's Anthology[12] being regarded as the proem to this supposed collection. But there is no external authority whatever for this hypothesis; nor is it necessary to regard this epigram as anything more than a poem commemorating the boys mentioned in it. Eros, not Meleager, is in this case the weaver of the garland.

The next compiler of an Anthology, more than a century after Meleager, was Philippus of Thessalonica. Of this also the proem is preserved.[13] It purports to be a collection of the epigrammatists since Meleager, and is dedicated to the Roman patron of the author, one Camillus. The proem runs thus:

"Having plucked for thee Heliconian flowers, and cut the first-blown blossoms of famous-forested Pieria, and reaped the ears from modern pages, I wove a rival garland, to be like those of Meleager; but do thou, noble Cantillus, who knowest the fame of the older poets, know likewise the short pieces of the younger. Antipater's corn-ear shall grace our garland, and Crinagoras like an ivy-cluster; Antiphilus shall glow like a grape-bunch, Tullius like melilote, Philodemus like marjoram: and Parmenio myrtle-berries: Antiphanes as a rose: Automedon ivy, Zonas lilies, Bianor oak, Antigonus olive, and Diodorus violet. Liken thou Euenus to laurel, and the multitude woven in with these to what fresh-blown flowers thou wilt."

One sees here the decline of the art from its first exquisiteness. There is no selection or appropriateness in the names of the flowers chosen, and the verse is managed baldly and clumsily. Philippus' own epigrams, of which over seventy are extant, are generally rather dull, chiefly school exercises, and, in the phrase of Jacobs, /imitatione magis quam inventione conspicua/. But we owe to him the preservation of a large mass of work belonging to the Roman period. The date of Philippus cannot be fixed very precisely. His own epigrams contain no certain allusion to any date other than the reign of Augustus. Of the poets named in his proem, Antiphanes, Euenus, Parmenio, and Tullius have no date determinable from internal evidence. Antigonus has been sometimes identified with Antigonus of Carystus, the author of the {Paradokon Sunagoge}, who lived in the third century B.C. under Ptolemy Philadelphus or Ptolemy Euergetes; but as this Anthology distinctly professes to be of poets since Meleager, he must be another author of the same name. Antipater of Thessalonica, Bianor, and Diodorus are of the Augustan period; Philodemus, Zonas, and probably Automedon, of the period immediately preceding it. The latest certain allusion in the poems of Antiphilus is to the enfranchisement of Rhodes by Nero in A.D. 53.[14] One of the epigrams under the name of Automedon in the Anthology[15] is on the rhetorician Nicetas, the teacher of the younger Pliny. But there are at least two poets of the name, Automedon of Aetolia and Automedon of Cyzicus, and the former, who is pre-Roman, may be the one included by Philippus. If so, we need not, with Jacobs, date this collection in the reign of Trajan, at the beginning of the second century, but may place it with greater probability half a century earlier, under Nero.

In the reign of Hadrian the grammarian Diogenianus of Heraclea edited an Anthology of epigrams,[16] but nothing is known of it beyond the name. The Anthology contains a good deal of work which may be referred to this period.

The first of the appendices to the Palatine Anthology is the {Paidike Mousa} of Strato of Sardis. The compiler apologises in a prefatory note for including it, excusing himself with the line of Euripides,[17] {e ge sopsron ou diapstharesetai}. It was a new Anthology of epigrams dealing with this special subject from the earliest period downwards. As we possess it, Strato's collection includes thirteen of the poets named in the Garland of Meleager (including Meleager himself), two of those named in the Garland of Philippus, and ten other poets, none of them of much mark, and most of unknown date; the most interesting being Alpheus of Mitylene, who from the style and contents of his epigrams seems to have lived about the time of Hadrian, but may possibly be an Augustan poet. Strato is mentioned by Diogenes Laërtius,[18] who wrote at the beginning of the third century; and his own epigram on the physician Artemidorus Capito,[19] who was a contemporary of Hadrian, fixes his approximate date.

How far we possess Strato's collection in its original form it is impossible to decide. Jacobs says he cannot attempt to determine whether Cephalas took it in a lump or made a selection from it, or whether he kept the order of the epigrams. As they stand they have no ascertainable principle of arrangement, alphabetical or of author or of subject. The collection consists of two hundred and fifty-nine epigrams, of which ninety-four are by Strato himself and sixty by Meleager. It has either been carelessly formed, or suffered from interpolation afterwards. Some of the epigrams are foreign to the subject of the collection. Six are on women;[20] and four of these are on women whose names end in the diminutive form, Phanion, Callistion, etc., which suggests the inference that they were inserted at a late date and by an ignorant transcriber who confused these with masculine forms. For all the epigrams of Strato's collection the Anthology is the only source.

In the three hundred years between Strato and Agathias no new Anthology is known to have been made.

The celebrated Byzantine poet and historian Agathias, son of Mamnonius of Myrina, came to Constantinople as a young man to study law in the year 554. In the preface to his History he tells us that he formed a new collection of recent and contemporary epigrams previously unpublished,[21] in seven books, entitled {Kuklos}. His proem to the Cyclus is extant.[22] It consists of forty-six iambics followed by eighty-seven hexameters, and describes the collection under the symbolism no longer of a flower-garden, but of a feast to which different persons bring contributions ({ou stepsanos alla sunagoge}), a metaphor which is followed out with unrelenting tediousness. The piece is not worth transcription here. He says he includes his own epigrams. After a panegyric on the greatness of the empire of Justinian, and the foreign and domestic peace of his reign, he ends by describing the contents of the collection. Book I. contains dedications in the ancient manner, {os proterois makaressin aneimena}: for Agathias was himself a Christian, and indeed the old religion had completely died out even before Justinian closed the schools of Athens. Book II. contains epigrams on statues, pictures, and other works of art; Book III., sepulchral epigrams; Book IV., epigrams "on the manifold paths of life, and the unstable scales of fortune," corresponding to the section of {Protreptika} in the Palatine Anthology; Book V., irrisory epigrams; Book VI. amatory epigrams; and Book VII., convivial epigrams. Agathias, so far as we know, was the first who made this sort of arrangement under subjects, which, with modifications, has generally been followed afterwards. His Anthology is lost; and probably perished soon after that of Cephalas was made.

Constantinus Cephalas, a grammarian unknown except from the Palatine MS., began again from the beginning. The scholiast to the Garland of Meleager in that MS., after saying that Meleager's Anthology was arranged in alphabetical order, goes on as follows:—"but Constantinus, called Cephalas, broke it up, and distributed it under different heads, viz., the love-poems separately, and the dedications and epitaphs, and epideictic pieces, as they are now arranged below in this book."[23] We must assume that with this rearranged Anthology he incorporated those of Philippus and Agathias, unless, which is not probable, we suppose that the Palatine Anthology is one enlarged from that of Cephalas by some one else completely unknown.

As to the date of Cephalas there is no certain indication. Suidas apparently quotes from his Anthology; but even were we certain that these quotations are not made from original sources, his lexicon contains entries made at different times over a space of several centuries. A scholium to one of the epigrams[24] of Alcaeus of Messene speaks of a discussion on it by Cephalas which took place in the School of the New Church at

Constantinople. This New Church was built by the Emperor Basil I. (reigned 867-876). Probably Cephalas lived in the reign of Constantine VII. Porphyrogenitus (911-959), who had a passion for art and literature, and is known to have ordered the compilation of books of excerpts. Gibbon gives an account of the revival of learning which took place under his influence, and of the relations of his Court with that of the Western Empire of Otto the Great.

The arrangement in the Anthology of Cephalas is founded on that of Agathias. But alongside of the arrangement under subjects we frequently find strings of epigrams by the same author with no particular connection in subject, which are obviously transcribed directly from a collected edition of his poems.

Maximus Planudes, theologian, grammarian, and rhetorician, lived in the early part of the fourteenth century; in 1327 he was appointed ambassador to the Venetian Republic by Andronicus II. Among his works were translations into Greek of Augustine's City of God and Caesar's Gallic War. The restored Greek Empire of the Palaeologi was then fast dropping to pieces. The Genoese colony of Pera usurped the trade of Constantinople and acted as an independent state; and it brings us very near the modern world to remember that while Planudes was the contemporary of Petrarch and Doria, Andronicus III., the grandson and successor of Andronicus II., was married, as a suitable match, to Agnes of Brunswick, and again after her death to Anne of Savoy.

Planudes made a new Anthology in seven books, founded on that of Cephalas, but with many alterations and omissions. Each book is divided into chapters which are arranged alphabetically by subject, with the exception of the seventh book, consisting of amatory epigrams, which is not subdivided. In a prefatory note to this book he says he has omitted all indecent or unseemly epigrams, {polla en to antigrapso onta}. This {antograpso} was the Anthology of Cephalas. The contents of the different books are as follows:

Book I.—{Epideiktika}, in ninety-one chapters; from the {Epideiktika} of Cephalas, with additions from his {Anathematika} and {Protreptika}, and twelve new epigrams on statues.

Book II.—{Skoptika}, in fifty-three chapters; from the {Sumpotika kai Skoptika} and the {Mousa Stratonos} of Cephalas, with six new epigrams.

Book III.—{Epitumbia}, in thirty-two chapters; from the {Epitumbia} of Cephalas, which are often transcribed in the original order, with thirteen new epigrams.

Book IV.—Epigrams on monuments, statues, animals, and places, in thirty-three chapters; some from the {Epideiktika} of Cephalas, but for the greater part new.

Book V.—Christodorus' description of the statues in the gymnasium called Zeuxippus, and a collection of epigrams in the Hippodrome at Constantinople; from appendices to the Anthology of Cephalas.

Book VI.—{Anathematika}, in twenty-seven chapters; from the {Anathematika} of Cephalas, with four new epigrams.

Book VII.—{Erotika}; from the {Erotika} of Cephalas, with twenty-six new epigrams.

Obviously then the Anthology of Planudes was almost wholly taken from that of Cephalas, with the exception of epigrams on works of art, which are conspicuously absent from the earlier collection as we possess it. As to these there is only one conclusion. It is impossible to account for Cephalas having deliberately omitted this class of epigrams; it is impossible to account for their re-appearance in Planudes, except on the supposition that we have lost a section of the earlier Anthology which included them. The Planudean Anthology contains in all three hundred and ninety-seven epigrams, which are not in the Palatine MS. of Cephalas. It is in these that its principal value lies. The vitiated taste of the period selected later and worse in preference to earlier and better epigrams; the compilation was made carelessly and, it would seem, hurriedly, the earlier part of the sections of Cephalas being largely transcribed and the latter part much less fully, as though the editor had been pressed for time or lost interest in the work as he went on. Not only so, but he mutilated the text freely, and made sweeping conjectural restorations where it was imperfect. The discrepancies too in the authorship assigned to epigrams are so frequent and so striking that they can only be explained by great carelessness in transcription; especially as internal evidence where it can be applied almost uniformly supports the headings of the Palatine Anthology.

Such as it was, however, the Anthology of Planudes displaced that of Cephalas almost at once, and remained the only MS. source of the anthology until the seventeenth century. The other entirely disappeared, unless a copy of it was the manuscript belonging to Angelo Colloti, seen and mentioned by the Roman scholar and antiquarian Fulvio Orsini (b. 1529, d. 1600) about the middle of the sixteenth century, and then again lost to view. The Planudean Anthology was first printed at Florence in 1484 by the Greek scholar, Janus Lascaris, from a good MS. It continued to be reprinted from time to time, the last edition being the five sumptuous quarto volumes issued from the press of Wild and Altheer at Utrecht, 1795-1822.

In the winter of 1606-7, Salmasius, then a boy of eighteen but already an accomplished scholar, discovered a manuscript of the Anthology of Cephalas in the library of the Counts Palatine at Heidelberg. He copied from it the epigrams hitherto unknown, and these began to be circulated in manuscript under the name of the Anthologia Inedita. The intention he repeatedly expressed of editing the whole work was never carried into effect. In 1623, on the capture of Heidelberg by the Archduke Maximilian of Bavaria in the Thirty Years' War, this with many other MSS. and books was sent by him to Rome as a present to Pope Gregory XV., and was placed in the Vatican Library. It remained there till it was taken to Paris by order of the French Directory in 1797, and was restored to the Palatine Library after the end of the war.

The description of this celebrated manuscript, the Codex Palatinus or Vaticanus, as it has been named from the different places of its abode, is as follows: it is a long quarto, on parchment, of 710 pages, together with a page of contents and three other pages glued on at the beginning. There are three hands in it. The table of contents and pages 1-452 and 645-704 in the body of the MS. are in a hand of the eleventh century; the middle of the MS., pages 453-644, is in a later hand; and a third, later than both, has written the last six pages and the three odd pages at the beginning, has added a few epigrams in blank spaces, and has made corrections throughout the MS.

The index, which is of great importance towards the history not only of the MS. but of the Anthology generally, runs as follows:—

{Tade enestin en tede te biblo ton epigrammaton
- A. Nonnou poirtou Panopolitou ekphrasis tou kata Ioannen agiou euaggeliou.
- B. Paulou poirtou selantiariou (sic) uiou Kurou ekphrasis eis ten megalen ekklesian ete ten agian Sophian.
- G. Sullogai epigrammaton Khristianikon eis te naous kai eikonas kai eis diaphora anathemata.
- D. Khristodorou poietou Thebaiou ekphrasis ton agalmaton ton eis to demosion gumnasion tou epikaloumenou Zeuxippou.
- E. Meleagou poietou Palaistinou stephanos diaphoron epigrammaton.
- S. Philippou poietou Thessalonikeos stephanos omoios diaphoron epigrammaton.
- Z. Agathiou skholastikou Asianou Murenaiou sulloge neon epigrammaton

ektethenton en Konstantinoupolei pros Theodoron Dekouriona. esti
de e taxis ton epigrammaton egoun diairesis outos.
a. prote men e ton Khristianon.
b. deutera de e ta Khristodorou periekhousa tou Thebaiou.
g. trete (sic) de arkhen men ekhousa ten ton erotikon epigrammaton
upothesin.
d. e ton anathematikon.
e. pempte e ton epitumbion.
s. e ton epideiktikon.
z. ebdome e ton pretreptikon.
e. e ton skoptikon.
th. ebdome e ton protreptikon.
i. diaphoron metron diaphora epigrammata.
ia. arithmetika kai grepha summikta.
ib. Ioannou grammatikou Gazes ekphrasis tou kosmikou pinakos tou en
kheimerio loutro.
ig. Surigx Theokritou kai pteruges Simmiou Dosiada bomos Besantinou
oon kai pelekus.
id. Anakreontos Teiou Sumposiaka emiambia kai Anakreontia kai
trimetra.
ie. Tou agiou Gregoriou tou theologou ek ton epon eklogai diaphorai
en ois kai ta Arethou kai Anastasiou kai Ignatiou kai
Konstantinou kai Theophanous keintai epigrammata.}

This index must have been transcribed from the index of an earlier MS. It differs from the actual contents of the MS. in the following respects:—

The hexameter paraphrase of S. John's Gospel by Nonnus is not in the MS., having perhaps been torn off from the beginning of it.

After the description of S. Sophia by Paulus Silentiarius, follow in the MS. select poems of S. Gregorius.

After the description by Christodorus of the statues in the gymnasium of Zeuxippus follows a collection of nineteen epigrams inscribed below carved reliefs in the temple of Apollonis, mother of Attalus and Eumenes kings of Pergamus, at Cyzicus.

After the proem to the Anthology of Agathias follows another epigram of his, apparently the colophon to his collection.

The book of Christian epigrams and that of poems by Christodorus of Thebes are wanting in the MS.

Between the /Sepulcralia/ and /Epideictica/ is inserted a collection of 254 epigrams by S. Gregorius.

John of Gaza's description of the Mappa Mundi in the winter baths is wanting in the MS.

After the miscellaneous Byzantine epigrams, which form the last entry in the index, is a collection of epigrams in the Hippodrome at Constantinople.

The Palatine MS. then is a copy from another lost MS. And the lost MS. itself was not the archetype of Cephalas. From a prefatory note to the /Dedicatoria/, taken in connection with the three iambic lines prefixed to the /Amatoria/, it is obvious that the /Amatoria/ formed the first section of the Anthology of Cephalas, preceded, no doubt, by the three proems of Meleager, Philippus, and Agathias as prefatory matter. The first four headings in the index, therefore, represent matter subsequently added. Whether all the small appendices at the end of the MS. were added to the Anthology by Cephalas or by a later hand it is not possible to determine. With or without these appendices, the work of

Cephalas consisted of six sections of {Erotika}, {Anathematika}, {Epitumbia}, {Epideiktica}, {Protreptika} and {Eumpotika kai Skoptika}, with the {Mousa Stratonos}, and probably, as we have already seen, a lost section containing epigrams on works of art. At the beginning of the sepulchral epigrams there is a marginal note in the MS., in the corrector's hand, speaking of Cephalas as then dead.[25] Another note, added by the same hand on the margin of vii. 432, says that our MS. had been collated with another belonging to one Michael Magister, which was copied by him with his own hand from the book of Cephalas.

The extracts made by Salmasius remained for long the only source accessible to scholars for the contents of the Palatine Anthology. Jacobs, when re-editing Brunck's /Analecta/, obtained a copy of the MS., then in the Vatican library, from Uhden, the Prussian ambassador at Rome; and from another copy, afterwards made at his instance by Spaletti, he at last edited the Anthology in its complete form. ⸻

[1] Cf. especially Hdt. v. 59, 60, 77; Thuc. i. 132, vi. 54, 59.

[2] Suid. s.v. {PHilokhoros}.

[3] Athen. x. 436 D., 442 E.

[4] Athen. xiii. 591 C, 594 D.

[5] Ibid. x. 454 F. The date of Neoptolemus is uncertain; he probably lived in the second century B.C.

[6] Anth. Pol. vii. 428; Cic. Or. iii. 194, Pis. 68-70.

[7] Ibid. iv. 1.

[8] Anth. Pal. xii. 257.

[9] Melanippides, however, also wrote epigrams according to Suidas, s.v., and the phrase of Meleager may mean "the epigrams of this poet who was celebrated as a hymn-writer".

[10] Anth. Pal. ix. 363.

[11] Ibid. ix. 440.

[12] Ibid. xii. 256.

[13] Anth. Pal. iv. 2.

[14] Anth. Pal. ix. 178.

[15] Ibid. x. 23.

[16] Suidas s.v. {Diogenianos}.

[17] Bacch. 318.

[18] v. 61.

[19] Anth. Pal. xi. 117.

[20] Anth. Pal. xvi. 53, 82, 114, 131, 147, 173.

[21] Agathias, Hist. i. 1: {ton epigrammaton ta artigene kai neotera oialanthanonti eti kai khuden outosi par eniois upophithurizomena}. Cf. also Suidas, s.v. {Agathias}.

[22] Anth. Pal. iv. 3.

[23] Schol. on Anth. Pal. iv. 1.

[24] Anth. Pal. vii. 429.

[25] {Konstantinos o Kephalas o makarios kai aeimnestos kai tripothetos anthrepos}.

V

When any selection of minor poetry is made, the principle of arrangement is one of the first difficulties. In dealing with the Greek epigram, the matter before us, as has been said already, consists of between five and six thousand pieces, all in the same metre, and varying in length from two to twenty-eight lines,[1] but rarely exceeding twelve. No principle of arrangement can therefore be based on the form of the poems. There are three other plans possible; a simply arbitrary order, an arrangement by authorship, or an arrangement by subject. The first, if we believe the note in the Palatine MS. already quoted, was adopted by Meleager in the alphabetical arrangement of his Garland; but beyond the uncommon variety it must give to the reader, it seems to have little to recommend it. The Anthologies of Cephalas and Planudes are both arranged by subject, but with considerable differences. The former, if we omit the unimportant sections and the Christian epigrams, consists of seven large sections in the following order:

(1) {Erotika}, amatory pieces. This heading requires no comment.

(2) {Anathematika}, dedicatory pieces, consisting of votive prayers and dedications proper.

(3) {Epitumbia}, sepulchral pieces: consisting partly of epitaphs real or imaginary, partly of epigrams on death or on dead persons in a larger scope. Thus it includes the epigram on the Lacedaemonian mother who killed her son for returning alive from an unsuccessful battle;[2] that celebrating the magnificence of the tomb of Semiramis;[3] that questioning the story as to the leap of Empedocles into Etna;[4] and a large number which might equally well come under the next head, being eulogies on celebrated authors and artists.

(4) {Epideiktika}, epigrams written as {epideixeis}, poetical exercises or show-pieces. This section is naturally the longest and much the most miscellaneous. There is indeed hardly any epigram which could not be included in it. Remarkable objects in nature or art, striking events, actual or imaginary, of present and past times, moral sentences, and criticisms on particular persons and things or on life generally; descriptive pieces; stories told in verse; imaginary speeches of celebrated persons on different occasions, with such titles as "what Philomela would say to Procne," "what Ulysses would say when he landed in Ithaca"; inscriptions for houses, baths, gardens, temples, pictures, statues, gems, clocks, cups: such are among the contents, though not exhausting them.

(5) {Protreptika}, hortatory pieces; the "criticism of life" in the direct sense.

(6) {Sumpotika kai Skoptika}, convivial and humorous epigrams.

(7) The {Mousa paidike Stratonos} already spoken of. Along with these, as we have seen, there was in all probability an eighth section now lost, containing epigrams on works of art.

Within each of these sections, the principle of arrangement, where it exists at all, is very loose; and either the compilation was carelessly made at first, or it has been considerably disordered in transcription. Sometimes a number of epigrams by the same author succeed one another, as though copied directly from a collection where each author's work was placed separately; sometimes, on the other hand, a number on the same subject by authors of different periods come together.[5] Epigrams occasionally are put under wrong headings. For example, a dedication by Leonidas of Alexandria is followed in the /Dedicatoria/ by another epigram of his on Oedipus;[6] an imaginary epitaph on Hesiod in the /Sepulcralia/ by one on the legendary contest between Hesiod and Homer;[7] and the lovely fragment of pastoral on Love keeping Thyrsis' sheep[8] comes oddly in among epitaphs. The epideictic section contains a number of epigrams which would be more properly placed in one or another of all the rest of the sections; and the /Musa Stratonis/ has several which happily in no way belong to it. There is no doubt a certain charm to the very confusion of the order, which gives great variety and unexpectedness; but for practical purposes a more accurate classification is desirable.

The Anthology of Planudes attempts, in a somewhat crude form, to supply this. Each of the six books, with the exception of the {Erotika}, which remain as is in the Palatine

Anthology, is subdivided into chapters according to subject, the chapters being arranged alphabetically by headings. Thus the list of chapters in Book I. begins, {eis agonas}, {eis ampelon}, {eis anathemata}, {eis anaperous}, and ends {eis phronesin}, {eis phrontidas}, {eis khronon}, {eis oras}.

On the other hand, Brunck, in his /Analecta/, the arrangement of which is followed by Jacobs in the earlier of his two great works, recast the whole scheme, placing all epigrams by the same author together, with those of unknown authorship at the end. This method presents definite advantages when the matter in hand is a complete collection of the works of the epigrammatists. With these smaller, as with the more important works of literature, it is still true that a poet is his own best commentator, and that by a complete single view of all his pieces we are able to understand each one of them better. A counter-argument is the large mass of {adespota} thus left in a heap at the end. In Jacobs there are upwards of 750 of these, most of them not assignable to any certain date; and they have to be arranged roughly by subject. Another is the fact that a difficulty still remains as to the arrangement of the authors. Of many of the minor epigrammatists we know absolutely nothing from external sources; and it is often impossible to determine from internal evidence the period, even within several centuries, at which an epigram was written, so little did the style and diction alter between the early Alexandrian and the late Byzantine period. Still the advantages are too great to be outweighed by these considerations.

But in a selection, an Anthology of the Anthology, the reasons for such an arrangement no longer exist, and some sort of arrangement by subject is plainly demanded. It would be possible to follow the old divisions of the Palatine Anthology with little change but for the epideictic section. This is not a natural division, and is not satisfactory in its results. It did not therefore seem worthwhile to adhere in other respects to the old classification except where it was convenient; and by a new and somewhat more detailed division, it has been attempted to give a closer unity to each section, and to make the whole of them illustrate progressively the aspect of the ancient world. Sections I., II., and VI. of the Palatine arrangement just given are retained, under the headings of Love, Prayers and Dedications, and the Human Comedy. It proved convenient to break up Section III., that of sepulchral epigrams, which would otherwise have been much the largest of the divisions, into two sections, one of epitaphs proper, the other dealing with death more generally. A limited selection from Section VII. has been retained under a separate heading, Beauty. Section V., with additions from many other sources, was the basis of a division dealing with the Criticism of Life; while Section IV., together with what was not already classed, fell conveniently under five heads: Nature, and in antithesis to it, Art and Literature; Family Life; and the ethical view of things under the double aspect of Religion on the one hand, and on the other, the blind and vast forces of Fate and Change.

---

[1] Single lines are excluded by the definition; Anth. Pal. ix. 482 appears to be the longest piece in the Anthology which can properly be called an epigram.

[2] Anth. Pal. vii. 433.

[3] Ibid. vii. 748.

[4] Ibid. vii. 124.

[5] Cf. especially Anth. Pal. vi. 179-187; ix. 713-742.

[6] Anth. Pal. vi. 322, 323.

[7] Ibid. vii. 52, 53.

[8] Ibid. vii. 703.

VI

The literary treatment of the passion of love is one of the matters in which the ancient stands furthest apart from the modern world. Perhaps the result of love in human lives differs but little from one age to another; but the form in which it is expressed (which is all that literature has to do with) was altered in Western Europe in the middle ages, and ever since then we have spoken a different language. And the subject is one in which the feeling is so inextricably mixed up with the expression that a new language practically means a new actual world of things. Of nothing is it so true that emotion is created by expression. The enormous volume of expression developed in modern times by a few great poets and a countless number of prose writers has reacted upon men and women; so certain is it that thought follows language, and life copies art. And so here more than elsewhere, though the rule applies to the whole sphere of human thought and action, we have to expect in Greek literature to find much latent and implicit which since then has become patent and prominent; much intricate psychology not yet evolved; much—as is the truth of everything Greek—stated so simply and directly, that we, accustomed as we are to more complex and highly organised methods of expression, cannot without some difficulty connect it with actual life, or see its permanent truth. Yet to do so is just the value of studying Greek; for the more simple the forms or ideas of life are, the better are we able to put them in relation with one another, and so to unify life. And this unity is the end which all human thought pursues.

Greek literature itself however may in this matter be historically subdivided. In its course we can fix landmarks, and trace the entrance and working of one and another fresh element. The Homeric world, the noblest and the simplest ever conceived on earth; the period of the great lyric poets; that of the dramatists, philosophers and historians, which may be called the Athenian period; the hardly less extraordinary ages that followed, when Greek life and language overspread and absorbed the whole Mediterranean world, mingling with East and West alike, making a common meeting-place for the Jew and the Celt, the Arab and the Roman; these four periods, though they have a unity in the fact that they are all Greek, are yet separated in other ways by intervals as great as those which divide Virgil from Dante, or Chaucer from Milton.

In the Iliad and Odyssey little is said about love directly; and yet it is not to be forgotten that the moving force of the Trojan war was the beauty of Helen, and the central interest of the return of Odysseus is the passionate fidelity of Penelope.[1] Yet more than this; when the poet has to speak of the matter, he never fails to rise to the occasion in a way that even now we can see to be unsurpassable. The Achilles of the Iliad may speak scornfully of Briseïs, as insufficient cause to quarrel on;[2] the silver-footed goddess, set above all human longings, regards the love of men and women from her icy heights with a light passionless contempt.[3] But in the very culminating point of the death-struggle between Achilles and Hector, it is from the whispered talk of lovers that the poet fetches the utmost touch of beauty and terror;[4] and it is in speaking to the sweetest and noblest of all the women of poetry that Odysseus says the final word that has yet been said of married happiness.[5]

In this heroic period love is only spoken of incidentally and allusively. The direct poetry of passion belongs to the next period, only known to us now by scanty fragments, "the spring-time of song,"[6] the period of the great lyric poets of the sixth and seventh centuries B.C. There human passion and emotion had direct expression, and that, we can judge from what is left to us, the fullest and most delicate possible. Greek life then must have been more beautiful than at any other time; and the Greek language, much as it afterwards gained in depth and capacity of expressing abstract thought, has never again the same freshness, as though steeped in dew and morning sunlight. Sappho alone, that unique instance of literature where from a few hundred fragmentary lines we know certainly that we are in face of one of the great poets of the world, expressed the passion of love in a way which makes the language of all other poets grow pallid: /ad quod cum iungerent purpuras suas, cineris specie decolorari videbantur ceterae divini comparatione fulgoris/.[7]

{eraman men ego sethen, Atthi, palai pota—}[8]
such simple words that have all sadness in their lingering cadences;

{Oion to glukumalon ereuthetai—
Er eti parthenias epiballomai;
Ou gar en atera pais, o gambre, toiauta—}[9]
the poetry of pure passion has never reached further than this.

But with the vast development of Greek thought and art in the fifth century B.C., there seems to have come somehow a stiffening of Greek life; the one overwhelming interest of the City absorbing individual passion and emotion, as the interest of logic and metaphysics absorbed history and poetry. The age of Thucydides and Antipho is not one in which the emotions have a change; and at Athens especially—of other cities we can only speak from exceedingly imperfect knowledge, but just at this period Athens means Greece—the relations between men and women are even under Pericles beginning to be vulgarised. In the great dramatic poets love enters either as a subsidiary motive somewhat severely and conventionally treated, as in the Antigone of Sophocles, or, as in the Phaedra and Medea of Euripides, as part of a general study of psychology. It would be foolish to attempt to defend the address of the chorus in the Antigone to Eros,[10] if regarded as the language of passion; and even if regarded as the language of criticism, it is undeniably frigid. Contrasted with the great chorus in the same play,[11] where Sophocles is dealing with a subject that he really cares about, it sounds almost artificial. And in Euripides, psychology occupies the whole of the interest that is not already preoccupied by logic and rhetoric; these were the arts of life, and with these serious writing dealt; with the heroism of Macaria, even with the devotion of Alcestis, personal passion has but little to do.

With the immense expansion of the Greek world that followed the political extinction of Greece Proper, there came a relaxation of this tension. Feeling grew humaner; social and family life reassumed their real importance; and gradually there grew up a thing till then unknown in the world, and one the history of which yet remains to be written, the romantic spirit. Pastoral poetry, with its passionate sense of beauty in nature, reacted on the sense of beauty in simple human life. The Idyls of Theocritus are full of a new freshness of feeling: {epei k esores tas parthenos oia gelanti}[12]—this is as alien from the Athenian spirit as it approaches the feeling of a medieval romance- writer: and in the Pharmaceutriae pure passion, but passion softened into exquisite forms, is once more predominant.[13] It is in this age then that we naturally find the most perfect examples of the epigram of love. In the lyric period the epigram was still mainly confined to its stricter sphere, that of inscriptions for tombs and dedicated offerings: in the great Athenian age the direct treatment of love was almost in abeyance. Just on the edge of this last period, as is usual in a time of transition, there are exquisite premonitions of the new art. The lovely hexameter fragment[14] preserved in the Anthology under the name of Plato, and not unworthy of so great a parentage, anticipates the manner and the cadences of Theocritus; and one or two of the amatory epigrams that are probably Plato's might be Meleager's, but for the severe perfection of language that died with Greek freedom. But it is in the Alexandrian period that the epigram of love flowers out; and it is at the end of that period, where the Greek spirit was touched by Oriental passion, that it culminates in Meleager.

We possess about a hundred amatory epigrams by this poet. Inferior perhaps in clearness of outline and depth of insight to those of the Alexandrian poet Asclepiades, they are unequalled in the width of range, the profusion of imagination, the subtlety of emotion with which they sound the whole lyre of passion. Meleager was born in a Syrian town and educated at Tyre in the last age of the Seleucid empire; and though he writes Greek with perfect mastery, it becomes in his hands almost a new language, full of dreams, at once more languid and more passionate. It was the fashion among Alexandrian poets to experiment in language; and Callimachus had in this way brought the epigram to the most elaborate jewel-finish; but in the work of Callimachus and his contemporaries the pure Greek tradition still survives. In Meleager, the touch of Asiatic blood creates a new type, delicate, exotic, fantastic. Art is no longer restrained and severe. The exquisite austerity of Greek poetry did not outlive the greatness of Athens; its perfect clearness of outline still survived in Theocritus; here both are gone. The atmosphere is loaded with a steam of perfumes, and with still unimpaired ease and perfection of hand there has come in a strain of the quality which of all qualities is the most remote from the Greek spirit, mysticism. Some of Meleager's epigrams are direct and simple, even to coarseness; but in all the best and most characteristic there is this vital difference from purely Greek art, that love has become a religion; the spirit of the East has touched them. It is this that makes Meleager so curiously akin to the medieval poets. Many of his turns of thought, many even of his actual expressions, have the closest parallel in poets of the fourteenth century who had never read a line of his work nor heard of his name. As in them, the religion of love is reduced to a theology; no subtlety, no fluctuation of fancy or passion is left unregistered, alike in their lighter and their graver moods. Sometimes the feeling is buried in masses of conceits, sometimes it is eagerly passionate, but even then always with an imaginative and florid passion, never directly as Sappho or Catullus is direct. Love appears in a hundred shapes amidst a shower of fantastic titles and attributes. Out of all the epithets that Meleager coins for him, one, set in a line of hauntingly liquid and languid rhythm, "delicate-sandalled,"[15] gives the key-note to the rest. Or again, he often calls him {glukupikros}, "bittersweet";[16] at first he is like wine mingled with honey for sweetness, but as he grows and becomes more tyrannous, his honey scorches and stings; and the lover, "set on fire and drenched to swooning with his ointments," drinks from a deeper cup and mingles his wine with burning tears.[17] Love the Reveller goes masking with the lover through stormy winter nights;[18] Love the Ball-player tosses hearts for balls in his hands;[19] Love the Runaway lies hidden in a lady's eyes;[20] Love the Healer soothes with a touch the wound that his own dart has made;[21] Love the Artist sets his signature beneath the soul which he has created;[22] Love the Helmsman steers the soul, like a winged boat, over the perilous seas of desire;[23] Love the Child, playing idly with his dice at sundawn, throws lightly for human lives.[24] Now he is a winged boy with childish bow and quiver, swift of laughter and speech and tears;[25] now a fierce god with flaming arrows, before whom life wastes away like wax in the fire, Love the terrible, Love the slayer of men.[26] The air all round him is heavy with the scent of flowers and ointments; violets and myrtle, narcissus and lilies, are woven into his garlands, and the rose, "lover-loving" as Meleager repeatedly calls it in one of his curious new compound epithets,[27] is perpetually about him, and rains its petals over the banqueting-table and the myrrh-drenched doorway.[28] For a moment Meleager can be piercingly simple; and then the fantastic mood comes over him again, and emotion dissolves in a mist of metaphors. But even when he is most fantastic the unfailing beauty of his rhythms and grace of his language remind us that we are still in the presence of a real art.

   The pattern set by Meleager was followed by later poets; and little more would remain to say were it not necessary to notice the brief renascence of amatory poetry in the sixth century. The poets of that period take a high place in the second rank; and one, Paulus Silentiarius, has a special interest among them as being at once the most antique in his workmanship and the most modern in his sentiment. One of his epigrams is like an early poem of Shakespeare's;[29] another has in a singular degree the manner and movement of a sonnet by Rossetti.[30] This group of epigrammatists brought back a phantom of freshness into the old forms; once more the epigram becomes full of pretty rhythms and fancies, but they are now more artificial; set beside work of the best period they come out clumsy and heavy. Language is no longer vivid and natural; the colour is a little dimmed, the tone a little forced. As the painter's art had disappeared into that of the worker in mosaic, so the language of poetry was no longer a living stream, but a treasury of glittering words. Verse- writers studied it carefully and used it cleverly, but never could make up for the want of free movement of hand by any laborious minuteness of tessellation. Yet if removed from the side of their great models they are graceful enough, with a prettiness that recalls and probably in many cases is copied from the novelists of the fourth century; and sometimes it is only a touch of the diffuseness inseparable from all Byzantine writing that separates their work in quality from that of an earlier period.

After Justinian the art practically died out. The pedantic rigour of Byzantine scholarship was little favourable to the poetry of emotion, and the spoken language had now fallen so far apart from the literary idiom that only scholars were capable of writing in the old classical forms. The popular love-poetry, if it existed, has perished and left no traces; henceforth, for the five centuries that elapsed till the birth of Provençal and Italian poetry, love lay voiceless, as though entranced and entombed. ———————

[1] Cf. Il. iii. 156; Anth. Pal. ix. 166.
[2] Il. i. 298.
[3] Il. xxiv. 130.
[4] Il. xxii. 126-8.
[5] Od. vi. 185.
[6] {ear umnon}, Anth. Pal. vii. 12.
[7] Vopisc. Aurel. c. 29.
[8] Frag. 33 Bergk.
[9] Fragg. 93, 102, 106 Bergk.
[10] ll. 781, foll.
[11] ll. 332, foll.
[12] Theocr. i. 85.
[13] ll. 105-110 of this poem set beside Sappho, Fr. ii. ll. 9-16, Bergk, are a perfect example of the pastoral in contrast with the lyrical treatment.
[14] App. Plan. 210.
[15] Anth. Pal. xii. 158, {soi me, Theokleis, abropedilos Eros gumnon upestoresen}.
[16] Ibid. xii. 109; cf. v. 163, 172; xii. 154.
[17] Ibid. xii. 132, 164.
[18] Ibid. xii. 167.
[19] Ibid. v. 214.
[20] Ibid. v. 177.
[21] Ibid. v. 225.
[22] Ibid. v. 155.
[23] Ibid. xii. 157.
[24] Anth. Pal. xii. 47.

[25] Ibid. v. 177.
[26] Ibid. v. 176, 180; xii. 72.
[27] Ibid. v. 136, 147.
[28] Ibid. v. 147, 198.
[29] Ibid. v. 241; cf. Passionate Pilgrim, xiv., xv.
[30] App. Plan. 278.

VII

Closely connected with the passion of love as conceived by Greek writers is a subject which continually meets us in Greek literature, and which fills so large a part of the Anthology that it can hardly be passed over without notice. The few epigrams selected from the Anthology of Strato and included in this collection under the heading of Beauty are not of course a representative selection. Of the great mass of those epigrams no selection is possible or desirable. They belong to that side of Greek life which is akin to the Oriental world, and remote and even revolting to the western mind. And on this subject the common moral sense of civilised mankind has pronounced a judgment which requires no justification as it allows of no appeal.

But indeed the whole conception of Eros the boy, familiar as it sounds to us from the long continued convention of literature, is, if we think of its origin or meaning, quite alien from our own habit of life and thought. Even in the middle ages it cohered but ill with the literary view of the relations between men and women in poetry and romance; hardly, except where it is raised into a higher sphere by the associations of religion, as in the friezes of Donatello, is it quite natural, and now, apart from what remains of these same associations, the natural basis of the conception is wholly obsolete. Since the fashion of squires and pages, inherited from the feudal system, ceased with the decay of the Renaissance, there has been nothing in modern life which even remotely suggests it. We still—such is the strength of tradition in art—speak of Love under the old types, and represent him under the image of a winged boy; but the whole condition of society in which this type grew up has disappeared and left the symbolism all but meaningless to the ordinary mind. In Greece it was otherwise. Side by side with the unchanging passions and affections of all mankind there was then a feeling, half conventional, and yet none the less of vital importance to thought and conduct, which elevated the mere physical charm of human youth into an object of almost divine worship. Beauty was the special gift of the gods, perhaps their choicest one; and not only so, but it was a passport to their favour. Common life in the open air, and above all the importance of the gymnasia, developed great perfection of bodily form and kept it constantly before all men's eyes. Art lavished all it knew on the reproduction of the forms of youthful beauty. Apart from the real feeling, the worship of this beauty became an overpowering fashion. To all this there must be added a fact of no less importance in historical Greece, the seclusion of women. Not that this ever existed in the Oriental sense; but, with much freedom and simplicity of relations inside the family, the share which women had in the public and external life of the city, at a time when the city meant so much, was comparatively slight. The greater freedom of women in Homer makes the world of the Iliad and Odyssey really more modern, more akin to our own, than that of the later poets. The girl in Theocritus, "with spring in her eyes,"[1] comes upon us as we read the Idyls almost like a modernism. It is in the fair shepherd boy, Daphnis or Thyrsis, that Greek pastoral finds its most obvious, one might almost say its most natural inspiration.

Much of what is most perplexing in the difference in this respect between Greek and western art has light thrown on it, if we think of the importance which angels have in medieval painting. Their invention, if one may call it so, was one of the very highest moment in art. Those lovely creations, so precisely drawn up to a certain point, so elusive beyond it, raised the feeling for pure beauty into a wholly ideal plane. The deepest longings of men were satisfied by the contemplation of a paradise in which we should be even as they. In that mystical portraiture of the invisible world an answer—perhaps the only answer—was found to the demand for an ideal of beauty. That remarkable saying preserved by S. Clement, of a kingdom in which "the two shall be one, and the male with the female neither male nor female,"[2] might form the text for a chapter of no small importance in human history. The Greek lucidity, which made all mysticism impossible in their art as it was alien from their life, did not do away with this imperious demand; and their cult of beauty was the issue of their attempt, imperfect indeed at best and at worst disastrous, to reunite the fragments of the human ideal.[3]

In much of this poetry too we are in the conventional world of pastoral; and pastoral, it must be repeated, does not concern itself with real life. The amount of latitude in literary expression varies no doubt with the prevalent popular morality of the period. But it would lead to infinite confusion to think of the poetry as a translation of conduct. A truer picture of Greek life is happily given us in those epigrams which deal with the material that history passes over and ideal poetry, at least in Greek literature, barely touches upon, the life of simple human relations from day to day within the circle of the family. ————

[1] {ear oroosa Nukheia}, Theocr. xiii. 42.

[2] Clem. Rom. II. 12: {eperototheis autos o Kurios upo tinos pote exei autou e basileia, eipen, otan estai ta duo en kai to exo os to eso kai to arsen meta tes theleias oute arsen oute thelu}. It is also quoted in almost the same words by Clem. Alex., Strom. xiii. 92, as from "the Gospel according to the Egyptians."

[3] Cf. Plato, Sympos. 191, 192.

VIII

Scattered over the sections of the Anthology are a number of epigrams touching on this life, which are the more valuable to us, because it is just this side of the ancient world of which the mass of Greek literature affords a very imperfect view. In Homer indeed this is not the case; but in the Athenian period the dramatists and historians give little information, if we accept the highly idealised burlesque of the Aristophanic Comedy. Of the New Comedy too little is preserved to be of much use, and even in it the whole atmosphere was very conventional. The Greek novel did not come into existence till too late; and, when it came, it took the form of romance, concerning itself more with the elaboration of sentiment and the excitement of adventure than with the portraiture of real manners and actual surroundings. For any detailed picture of common life, like that which would be given of our own day to future periods by the domestic novel, we look to ancient literature in vain. Thus, when we are admitted by a fortunate chance into the intimacy of private life, as we are by some of the works of Xenophon and Plutarch or by the letters of the younger Pliny, the charm of the picture is all the greater: and so it is with the epigrams that record birthdays and bridals, the toys of children, the concord of quiet homes. We see the house of the good man,[1] an abiding rest from the labours of a busy life, bountiful to all, masters and servants, who dwell under its shelter, and extending a large hospitality to the friend and the stranger. One generation after another grows up in it under all good and gracious influences; a special providence, under the symbolic forms of Cypris Urania or Artemis the Giver of Light, holds the house in keeping, and each new year brings increased blessing from the gods of the household in recompense of piety and duty.[2] Many dedications bring vividly before us the humbler life of the country cottager, no man's servant or master, happy in the daily labour over his little plot of land, his corn-field and vineyard and coppice; of the fowler with his boys in the woods, the forester and the beekeeper, and the fisherman in his thatched hut on the beach.[3] And in these contrasted pictures the "wealth that makes men kind" seems not to jar with the "poverty that lives with freedom."[4] Modern poetry dwells with more elaboration, but not with the truer or more delicate feeling than those ancient epigrams, on the pretty ways of children, the freshness of school-days, the infinite beauty of the girl as she passes into the woman; or even such slight things as the school-prize for the best copy-book, and the child's doll in the well.[5] A shadow passes over the picture in the complaint of a girl sitting indoors, full of dim thoughts, while the boys go out to their games and enjoy unhindered the colour and movement of the streets.[6] But this is the melancholy of youth, the shadow of the brightness that passes before the maiden's eyes as she sits, sunk in day-dreams, over her loom;[7] it passes away again in the portrait of the girl growing up with the sweet eyes of her mother, the budding rose that will soon unfold its heart of flame;[8] and once more the bride renders thanks for perfect felicity to the gods who have given her "a stainless youth and the lover whom she desired."[9] Many of the most beautiful of the dedicatory epigrams are thanksgivings after the birth of children; in one a wife says that she is satisfied with the harmonious life that she and her husband live together, and asks no further good.[10] Even death coming at the end of such a life is disarmed of terror. In one of the most graceful epitaphs of the Roman period[11] the dead man sums up the happiness of his long life by saying that he never had to weep for any of his children, and that their tears over him had no bitterness. The inscription placed by Androtion over the yet empty tomb, which he has built for himself and his wife and children, expresses that placid acceptance which finds no cause of complaint with life.[12] Family affection in an unbroken home; long and happy life of the individual, and still longer, that of the race which remains; the calm acquiescence in the law of life which is also the law of death, and the desire that life and death alike may have their ordinary place and period, not breaking use and wont; all this is implied here rather than expressed, in words so simple and straightforward that they seem to have fallen by accident, as it were, into verse. Thus too in another epigram the dying wife's last words are praise to the gods of marriage that she has had even such a husband, and to the gods of death that he and their children survive her.[13] Or again, where there is a cry of pain over severance, it is the sweetness of the past life that makes parting so bitter; "what is there but sorrow," says Marathonis over the tomb of Nicopolis,[14] "for a man alone upon earth when his wife is gone?" ———

[1] Anth. Pal. ix. 649.

[2] Ibid. vi. 267, 280, 340.

[3] Ibid. vi. 226, vii. 156.

[4] {Dunatai to ploutein kai philanthropous poiein}, Menand., {Alieis} fr. 7; Anth. Pal. ix. 172.

[5] Anth. Pal. vi. 308, ix. 326.

[6] Ibid. v. 297.

[7] Ibid. vi. 266.

[8] Ibid. vi. 353, v. 124.

[9] Ibid. vi. 59.

[10] Ibid. vi. 209.

[11] Ibid. vii. 260.

[12] Ibid. vii. 228.

[13] Anth. Pal. vii. 555.

[14] Ibid. vii. 340.

IX

"Even this stranger, I suppose, prays to the immortals," says Nestor in the Odyssey,[1] "since all men have need of gods." When the Homeric poems were written the Greek temper had already formed and ripened; and so long as it survived, this recognition of religious duty remained part of it. The deeper and more violent forms of religious feeling were indeed always alien, and even to a certain degree repugnant, to the Greek peoples. Mysticism, as has already been observed, had no place with them; demons and monsters were rejected from their humane and rationalised mythology, and no superstitious terrors forced them into elaboration of ritual. There was no priestly caste; each city and each citizen approached the gods directly at any time and place. The religious life, as a life distinct from that of an ordinary citizen, was unknown in Greece. Even at Rome the perpetual maidenhood of the Vestals was a unique observance; and they were the keepers of the hearth-fire of the city, not the intermediaries between it and its gods. But the Vestals have no parallel in Greek life. Asiatic rites and devotions, it is true, from an early period obtained a foothold among the populace; but they were either discountenanced, or by being made part of the civic ritual were disarmed of their mystic or monastic elements. An epitaph in the Anthology commemorates two aged priestesses as having been happy in their love for their husbands and children;[2] nothing could be further from the Eastern or the medieval sentiment of a consecrated life. Thus, if Greek religion did not strike deep, it spread wide; and any one, as he thought fit, might treat his whole life, or any part of it, as a religious act. And there was a strong feeling that the observance of such duties in a reasonable manner was proper in itself, besides being probably useful in its results; no gentleman, if we may so translate the idea into modern terms, would fail in due courtesy to the gods. That piety sometimes met with strange returns was an undoubted fact, but that it should be so inexplicable and indeed shocking even to the least superstitious and most dispassionate minds.[3]

With the diffusion of a popularised philosophy religious feeling became fainter among the educated classes, and correspondingly more uncontrolled in the lower orders. The immense mass of dedicatory epigrams written in the Alexandrian and Roman periods are in the main literary exercises, though they were also the supply of a real and living demand. The fashion outlived the belief; even after the suppression of pagan worship scholars continued to turn out imitations of the old models. One book of the Anthology of Agathias[4] consisted entirely of contemporary epigrams of this sort, "as though dedicated to former gods." But of epigrams dealing with religion in its more intimate sense there are, as one would expect, very few in the Anthology until we come to collections of Christian poetry. This light form of verse was not suited to the treatment of the deepest subjects. For the religious poetry of Greece one must go to Pindar and Sophocles.

But the small selection given here throws some interesting light on Greek thought with regard to sacred matters. Each business of life, each change of circumstance, calls for worship and offering. The sailor, putting to sea with spring, is to pay his sacrifice to the harbour-god, a simple offering of cakes or fish.[5] The seafarer should not pass near a great shine without turning aside to pay it reverence.[6] The traveller, as he crosses a hill-pass or rests by the wayside fountain, is to give the accustomed honour to the god of the ground, Pan or Hermes, or whoever holds the spot in special protection.[7] Each shaded well in the forest, each jut of cliff on the shore, has its tutelar deity, if only under the form of the rudely-carved stake set in a garden or on a lonely beach where the sea-gulls hover; and with their more sumptuous worship the houses of great gods, all marble and gold, stand overlooking the broad valley or the shining spaces of sea.[8] Even the wild thicket has its rustic Pan, to whom the hunter and fowler pray for success in their day's work, and the image of Demeter stands by the farmer's threshing-floor.[9] And yet close as the gods come in their daily dealings with men, scorning no offering, however small, that is made with clean hands, finding no occasion too trifling for their aid, there is a yet more homely worship of "little gods"[10] who take the most insignificant matters in their charge. These are not mere abstractions, like the lesser deities of the Latin religion, Bonus Eventus, Tutilina, Iterduca and Domiduca, but they occupy much the same place in worship. By their side are the heroes, the saints of the ancient world, who from their graves have some power of hearing and answering. Like the saints, they belong to all times, from the most remote to the most recent. The mythical Philopregmon, a shadowy being dating back to times of primitive worship, gives luck from his monument on the roadside by the gate of Potidaea.[11] But the traveller who had prayed to him in the morning as he left the town might pay the same duty next evening by the tomb of Brasidas in the market-place of Amphipolis.[12]

But alongside of the traditional worship of these multitudinous and multiform deities, a grave and deep religious sense laid stress on the single quality of goodness as being essentially akin to divinity, and spoke with aversion of complicated ritual and extravagant sacrifice. A little water purifies the good man; the whole ocean is not sufficient to wash away the guilt of the sinner.[13] "Holiness is a pure mind," said the inscription over the doorway of a great Greek temple.[14] The sanctions of religion were not indeed independent of rewards and punishments, in this or in a future state. But the highest Greek teachings never laid great stress on these; and even where they are adduced as a motive for good living, they are always made secondary to the excellence of piety here and in itself. Through the whole course of Greek thought the belief in a future state runs in an undercurrent. A striking fragment of Sophocles[15] speaks of the initiated alone as being happy, since their state after death is secure. Plato, while he reprobates the teaching which would make men good in view of the other world, and insists on the natural excellence of goodness for its own sake, himself falls back on the life after death, as affected for good or evil by our acts here, in the visions, "no fairy-tales,"[16] which seem to collect and reinforce the arguments of the /Phaedo/ and the /Republic/. But the ordinary thought and practice ignored what might happen after death. Life was what concerned men and absorbed them; it seemed sufficient for them to think about what they knew of.[17] The revolution which Christianity brought into men's way of thinking as regards life and death was that it made them know more certainly, or so it seemed, about the latter than about the former. Who knows, Euripides had long ago asked, if life be not death, and death life? and the new religion answered his question with an emphatic affirmation that it was so; that this life was momentary and shadowy, was but a death, in comparison of the life unchangeable and eternal.

The dedicatory epigram was one of the earliest forms of Greek poetry. Herodotus quotes verses inscribed on offerings at Thebes, written in "Cadmean letters," and dating back to a mythical antiquity;[18] and actual dedications are extant which are at least as early as 600 B.C.[19] In this earlier period the verses generally contained nothing more than a bare record of the act. Even at a later date, the anathematic epigrams of Simonides are for the most part rather stiff and formal when set beside his epitaphs. His nephew Bacchylides brought the art to perfection, if it is safe to judge from a single flawless specimen.[20] But it is hardly till the Alexandrian period that the dedication has elaborate pains bestowed upon it simply for the feeling and expression as a form of poetry; and it is to this period that the mass of the best prayers and dedications belong.

Ranging as they do over the whole variety of human action, these epigrams show us the ancient world in its simplest and most pleasant aspect. Family life has its offerings for the birth of a child, for return from travel, for recovery from sickness. The eager and curious spirit of youth, and old age to which nothing but rest seems good, each offer prayer to the guardians of the traveller or of the home.[21] The most numerous and the most beautiful are those where, towards the end of life, dedications are made with thanksgiving for the past and prayer for what remains. The Mediterranean merchantman retires to his native town and offers prayer to the protector of the city to grant him a quiet age there, or dedicates his ship, to dance no more "like a feather on the sea," now that its master has set his weary feet on land.[22] The fisherman, ceasing his labours, hangs up his fish-spear to Poseidon, saying, "Thou knowest I am tired." The old hunter, whose hand has lost its suppleness, dedicates his nets to the Nymphs, as all that he has to give. The market-gardener, when he has saved a competence, lays his worn tools before Priapus the Garden- Keeper. Heracles and Artemis receive the aged soldier's shield into their temples, that it may grow old there amid the sound of hymns and the dances of maidens.[23] Quiet peace, as of the greyness of a summer evening, is the desired end.

The diffusion of Greece under Alexander and his successors, as at a later period the diffusion of Rome under the Empire, brought with the decay of civic spirit a great increase of humanity. The dedication written by Theocritus for his friend Nicias of Miletus[24] gives a vivid picture of the gracious atmosphere of a rich and cultured Greek home, of the happy union of science and art with harmonious family life and kindly helpfulness and hospitality. Care for others was a more controlling motive in life than before. The feeling grew that we are all one family, and owe each other the service and thoughtfulness due to kinsfolk, till Menander could say that true life was living for others.[25] In this spirit the sailor, come safe ashore, offers prayer to Poseidon that others who cross the sea may be as fortunate; so too, from the other side of the matter, Pan of the sea-cliff promises a favourable wind to all strangers who sail by him, in remembrance of the pious fisherman who set his statue there, as guardian of their trawling-nets and eel-baskets.[26]

In revulsion from the immense accumulation of material wealth in this period, a certain refined simplicity was then the ideal of the best minds, as it was afterwards in the early Roman Empire, as it is in our own day. The charm of the country was, perhaps for the first time, fully realised; the life of gardens became a passion, and hardly less so the life of the opener air, of the hill and meadow, of the shepherd and hunter, the farmer and fisherman. The rules of art, like the demands of heaven, were best satisfied with small and simple offerings. "The least of a little"[27] was sufficient to lay before gods who had no need of riches; and as the art of the epigrammatist grew more refined, the poet took pride in working with the slightest materials. The husbandman lays a handful of corn-ears before Demeter, the gardener a basket of ripe fruit at the feet of Priapus; the implements of their craft are dedicated by the carpenter and the goldsmith; the young girl and the aged woman offer their even slighter gift, the spindle and distaff, the reel of wool, and the rush-woven basket.[28] A staff of wild-olive cut in the coppice is accepted by the lord of the myriad-boughed forest; the Muses are pleased with their bunch of roses wet with morning dew.[29] The boy Daphnis offers his fawnskin and scrip of apples to the great divinity of Pan;[30] the young herdsman and his newly-married wife, still with the rose-garland on her hair, make prayer and thanksgiving with a cream cheese and a piece of honeycomb to the mistress of a hundred cities, Aphrodite with her house of gold.[31] The hard and laborious life of the small farmer was touched with something of the natural magic that saturates the Georgics; "rich with fair fleeces, and fair wine, and fair fruit of corn," and blessed by the gracious Seasons whose feet pass over the furrows.[32] On the green slope Pan himself makes solitary music to the shepherd in the divine silence of the hills.[33] The fancy of three brothers, a hunter, a fowler, and a fisherman, meeting to make dedication of the spoils of their crafts to the country-god, was one which had a special charm for epigrammatists; it is treated by no less than nine poets, whose dates stretch over as many centuries.[34] Sick of cities, the imagination turned to an Arcadia that thenceforth was to fill all poetry with the music of its names and the fresh chill of its pastoral air; the lilied banks of Ladon, the Erymanthian water, the deep woodland of Pholoë and the grey steep of Cyllene.[35] Nature grew full of a fresh and lovely divinity. A spirit dwells under the sea, and looks with kind eyes on the creatures that go up and down in its depths; Artemis flashes by in the rustle of the windswept oakwood, and the sombre shade of the pines makes a roof for Pan; the wild hill becomes a sanctuary, for ever unsown and unmown, where the Spirit of Nature, remote and invisible, feeds his immortal flock and fulfils his desire.[36] ———

[1] Od. iii. 47.
[2] Anth. Pal. vii. 733; cf. also v. 14 in this selection.
[3] Cf. Thuc. vii. 86.
[4] Anth. Pal. iv. 3, ll. 113-116.
[5] Ibid. vi. 105; x. 14.
[6] Ibid. vi. 251; cf. v. 3 in this selection.
[7] App. Plan. 227; Anth. Pal. x. 12.
[8] App. Plan. 291; Anth. Pal. vi. 22, 119, ix. 144, x. 8, 10.
[9] Anth. Pal. x. 11, vi. 98.
[10] Ibid. ix. 334.
[11] Ibid. vii. 694.
[12] Thuc. v. 11; Arist. Eth. v. 7.
[13] Anth. Pal. xiv. 71.
[14] v. 15 in this selection.
[15] Fr. anon. 719.
[16] {ou mentoi soi Alkinou ge apologon ero}, Plato, Rep. 614 B.
[17] {To zen gar ismen tou thanein d apeiria Pas tis phobeitai phos lipein tod eliou}— Eurip. Phoenix, fr. 9.
[18] Hdt. v. 60, 61.
[19] See Kaibel, Epigr. Gr. 738-742.
[20] Anth. Pal. vi. 53.
[21] Anth. Pal. x. 6, vi. 70.
[22] Ibid. ix. 7, vi. 70.
[23] Ibid. vi. 30, 25, 21, 178, 127.
[24] Ibid. vi. 337; cf. Theocr. Idyl xxii.
[25] Frag. incert. 257, {tout esti to zen oukh eauto zen monon}.
[26] Anth. Pal. x. 10, 24.
[27] Ibid. vi. 98, {ek mikron oligista}.
[28] Ibid. vi. 98, 102; 103, 92; 174, 247.
[29] Ibid. vi. 3, 336.
[30] Ibid. vi. 177.
[31] Ibid. vi. 55; cf. vi. 119, xii. 131.
[32] Anth. Pal. vi. 31, 98.
[33] App. Plan. 17; cf. Lucret. v. 1387.
[34] Anth. Pal. vi. 11-16, and 179-187. The poets are Leonidas of Tarentum, Alcaeus of Messene, Antipater of Sidon, Alexander, Julius Diocles, Satyrus, Archias, Zosimus and Julianus Aegyptius.
[35] Anth. Pal. vi. 111, App. Plan. 188: compare Song iii. in Milton's /Arcades/.

[36] Anth. Pal. x. 8; vi. 253, 268; vi. 79.

X

Though the section of the Palatine Anthology dealing with works of art, if it ever existed, is now completely lost, we have still left a considerable number of epigrams which come under this head. Many are preserved in the Planudean Anthology. Many more, on account of the cross-division of subjects that cannot be avoided in arranging any collection of poetry, are found in other sections of the Palatine Anthology. It was a favourite device, for example, to cast a criticism or eulogy of an author or artist into the form of an imaginary epitaph; and this was often actually inscribed on a monument, or beneath a bust, in the galleries or gardens of a wealthy /virtuoso/. Thus the sepulchral epigrams include inscriptions of this sort of many of the most distinguished names of Greek literature. They are mainly on poets and philosophers; Homer and Hesiod, the great tragedians and comedians, the long roll of the lyric poets, most frequently among them Sappho, Alcman, Erinna, Archilochus, Pindar, and the whole line of philosophers from Thales and Anaxagoras down to the latest teachers in the schools of Athens. Often in those epigrams some vivid epithet or fine touch of criticism gives a real value to them even now; the "frowning towers" of the Aeschylean tragedy, the trumpet-note of Pindar, the wealth of lovely flower and leaf, crisp Archanian ivy, rose and vine, that clusters round the tomb of Sophocles.[1] Those on the philosophers are, as one would expect, generally of inferior quality.

Many again are to be found among the miscellaneous section of epideictic epigrams. Instances which deal with literature directly are the noble lines of Alpheus on Homer, the interesting epigram on the authorship of the /Phaedo/, the lovely couplet on the bucolic poets.[2] Some are inscriptions for libraries or collections;[3] others are on particular works of art. Among these last, epigrams on statues or pictures dealing with the power of music are specially notable; the conjunction, in this way, of the three arts seems to have given peculiar pleasure to the refined and eclectic culture of the Graeco-Roman period. The contest of Apollo and Marsyas, the piping of Pan to Echo, and the celebrated subject of the Faun listening for the sound of his own flute,[4] are among the most favourite and the most gracefully treated of this class. Even more beautiful, however, than these, and worthy to take rank with the finest "sonnets on pictures" of modern poets, is the epigram ascribed to Theocritus, and almost certainly written for a picture,[5] which seems to place the whole world of ancient pastoral before our eyes. The grouping of the figures is like that in the famous Venetian Pastoral of Giorgione; in both alike are the shadowed grass, the slim pipes, the hand trailing upon the viol-string. But the execution has the matchless simplicity, the incredible purity of outline, that distinguishes Greek work from that of all other races.

A different view of art and literature, and one which adds considerably to our knowledge of the ancient feeling about them, is given by another class of pieces, the irrisory epigrams of the Anthology. Then, as now, people were amused by bad and bored by successful artists, and delighted to laugh at both; then, as now, the life of the scholar or the artist had its meaner side, and lent itself easily to ridicule from without, to jealousy and discontent from within. The air rang with jeers at the portrait-painter who never got a likeness, the too facile composer whose body was to be burned on a pile of five-and-twenty chests all filled with his own scores, the bad grammar of the grammarian, the supersubtle logic and the cumbrous technical language of the metaphysician, the disastrous fertility of the authors of machine-made epics.[6] The poor scholar had become proverbial; living in a garret where the very mice were starved, teaching the children of the middle classes for an uncertain pittance, glad to buy a dinner with a dedication, and gradually petrifying in the monotony of a thousand repetitions of stock passages and lectures to empty benches.[7] Land and sea swarmed with penniless grammarians.[8] The epigrams of Palladas of Alexandria bring before us vividly the miseries of a schoolmaster. Those of Callimachus shew with as painful clearness how the hatred of what was bad in literature might end in embittering the whole nature.[9] Many epigrams are extant which indicate that much of a scholar's life, even when he had not to earn bitter bread on the stairs of patrons, was wasted in laborious pedantry or in personal jealousies and recriminations.[10]

Of epigrams on individual works of art it is not necessary to say much. Their numbers must have been enormous. The painted halls and colonnades, common in all Greek towns, had their stories told in verse below; there was hardly a statue or picture of any note that was not the subject of a short poem. A collected series of works of art had its corresponding series of epigrams. The Anthology includes, among other lists, a description of nineteen subjects carved in relief on the pedestals of the columns in a temple at Cyzicus, and another of seventy-three bronze statues which stood in the great hall of a gymnasium at Constantinople.[11] Any celebrated work like the Niobe of Praxiteles, or the bronze heifer of Myron, was the practising-ground for every tried or untried poet, seeking new praise for some clever conceit or neater turn of language than had yet been invented. Especially was this so with the trifling art of the decadence and its perpetual round of childish Loves: Love ploughing, Love holding a fish and a flower as symbols of his sovereignty over sea and land, Love asleep on a pepper-castor, Love blowing a torch, Love grasping or breaking the thunderbolt, Love with a helmet, a shield, a quiver, a trident, a club, a drum.[12] Enough of this class of epigrams are extant to be perfectly wearisome, were it not that, like the engraved gems from which their subjects are principally taken, they are all, however trite in subject or commonplace in workmanship, wrought in the same beautiful material, in that language which is to all other languages as a gem to an ordinary pebble.

From these sources we are able to collect a body of epigrams which in a way cover the field of ancient art and literature. Sometimes they preserve fragments of direct criticism, verbal or real. We have epigrams on fashions in prose style, on conventional graces of rhetoric, on the final disappearance of ancient music in the sixth century.[13] Of art-criticism in the modern sense there is but little. The striking epigram of Parrhasius, on the perfection attainable in painting,[14] is almost a solitary instance. Pictures and statues are generally praised for their actual or imagined realism. Silly stories like those of the birds pecking at the grapes of Zeuxis, or the calf who went up to suck the bronze cow of Myron, represent the general level of the critical faculty. Even Aristotle, it must be remembered, who represents the most finished Greek criticism, places the pleasure given by works of art in the recognition by the spectator of things which he has already seen. "The reason why people enjoy seeing pictures is that the spectators learn and infer what each object is; /this/, they say, /is so and so/; while if one has not seen the thing before, the pleasure is produced not by the imitation,"—or by the art, for he uses the two terms convertibly—"but by the execution, the colour, or some such cause."[15] And Plato (though on this subject one can never be quite sure that Plato is serious) talks of the graphic art as three times removed from realities, being only employed to make copies of semblances of the external objects which are themselves the copies or shadows of the ideal truth of things.[16] So far does Greek thought seem to be from the conception of an ideal art which is nearer truth than nature is, which nature itself indeed tries with perpetual striving, and ever incomplete success, to copy, which, as Aristotle does in one often quoted passage admit with regard to poetry, has a higher truth and a deeper seriousness than that of actual things.

But this must not be pressed too far. The critical faculty, even where fully present, may be overpowered by the rhetorical impulse; and of all forms of poetry the epigram has the greatest right to be fanciful. "This is the Satyr of Diodorus; if you touch it, it will awake;

the silver is asleep,"[17]—obviously this play of fancy has nothing to do with serious criticism. And of a really serious feeling about art there is sufficient evidence, as in the pathos of the sculptured Ariadne, happy in sleeping and being stone, and even more strongly in the lines on the picture of the Faun, which have the very tone and spirit of the /Ode on a Grecian Urn/.[18]

Two epigrams above all deserve special notice; one almost universally known, that written by Callimachus on his dead friend, the poet Heraclitus of Halicarnassus; the other, no less noble, though it has not the piercing tenderness of the first, by Claudius Ptolemaeus, the great astronomer, upon his own science, a science then not yet divorced from art and letters. The picture touched by Callimachus of that ancient and brilliant life, where two friends, each an accomplished scholar, each a poet, saw the summer sun set in their eager talk, and listened through the dusk to the singing nightingales, is a more exquisite tribute than all other ancient writings have given to the imperishable delight of literature, the mingled charm of youth and friendship, and the first stirring of the blood by poetry, and the first lifting of the soul by philosophy.[19] And on yet a further height, above the nightingales, under the solitary stars alone, Ptolemy as he traces the celestial orbits is lifted above the touch of earth, and recognises in man's mortal and ephemeral substance a kinship with the eternal. /Man did eat angels' food: he opened the doors of heaven./[20] ———————

[1] Anth. Pal. vii. 39, 34, 21, 22.
[2] Ibid. ix. 97, 358, 205.
[3] Cf. iv. 1 in this selection.
[4] Anth. Pal. vii. 696, App. Plan. 8, 225, 226, 244.
[5] Anth. Pal. ix. 433. On this epigram Jacobs says, /Frigide hoc carmen interpretantur qui illud tabulae pictae adscriptum fuisse existimant/. But the art of poems on pictures, which flourished to an immense degree in the Alexandrian and later periods, had not then been revived. One can fancy the same note being made hundreds of years hence on some of Rossetti's sonnets.
[6] Anth. Pal. xi. 215, 133, 143, 354, 136.
[7] Ibid. vi. 303, ix. 174, vi. 310; cf. also x. 35 in this selection.
[8] Ibid. xi. 400.
[9] Compare Anth. Pal. xii. 43 with ix. 565.
[10] Ibid. xi. 140, 142, 275.
[11] Anth. Pal. ii., iii.
[12] App. Plan. 200, 207, 208, 209, 214, 215, 250.
[13] Anth. Pal. xi. 141, 142, 144, 157; vii. 571.
[14] iv. 46 in this selection.
[15] Poet. 1448 b. 15-20.
[16] Republic, x. 597.
[17] App. Plan. 248.
[18] App. Plan. 146, 244.
[19] Anth. Pal. vii. 80. Cf. In Memoriam, xxiii.
[20] Anth. Pal. ix. 577; notice especially {theies pimplamai ambrosies}.

XI

That the feeling for Nature is one of the new developments of the modern spirit, is one of those commonplaces of criticism which express vaguely and loosely a general impression gathered from the comparison of ancient with modern poetry. Like most of such generalisations it is not of much value unless defined more closely; and as the definition of the rule becomes more accurate, the exceptions and limitations to be made grow correspondingly numerous. The section which is here placed under this heading is obviously different from any collection which could be made of modern poems, professing to deal with Nature and not imitated from the Greek. But when we try to analyse the difference, we find that the word Nature is one of the most ambiguous possible. Man's relation to Nature is variable not only from age to age, and from race to race, but from individual to individual, and from moment to moment. And the feeling for Nature, as expressed in literature, varies not only with all these variations but with other factors as well, notably with the prevalent mode of poetical expression, and with the condition of the other arts. The outer world lies before us all alike, with its visible facts, its demonstrable laws, /Natura daedala rerum/; but with each of us the /species ratioque naturae/, the picture presented by the outer world and the meaning that underlies it, are created in our own minds, the one by the apprehensions of our senses (and the eye sees what it brings the power to see), the other by our emotions, our imagination, our intellectual and moral qualities, as all these are affected by the pageant of things, and affect it in turn. And in no case can we express in words the total impression made upon us, but only that amount of it for which we possess a language of sufficient range and power and flexibility. For an impression has permanence and value— indeed one may go further and say has reality—only in so far as it is fixed and recorded in language, whether in the language of words or that of colours, forms, and sounds.

First in the natural order comes that simply sensuous view of the outer world, where combination and selection have as yet little or no part. Objects are distinct from one another, each creates a single impression, and the effect of each is summed up in a single phrase. The "constant epithet" of early poetry is a survival of this stage of thought; nature is a series of things, every one of which has its special note; "green grass," "wet water." Here the feeling for Nature likewise is simple and sensuous; the pleasure of shade and cool water in summer, of soft grass to lie on, of the flowers and warm sunshine of spring.

Then out of this infancy of feeling rises the curiosity of childhood; no longer content with noting and recording the obvious aspects of Nature, man observes and inquires and pays attention. The more attention is paid, the more is seen: and an immense growth follows in the language of poetry. To express the feeling for nature description becomes necessary, and this again involves, in order that the work may not be endless, selection and composition.

Again, upon this comes the sentimental feeling for Nature, a sort of sympathy created by interest and imagination. Among early races this, like other feelings, expresses itself in the forms of mythology, and half personifies the outer world, giving the tree her Dryad and the fountain her Nymph, making Pan and Echo meet in the forest glade. When the mythological instinct has ceased to be active, it results in sentimental description, sometimes realistic in detail, sometimes largely or even wholly conventional. It has always in it something of a reaction, real or affected, from crowds and the life of cities, an attempt to regain simplicity by isolation from the complex fabric of society.

Once more, the feeling for Nature may go deeper than the senses and the imagination, and become moral. The outer world is then no more a spectacle only, but the symbol of a meaning, the embodiment of a soul. Earth, the mother and fostress, receives our sympathy and gives us her own. The human spirit turns away from itself to seek sustenance from the mountains and the stars. The whole outer universe becomes the visible and sensible language of an ideal essence; and dawn or sunset, winter or summer, is of the nature of a sacrament.

There is over and above all these another sense in which we may speak of the feeling for Nature; and in regard to poetry it is perhaps the most important of all. But it no longer follows, like the rest, a sort of law of development in human nature generally; it is confined to art, and among the arts is eminent in poetry beyond the rest. This is the romantic or magical note. It cannot be analysed, perhaps it cannot be defined; the insufficiency of all attempted definitions of poetry is in great part due to the impossibility of their including this final quality, which, like some volatile essence, escapes the moment the phial is touched. In the poetry of all ages, even in the periods where it has been most intellectual and least imaginative, come sudden lines like the /Cette obscure clarté qui tombe des étoiles/ of Corneille, like the /Placed far amid the melancholy main/ of Thomson, where the feeling for Nature cannot be called moral, and yet stirs us like the deepest moral criticism upon life, rising as far beyond the mere idealism of sentiment as it does beyond the utmost refinement of realistic art.

    In all these different forms the feeling for Nature may be illustrated from Greek poetry; but the broad fact remains that Nature on the whole has a smaller part than it has with modern poets. Descriptive pieces are executed in a slighter manner, and on the whole with a more conventional treatment. Landscapes, for example, are always a background, never (or hardly ever) the picture itself. The influence of mythology on art was so overwhelming that, down to the last, it determined the treatment of many subjects where we should now go directly to the things themselves. Especially is this so with what has been described as the moral feeling for nature. Among "the unenlightened swains of Pagan Greece," as Wordsworth says, the deep effect of natural beauty on the mind was expressed under the forms of a concrete symbolism, a language to which literature had grown so accustomed that they had neither the power nor the wish to break free from it. The appeal indeed from man to Nature, and especially the appeal to Nature as knowing more about man's destiny than he knows himself, was unknown to the Greek poets. But this feeling is sentimental, not moral; and with them too "something far more deeply interfused" stirred the deepest sources of emotion. The music of Pan, at which the rustle of the oakwood ceases and the waterfall from the cliff is silent and the faint bleating of the sheep dies away,[1] is the expression in an ancient language of the spirit of Nature, fixed and embodied by the enchanting touch of art.

    Of the epigrams which deal primarily with the sensuous feeling for Nature, the most common are those on the delight of summer, rustling breezes and cold springs and rest under the shadow of trees. In the ardours of midday the traveller is guided from the road over a grassy brow to an ice-cold spring that gushes out of the rock under a pine; or lying idly on the soft meadow in the cool shade of the plane, is lulled by the whispering west wind through the branches, the monotone of the cicalas, the faint sound of a far-off shepherd's pipe floating down the hills; or looking up into the heart of the oak, sees the dim green roof, layer upon layer, mount and spread and shut out the sky.[2] Or the citizen, leaving the glare of town, spends a country holiday on strewn willow-boughs with wine and music,[3] as in that most perfect example of the poetry of a summer day, the /Thalysia/ of Theocritus. Down to a late Byzantine period this form of poetry, the nearest approach to pure description of nature in the old world, remained alive; as in the picture drawn by Arabius of the view from a villa on the shore of the Propontis, with its gardens set between wood and sea, where the warbling of birds mingled with the distant songs of the ferrymen.[4] Other landscape poems, as they may be called, remarkable for their clear and vivid portraiture, are that of Mnasalcas,[5] the low shore with its bright surf, and the temple with its poplars round which the sea-fowl hover and cry, and that of Anyte,[6] the windy orchard-close near the grey colourless coast, with the well and the Hermes standing over it at the crossways. But such epigrams always stop short of the description of natural objects for their own sake, for the mere delight in observing and speaking about them. Perhaps the nearest approach that Greek poetry makes to this is in a remarkable fragment of Sophocles,[7] describing the shiver that runs through the leaves of a poplar when all the other trees stand silent and motionless.

The descriptions of Nature too are, as a rule, not only slightly sketched, but kept subordinate to a human relation. The brilliance and loveliness of spring is the background for the picture of the sailor again putting to sea, or the husbandman setting his plough at work in the furrow; the summer woods are a resting-place for the hot and thirsty traveller; the golden leaves of autumn thinning in the frosty night, making haste to be gone before the storms of rough November, are a frame for the boy beneath them.[8] The life of earth is rarely thought of as distinct from the life of man. It is so in a few late epigrams. The complaint of the cicala, torn away by shepherds from its harmless green life of song and dew among the leaves, and the poem bidding the blackbird leave the dangerous oak, where, with its breast against a spray, it pours out its clear music,[9] are probably of Roman date; another of uncertain period but of great beauty, an epitaph on an old bee-keeper who lived alone on the hills with the high woods and pastures for his only neighbours, contrasts with a strangely modern feeling the perpetuity of nature and the return of the works of spring with the brief life of man that ends once for all on a cold winter night.[10]

Between the simply sensuous and the deep moral feeling for nature lies the broad field of pastoral. This is not the place to enter into the discussion of pastoral poetry; but it must be noted in passing that it does not imply of necessity any deep love, and still less any close observation, of nature. It looks on nature, as it looks on human life, through a medium of art and sentiment; and its treatment of nature depends less on the actual world around it than on the prevalent art of the time. Greek art concentrated its efforts on the representation of the human figure, and even there preferred the abstract form and the rigid limitations of sculpture; and the poetry that saw, as it were, through the eyes of art sought above all things simplicity of composition and clearness of outline. The scanty vocabulary of colour in Greek poetry, so often noticed, is a special and patent example of this difference in the spirit with which Nature was regarded. As the poetry of Chaucer corresponds, in its wealth and intimacy of decoration, to the illuminations and tapestries of the middle ages, so the epigrams given under this section constantly recall the sculptured reliefs and the engraved gems of Greek art.

But any such general rules must be taken with their exceptions. As there is a risk of reading modern sentiment into ancient work, and even of fixing on the startling modernisms that occur in Greek poetry,[11] and dwelling on them till they assume an exaggerated importance, so there is a risk perhaps as great of slurring over the inmost quality, the poetry of the poetry, where it has that touch of romance or magic that sets it beyond all our generalisations. The magical charm is just what cannot be brought under any rules; it is the result less of art than of instinct, and is almost independent of time and place. The lament of the swallow in an Alexandrian poet[12] touches the same note of beauty and longing that Keats drew from the song of the nightingale; the couplet of Satyrus, where echo repeats the lonely cry of the birds,[13] is, however different in tone, as purely romantic as the opening lines of /Christabel/. ———

[1] Anth. Pal. ix. 823.

[2] App. Plan. 230, 227; Anth. Pal. ix. 71.

[3] vi. 28 in this selection.

[4] Anth. Pal. ix. 667.

[5] Ibid. ix. 333.

[6] Ibid. ix. 314.

[7] Aegeus, fr. 24; cf. the celebrated simile in /Hyperion/, beginning, /As when upon a tranced summer night/.

[8] Anth. Pal. xii. 138.
[9] Ibid. ix. 373, 87.
[10] Ibid. vii. 717.
[11] A curious instance is in an epigram by Mnasalcas (Anth. Pal. vii. 194), where he speaks of the evening hymn ({panesperon umnon}) of the grasshopper. This, it must be remembered, was written in the third century B.C.
[12] Pamphilus in Anth. Pal. ix. 57.
[13] App. Plan. 153.

XII

Though fate and death make a dark background against which the brilliant colouring of Greek life glitters out with heightened magnificence, the comedy of men and manners occupies an important part of their literature, and Aristophanes and Menander are as intimately Greek as Sophocles. It is needless to speak of what we gain in our knowledge of Greece from the preserved comedies of Aristophanes; and if we follow the best ancient criticism, we must conclude that in Menander we have lost a treasury of Greek life that cannot be replaced. Quintilian, speaking at a distance from any national or contemporary prejudice, uses terms of him such as we should not think unworthy of Shakespeare.[1] These Attic comedians were the field out of which epigrammatists, from that time down to the final decay of literature, drew some of their graver and very many of their lighter epigrams. Of the convivial epigrams in the Anthology a number are imitated from extant fragments of the New Comedy; one at least[2] transfers a line of Menander's unaltered; and short fragments of both Menander and Diphilus are included in the Anthology as though not materially differing from epigrams themselves.[3]

Part of this section might be classed with the criticism of life from the Epicurean point of view. Some of the convivial epigrams are purely unreflective; they speak only of the pleasure of the moment, the frank joy in songs and wine and roses, at a vintage-revel, or in the chartered licence of a public festival, or simply without any excuse but the fire in the blood, and without any conclusion but the emptied jar.[4] Some bring in a flash of more vivid colour where Eros mingles with Bromius, and, on a bright spring day, Rose-flower crosses the path, carrying her fresh-blown roses.[5] Others, through their light surface, show a deeper feeling, a claim half jestingly but half seriously made for dances and lyres and garlands as things deeply ordained in the system of nature, a call on the disconsolate lover to be up and drink, and rear his drooping head, and not lie down in the dust while he is yet alive.[6] Some in complete seriousness put the argument for happiness with the full force of logic and sarcasm. "All the ways of life are pleasant," cries Julianus in reply to the weariness expressed by an earlier poet;[7] "in country or town, alone or among fellow-men, dowered with the graciousness of wife and children, or living on in the free and careless life of youth; all is well, live!" And the answer to melancholy has never been put in a concrete form with finer and more penetrating wit than in the couplet of Lucian on the man who must needs be sober when all were drinking, and so appeared in respect of his company to be the one drunk man there.[8]

It is here that the epigrams of comedy reach their high-water mark; in contrast to them is another class in which the lightness is a little forced and the humour touches cynicism. In these the natural brutality of the Roman mind makes the Latin epigram heavier and keener-pointed; the greater number indeed of the Greek epigrams of this complexion are of the Roman period; and many of them appear to be directly imitated from Martial and Juvenal, though possibly in some cases it is the Latin poet who is the copyist.

Though they are not actually kept separate—nor indeed would a complete separation be possible—the heading of this section of the Palatine Anthology distinguishes the {sumpotika}, the epigrams of youth and pleasure, from the {skoptika}, the witty or humorous verses which have accidentally in modern English come almost to absorb the full signification of the word epigram. The latter come principally under two heads: one, where the point of the epigram depends on an unexpected verbal turn, the other, where the humour lies in some gross exaggeration of statement. Or these may be combined; in some of the best there is an accumulation of wit, a second and a third point coming suddenly on the top of the first.[9]

Perhaps the saying, so often repeated, that ancient humour was simpler than modern, rests on a more sufficient basis than most similar generalisations; and indeed there is no single criterion of the difference between one age and another more easy and certain of application, where the materials for applying it exist, than to compare the things that seem amusing to them. A certain foundation of humour seems to be the common inheritance of mankind, but on it different periods build differently. The structure of a Greek joke is generally very simple; more obvious and less highly elliptical in thought than the modern type, but, on the other hand, considerably more subtle than the wit of the middle ages. There was a store of traditional jests on the learned professions, law, astrology, medicine —the last especially; and the schools of rhetoric and philosophy were, from their first beginning, the subject of much pleasantry. Any popular reputation, in painting, music, literature, gave material for facetious attack; and so did any bodily defect, even those, it must be added, which we think of now as exciting pity or as to be passed over in silence.[10] Many of these jokes, which even then may have been of immemorial antiquity, are still current. The serpent that bit a Cappadocian and died of it, the fashionable lady whose hair is all her own, and paid for,[11] are instances of this simple form of humour that has no beginning nor end. Some Greek jests have an Irish inconsequence, some the grave and logical monstrosity of American humour.

Naïve, crude, often vulgar; such is the general impression produced by the mass of these lighter epigrams. The bulk of them are of late date; and the culture of the ancient world was running low when its /vers de société/ reached no higher level than this. Of course they can only be called poetry by a large stretch of courtesy. In a few instances the work is raised to the level of art by a curious Dutch fidelity and minute detail. In one given in this selection,[12] a great poet has bent to this light and trivial style. The high note of Simonides is as clear and certain here as in his lines on the Spartans at Thermopylae or in the cry of grief over the young man dead in the snow-clogged surf of the Saronic sea. With such exceptions, the only touch of poetry is where a graver note underlies their light insolence. "Drink with me," runs the Greek song, "be young with me; love with me, wear garlands with me; be mad with me in my madness; I will be serious with you in your seriousness."[13] And so behind the flutes and flowers change comes and the shadow of fate stands waiting, and through the tinkling of the rose-hung river is heard in undertone the grave murmur of the sea. ———

[1] /Omnem vitae imaginem expressit . . . omnibus rebus, personis, adfectibus accomodatus/: see the whole passage, Inst. Rhet. x. i. 69-72.

[2] Anth. Pal. xi. 286.

[3] Ibid. xi. 438, 439.

[4] Ibid. v. 134, 135; xi. 1.

[5] Ibid. v. 81; xi. 64.

[6] Anth. Pal. ix. 270; xii. 50.

[7] Ibid. ix. 446.

[8] Ibid. xi. 429.

[9] Cf. ibid. xi. 85, 143.
[10] Cf. Anth. Pal. xi. 342, 404.
[11] Ibid. xi. 68, 237.
[12] Infra, x. 5.
[13] Athenaeus, 695, d.

XIII

For over all Greek life there lay a shadow. Man, a weak and pitiable creature, lay exposed to the shafts of a grim and ironic power that went its own way careless of him, or only interfered to avenge its own slighted majesty. "God is always jealous and troublesome"; such is the reflection which Herodotus, the pious historian of a pious age, puts in the mouth of the wisest of the Greeks.[1] Punishment will sooner or later follow sin; that is certain; but it is by no means so certain that the innocent will not be involved with the guilty, or that offence will not be taken where none was meant. The law of /laesa majestas/ was executed by the ruling powers of the universe with unrelenting and undiscriminating severity. Fate seemed to take a sardonic pleasure in confounding expectation, making destruction spring out of apparent safety, and filling life with dramatic and memorable reversals of fortune.

And besides the bolts launched by fate, life was as surely if more slowly weighed down by the silent and ceaseless tide of change against which nothing stood fixed or permanent, and which swept the finest and most beautiful things away the soonest. The garland that blooms at night withers by morning; and the strength of man and the beauty of women are no longer-lived than the frail anemone, the lily and violet that flower and fall.[2] Sweetness is changed to bitterness; where the rose has spread her cup, one goes by and the brief beauty passes; returning, the seeker finds no rose, but a thorn. Swifter than the flight of a bird through the air the light-footed Hours pass by, leaving nothing but scattered petals and the remembrance of youth and spring.[3] The exhortation to use the brief space of life, to realise, and, so far as that may be, to perpetuate in action the whole of the overwhelming possibilities crowded into a minute's space[4] comes with a passion like that of Shakespeare's sonnets. "On this short day of frost and sun to sleep before evening" is the one intolerable misuse of life.[5] Sometimes the feeling is expressed with the vivid passion of a lyric:—"To what profit? for thou wilt not find a lover among the dead, O girl";[6] sometimes with the curiously impersonal and incomparably direct touch that is peculiar to Greek, as in the verses by Antipater of Sidon,[7] that by some delicate magic crowd into a few words the fugitive splendour of the waning year, the warm lingering days and sharp nights of autumn, and the brooding pause before the rigours of winter, and make the whole masque of the seasons a pageant and metaphor of the lapse of life itself. Or a later art finds in the harsh moralisation of ancient legends the substance of sermons on the emptiness of pleasure and the fragility of loveliness; and the bitter laugh over the empty casket of Pandora[8] comes from a heart wrung with the sorrow that beauty is less strong than time. Nor is the burden of these poems only that pleasant things decay; rather that in nothing good or bad, rich or mean, is there permanence or certitude, but everywhere and without selection Time feeds oblivion with decay of things. All things flow and nothing abides; shape and name, nature and fortune yield to the dissolving touch of time.[9]

Even then the world was old. The lamentations over decayed towns and perished empires remind us that the distance which separates the age of the Caesars from our own is in relation to human history merely a chapter somewhere in the middle of a great volume. Then, no less than now, men trod daily over the ruins of old civilisations and the monuments of lost races. One of the most striking groups of poems in the Anthology is the long roll of the burdens of dead cities; Troy, Delos, Mycenae, Argos, Amphipolis,

Corinth, Sparta.[10] The depopulation of Greece brought with it a foreshadowing of the wreck of the whole ancient world. With the very framework of human life giving way daily before their eyes, men grew apt to give up the game. The very instability of all things, once established as a law, brought a sort of rest and permanence with it; "there is nothing strictly immutable," they might have said, "but mutability." Thus the law of change became a permanent thread in mortal affairs, and, with the knowledge that all the old round would be gone over again by others, grew the sense that in the acceptance of this law of nature there was involved a conquest of nature, an overcoming of the world.

For the strength of Fate was not otherwise to be contended with, and its grim irony went deeper than human reach. Nemesis was merciless; an error was punished like a crime, and the more confident you had been that you were right, the most severe was the probable penalty. But it was part of Fate's malignity that, though the offender was punished, though Justice took care that her own interests were not neglected nor her own majesty slighted, even where a humane judge would have shrunk from inflicting a disproportionate penalty,[11] yet for the wronged one himself she provided no remedy; he suffered at his own risk. For falseness in friendship, for scorn of poverty, for wanton cruelty and torture, the wheel of fortune brought round some form of retribution, but the sufferers were like pieces swept off the board, once and for all.

And Fate seemed to take a positive pleasure in eluding anticipation and constructing dramatic surprises. Through all Greek literature this feeling shows itself; and later epigrams are full of incidents of this sort, recounted and moralised over with the wearisomeness of a tract, stories sometimes obviously invented with an eye to the moral, sometimes merely silly, sometimes, though rarely, becoming imaginative. The contrast of a youth without means to indulge its appetites and an age without appetites to exhaust its means; the story of the poor man who found treasure and the rich man who hanged himself; the fable of the vine's revenge upon the goat, are typical instances of the prosaic epigram.[12] The noble lines inscribed upon the statue of Memnon at Thebes[13] are an example of the vivid imaginative touch lighting up a sufficiently obvious theme for the rhetorician. Under the walls of Troy, long ages past, the son of Dawn had fallen under Achilles' terrible spear; yet now morning by morning the goddess salutes her son and he makes answer, while Thetis is childless in her sea-halls, and the dust of Achilles moulders silently in the Trojan plain. The Horatian maxim of /nulli satis cautum/ recurs in the story of the ship, that had survived its sea-perils, burnt at last as it lay on shore near its native forest, and finding the ocean less faithless than the land.[14] In a different vein is the sarcastic praise of Fortune for her exaltation of a worthless man to high honour, "that she might shew her omnipotence."[15] At the root of all there is the sense, born of considering the flux of things and the tyranny of time, that man plays a losing game, and that his only success is in refusing to play. For the busy and idle, for the fortunate and unhappy alike, the sun rises one morning for the last time;[16] he only is to be congratulated who is done with hope and fear;[17] how short-lived soever he be in comparison with the world through which he passes, yet no less through time Fate dries up the holy springs, and the mighty cities of old days are undecipherable under the green turf;[18] it is the only wisdom to acquiesce in the forces, however ignorant or malign in their working, that listen to no protest and admit no appeal, that no force can affect, no subtlety elude, no calculation predetermine. ———

[1] {to theion pan phthoneron te kai tarakhodes}, Hdt. i. 32.

[2] Anth. Pal. v. 74, 118.

[3] Ibid. xi. 53; xii. 32, 234.

[4] Anth. Pal. vii. 472.

[5] Ibid. xi. 25; xii. 50.

[6] Ibid. v. 85.
[7] Ibid. xi. 37.
[8] Ibid. x. 71.
[9] Ibid. ix. 51.
[10] Ibid. vii. 705, 723; ix. 28, 101-4, 151-6, 408.
[11] Anth. Pal. ix. 269.
[12] Ibid. ix. 138, 44, 75.
[13] ix. 19 in this selection.
[14] Anth. Pal. ix. 106.
[15] Ibid. ix. 530.
[16] Ibid. ix. 8.
[17] Ibid. ix. 172; xi. 282.
[18] Ibid. ix. 101, 257.

XIV

Of these prodigious natural forces the strongest and the most imposing is Death. Here, if anywhere, the Greek genius had its fullest scope and most decisive triumph; and here it is that we come upon the epigram in its inmost essence and utmost perfection. "Waiting to see the end" as it always did, the Greek spirit pronounced upon the end when it came with a swiftness, a tact, a certitude that leave all other language behind. For although Latin and not Greek is pre-eminently and without rival the proper and, one might almost say, the native language of monumental inscription, yet the little difference that fills inscriptions with imagination and beauty, and will not be content short of poetry, is in the Greek temper alone. The Roman sarcophagus, square hewn of rock, and bearing on it, incised for immortality, the haughty lines of rolling Republican names, represents to us with unequalled power the abstract majesty of human States and the glory of law and government; and the momentary pause in the steady current of the life of Rome, when one citizen dropped out of rank and another succeeded him, brings home to us with crushing effect, like some great sentence of Tacitus, the brief and transitory worth of a single life. /Qui apicem gessisti, mors perfecit tua ut essent omnia brevia, honos fama virtusque, gloria atque ingenium/[1]—words like these have a melancholy majesty that no other human speech has known; nor can any greater depth of pathos be reached than is in the two simple words /Bene merenti/ on a hundred Roman tombs. But the Greek mind here as elsewhere came more directly than any other face to face with the truth of things, and the Greek genius kindled before the vision of life and death into a clearer flame. The sepulchural reliefs show us many aspects of death; in all of the best period there is a common note, mingled of a grave tenderness, simplicity, and reserve. The quiet figures there take leave of one another with the same grace that their life had shown. There is none of the horror of darkness, none of the ugliness of dying; with calm faces and undisordered raiment they rise from their seats and take the last farewell. But the sepulchural verses show us more clearly how deep the grief was that lay beneath the quiet lines of the marble and the smooth cadence of the couplets. They cover and fill the whole range of emotion: household grief, and pain for the dead baby or the drowned lover, and the bitter parting of wife and husband, and the chill of distance and the doubt of the unknown nether world; and the thoughts of the bright and brief space of life, and the merciless continuity of nature, and the resolution of body and soul into the elements from which they came; and the uselessness of Death's impatience, and the bitter cry of a life gone like spilt water; and again, comfort out of the grave, perpetual placidity, "holy sleep," and earth's gratitude to her children, and beyond all, dimly and lightly drawn, the flowery meadows of Persephone, the great simplicity and rest of the other world, and far away a shadowy and beautiful country to which later men were to give the name of Heaven.

The famous sepulchral epigrams of Simonides deserve a word to themselves; for in them, among the most finished achievements of the greatest period of Greece, the art not only touches its highest recorded point, but a point beyond which it seems inconceivable that art should go. They stand with the odes of Pindar and the tragedies of Sophocles as the symbols of perfection in literature; not only from the faultlessness of their form, but from their greatness of spirit, the noble and simple thought that had then newly found itself so perfect a language to commemorate the great deeds which it inspired. Foremost among them are those on the men whose fame they can hardly exalt beyond the place given them by history; on the three hundred of Thermopylae, the Athenian dead at Marathon, the Athenian and Lacedaemonian dead at Plataea.[2] "O stranger, tell the Lacedaemonians that we lie here obeying their orders"—the words have grown so famous that it is only by sudden flashes that we can appreciate their greatness. No less noble are others somewhat less widely known: on the monument erected by the city of Corinth to the men who, when all Greece stood as near destruction as a knife's edge, helped to win her freedom at Salamis; on the Athenians, slain under the skirts of the Euboean hills, who lavished their young and beautiful lives for Athens; on the soldiers who fell, in the full tide of the Greek glory, at the great victory of the Eurymedon.[3] In all the epitaphs of this class the thought of the city swallows up individual feeling; for the city's sake, that she may be free and great, men offer their death as freely as their life; and the noblest end for a life spent in her service is to die in the moment of her victory. The funeral speech of Pericles dwells with all the amplitude of rhetoric on the glory of such a death; "having died they are not dead" are the simpler words of Simonides.[4]

Not less striking than these in their high simplicity are his epitaphs on private persons: that which preserves the fame of the great lady who was not lifted up to pride, Archedice daughter of Hippias; that on Theognis of Sinope, so piercing and yet so consoling in its quiet pathos, or that on Brotachus of Gortyn, the trader who came after merchandise and found death; the dying words of Timomachus and the eternal memory left to his father day by day of the goodness and wisdom of his dead child; the noble apostrophe to mount Gerania, where the drowned and nameless sailor met his doom, the first and one of the most magnificent of the long roll of poems on seafarers lost at sea.[5] In all of them the foremost quality is their simplicity of statement. There are no superlatives. The emotion is kept strictly in the background, neither expressed nor denied. Great minds of later ages sought a justification of the ways of death in denying that it brought any reasonable grief. To the cold and profound thought of Marcus Aurelius death is "a natural thing, like roses in spring or harvest in autumn."[6] But these are the words of a strange language. The feeling of Simonides is not, like theirs, abstract and remote; he offers no justification, because none is felt to be needed where the pain of death is absorbed in the ardour of life.

That great period passed away; and in those which follow it, the sepulchural inscription, while it retains the old simplicity, descends from those heights into more common feelings, lets loose emotion, even dallies with the ornaments of grief. The sorrow of death is spoken of freely; nor is there any poetry more pathetic than those epitaphs which, lovely in their sadness, commemorate the lost child, the sundered lovers, the disunited life. Among the most beautiful are those on children: on the baby that just lived, and, liking it not, went away again before it had known good or evil;[7] on the children of a house all struck down in one day and buried in one grave;[8] on the boy whom his parents could not keep, though they held both his little hands in theirs, led downward by the Angel of Death to the unsmiling land.[9] Then follows the keener sadness of the young life, spared till it opened into flower only to be cut down before noon; the girl who, sickening for her baby-brother, lost care for her playmates, and found no peace till she went to rejoin him;[10] the boy of twelve, with whom his father, adding no words of lamentation, lays his whole hope in the grave;[11] the cry of the mourning mother over her son, Bianor or Anticles, an only child laid on the funeral pyre before an only parent's eyes, leaving dawn thenceforth disadorned of her sweetness, and no comfort in the sun.[12] More piercing still in their sad sweetness are the epitaphs on young wives; on Anastasia, dead at sixteen, in the first year of her marriage, over whom the ferryman of the dead must needs mingle his own with her father's and her husband's tears; on Atthis of Cnidos, the wife who had never left her husband till this the first and last sundering came; on Paulina of Ravenna, holy of life and blameless, the young bride of the physician whose skill could not save her, but whose last testimony to her virtues has survived the wreck of the centuries that have made the city crumble and the very sea retire.[13] The tender feeling for children mingles with the bitter grief at their loss, a touch of fancy, as though they were flowers plucked by Persephone to be worn by her and light up the greyness of the underworld. Cleodicus, dead before the festival of this third birthday, when the child's hair was cut and he became a boy, lies in his little coffin; but somewhere by unknown Acheron a shadow of him grows fair and strong in youth, though he never may return to earth again.[14]

With the grief for loss comes the piercing cry over crushed beauty. One of the early epitaphs, written before the period of the Persian wars, is nothing but this cry: "pity him who was so beautiful and is dead."[15] In the same spirit is the fruitless appeal so often made over the haste of Death; /mais que te nuysoit elle en vie, mort?/ Was he not thine, even had he died an old man? says the mourner over Attalus.[16] A subject whose strange fascination drew artist after artist to repeat it, and covered the dreariness of death as with a glimmer of white blossoms, was Death the Bridegroom, the maiden taken away from life just as it was about to be made complete. Again and again the motive is treated with delicate profusion of detail, and lingering fancy draws out the sad likeness between the two torches that should hold such a space of lovely life between them,[17] now crushed violently together and mingling their fires. Already the bride-bed was spread with saffron in the gilded chamber; already the flutes were shrill by the doorway, and the bridal torches were lit, when Death entered, masked as a reveller, and the hymeneal song suddenly changed into the death-dirge; and while the kinsfolk were busy about another fire, Persephone lighted her own torch out of their hands; with hardly an outward change—as in a processional relief on a sarcophagus—the bridal train turns and moves to the grave with funeral lights flaring through the darkness and sobbing voices and wailing flutes.[18]

As tender in their fancy and with a higher note of sincerity in their grief are the epitaphs on young mothers, dead in childbirth: Athenaïs of Lesbos, the swift-footed, whose cry Artemis was too busy with her woodland hounds to hear; Polyxena, wife of Archelus, not a year's wife nor a month's mother, so short was all her time; Prexo, wife of Theocritus, who takes her baby with her, content with this, and gives blessings from her grave to all who will pray with her that the boy she leaves on earth may live into a great old age.[19] Here tenderness outweighs sorrow; in others a bitterer grief is uttered, the grief of one left alone, forsaken and cast off by all that had made life sweet; where the mother left childless among women has but the one prayer left, that she too may quickly go whence she came, or where the morbid imagination of a mourner over many deaths invents new forms of self-torture in the idea that her very touch is mortal to those whom she loves, and that fate has made her the instrument of its cruelty; or where Theano, dying alone in Phocaea, sends a last cry over the great gulfs of sea that divide her from her husband, and goes down into the night with the one passionate wish that she might have but died with her hand clasped in his hand.[20]

Into darkness, into silence: the magnificent brilliance of that ancient world, its fulness of speech and action, its copiousness of life, made the contrast more sudden and appalling; and it seems to be only at a later period, when the brightness was a little dimmed and the tide of life did not run so full, that the feeling grew up which regarded death as the giver of rest. With a last word of greeting to the bright earth the dying man departs, as into a mist.[21] In the cold shadows underground the ghost will not be comforted by ointments and garlands lavished on the tomb; though the clay covering be drenched with wine, the dead man will not drink.[22] On an island of the Aegean, set like a gem in the splendid sea, the boy lying under earth, far away from the sweet sun, asks a word of pity from those who go up and down, busy in the daylight, past his grave. Paula of Tarentum, the brief-fated, cries out passionately of the stone chambers of her night, the night that has hidden her. Samian girls set up a monument over their playfellow Crethis, the chatterer, the story-teller, whose lips will never open in speech again. Musa, the singing-girl, blue-eyed and sweet-voiced, suddenly lies voiceless, like a stone.[23] With a jarring shock, as of closed gates, the grave closes over sound and colour; /moved round in Earth's diurnal course with rocks, and stones, and trees./

Even thus there is some little comfort in lying under known earth; and the strangeness of a foreign grave adds a last touch to the pathos of exile. The Eretrians, captured by the Persian general Datis, and sent from their island home by endless marches into the heart of Asia, pine in the hot Cassian plains, and with their last voice from the tomb send out a greeting to the dear and distant sea.[24] The Athenian laid in earth by the far reaches of Nile, and the Egyptian whose tomb stands by a village of Crete, though from all places the descent to the house of Hades is one, yet grieve and fret at their strange resting-places.[25] No bitterer pang can be added to death than for the white bones of the dead to lie far away, washed by chill rains, or mouldering on a strange beach with the screaming seagulls above them.[26]

This last aspect of death was the one upon which the art of the epigrammatist lavished its utmost resources. From first to last the Greeks were a seafaring people, and death at sea was always present to them as a common occurrence. The Mediterranean was the great highway of the world's journeying and traffic. All winter through, travel almost ceased on it except for those who could not avoid it, and whom desire or gain or urgence of business drove forth across stormy and perilous waters; with spring there came, year by year, a sort of breaking-up of the frost, and the seas were all at once covered with a swarm of shipping. From Egypt and Syria fleets bore the produce of the East westward; from the pillars of Hercules galleys came laden with the precious ores of Spain and Britain; through the Propontis streamed the long convoys of corn-ships from the Euxine with their loads of wheat. Across the Aegean from island to island, along its shores from port to port, ran continually the tide of local commerce, the crowds of tourists and emigrants, the masses of people and merchandise drawn hither and thither in the track of armies, or bound to and from shows and festivals and markets. The fishing industry, at least in the later Greek period, employed the whole population of small islands and seaside towns. Among those thousands of vessels many must, every year, have come to harm in those difficult channels and treacherous seas. And death at sea had a great horror and anguish attached to it; the engulfing in darkness, the vain struggles for life, the loss of burial rites and all the last offices that can be paid to death, made it none the less terrible that it was so common. From the Odyssey downward tales of sea-peril and shipwreck had the most powerful fascination. Yet to that race of sailors the sea always remained in a manner hateful; "as much as a mother is sweeter than a stepmother," says Antipater,[27] "so much is earth dearer than the dark sea." The fisherman tossing on the waves looked back with envy to the shepherd, who, though his life was no less hard, could sit in quiet piping to his flock on the green hillside; the great merchantman who crossed the whole length of the Mediterranean on his traffic, or even ventured out beyond Calpe into the unknown ocean, hungered for the peace of broad lands, the lowing of herds.[28] /Cedet et ipse mari vector, nec nautica pinus mutabit merces/: all dreams of a golden age, or of an ideal life in an actual world, included in them the release from this weary and faithless element. Even in death it would not allow its victims rest; the cry of the drowned man is that though kind hands have given him burial on the beach, even there the ceaseless thunder of the surge is in his ears, and the roar of the surf under the broken reef will not let him be quiet; "keep back but twelve feet from me," is his last prayer, "and there billow and roar as much as thou wilt."[29] But even the grace of a tomb was often denied. In the desolation of unknown distances the sailor sank into the gulfs or was flung on a desert beach. Erasippus, perished with his ship, has all the ocean for his grave; somewhere far away his white bones moulder on a spot that the seagulls alone can tell. Thymodes rears a cenotaph to his son, who on some Bithynian beach or island of the Pontic lies a naked corpse on an inhospitable shore. Young Seleucus, wrecked in the distant Atlantic, has long been dead on the trackless Spanish coasts, while yet at home in Lesbos they praise him and look forward to his return. On the thirsty uplands of Dryopia the empty earth is heaped up that does not cover Polymedes, tossed up and down far from stony Trachis on the surge of the Icarian sea. "Also thee, O Cleanoridas," one abruptly opens, the thought of all those many others whom the sea had swallowed down overwhelming him as he tells the fate of the drowned man.[30] The ocean never forgot its cruelty. {Pasa thalassa thalassa}, "everywhere the sea is the sea," wails Aristagoras,[31] past the perilous Cyclades and the foaming narrows of the Hellespont only to be drowned in a little Locrian harbour; the very sound of the words echoes the heavy wash of blind waves and the hissing of eternal foam. Already in sight of home, like Odysseus on his voyage from Aeolia, the sailor says to himself, "to-morrow the long battle against contrary winds will be over," when the storm gathers as the words leave his lips, and he is swept back to death.[32] The rash mariner who trusts the gale of winter draws fate on himself with his own hands; Cleonicus, hastening home to Thasos with his merchandise from Hollow Syria at the setting of the Pleiad, sinks with the sinking star.[33] But even in the days of the halcyons, when the sea should stand like a sheet of molten glass, the terrible straits swallow Aristomenes, with ship and crew; and Nicophemus perishes, not in wintry waves, but of thirst in a calm on the smooth and merciless Lybian sea.[34] By harbours and headlands stood the graves of drowned men with pathetic words of warning or counsel. "I am the tomb of one shipwrecked"; in these words again and again the verses begin. What follows is sometimes an appeal to others to take example: "let him have only his own hardihood to blame, who looses moorings from my grave"; sometimes it is a call to courage: "I perished; yet even then other ships sailed safely on." Another, in words incomparable for their perfect pathos and utter simplicity, neither counsels nor warns: "O mariners, well be with you at sea and on land; but know that you pass the tomb of a shipwrecked man." And in the same spirit another sends a blessing out of his nameless tomb: "O sailor, ask not whose grave I am, but be thine own fortune a kinder sea."[35]

Beyond this simplicity and pathos cannot reach. But there is a group of three epigrams yet unmentioned[36] which, in their union of these qualities with the most severe magnificence of language and with the poignant and vivid emotion of a tragical Border ballad, reach an even more amazing height: that where Ariston of Cyrene, lying dead by the Icarian rocks, cries out in passionate urgency on mariners who go sailing by to tell Meno how his son perished; that where the tomb of Biton in the morning sun, under the walls of Torone, sends a like message by the traveller to the childless father, Nicagoras of Amphipolis; and most piercing of all in their sorrow and most splendid in their cadences, the stately lines that tell the passer-by of Polyanthus, sunk off Sciathus in the stormy

Aegean, and laid in his grave by the young wife to whom only a dead body was brought home by the fishermen as they sailed into harbour under a flaring and windy dawn.

Less numerous than these poems of sea-sorrow, but with the same trouble of darkness, the same haunting chill, are others where death comes through the gloom of wet nights, in the snowstorm or the thunderstorm or the autumn rains that drown the meadow and swell the ford. The contrast of long golden summer days may perhaps make the tidings of death more pathetic, and wake a more delicate pity; but the physical horror, as in the sea-pieces, is keener at the thought of lonely darkness, and storm in the night. Few pictures can be more vivid than that of the oxen coming unherded down the hill through the heavy snow at dusk, while high on the mountain side their master lies dead, struck by lightning; or of Ion, who slipped overboard, unnoticed in the darkness, while the sailors drank late into night at their anchorage; or of the strayed revellers, Orthon and Polyxenus, who, bewildered in the rainy night, with the lights of the banquet still flaring in their eyes, stumbled on the slippery hill-path and lay dead at the foot of the cliff.[37]

/O Charides, what is there beneath?/ cries a passer-by over the grave of one who had in life nursed his hopes on the doctrine of Pythagoras; and out of the grave comes the sombre answer, /Great darkness/.[38] It is in this feeling that the brooding over death in later Greek literature issues; under the Roman empire we feel that we have left the ancient world and are on the brink of the Middle Ages with their half hysterical feeling about death, the piteous and ineffectual revolt against it, and the malign fascination with which it preys on men's minds and paralyses their action. To the sombre imagination of an exhausted race the generations of mankind were like bands of victims dragged one after another to the slaughter-house; in Palladas and his contemporaries the medieval dance of death is begun.[39] The great and simple view of death is wholly broken up, with the usual loss and gain that comes of analysis. On the one hand is developed this tremulous and cowardly shrinking from the law of nature. But on the other there arises in compensation the view of death as final peace, the release from trouble, the end of wandering, the resolution of the feverous life of man into the placid and continuous life of nature. With a great loss of strength and directness comes an increased measure of gentleness and humanity. Poetry loves to linger over the thought of peaceful graves. The dead boy's resting-place by the spring under the poplars bids the weary wayfarer turn aside and drink in the shade, and remember the quiet place when he is far away.[40] The aged gardener lies at peace under the land that he had laboured for many a year, and in recompence of his fruitful toil over vine and olive, corn-field and orchard-plot, grateful earth lies lightly over his grey temples, and the earliest flowers of spring blossom above his dust.[41] The lovely lines of Leonidas,[42] in which Clitagoras asks that when he is dead the sheep may bleat over him, and the shepherd pipe from the rock as they graze softly along the valley, and that the countryman in spring may pluck a posy of meadow flowers and lay it on his grave, have all the tenderness of an English pastoral in a land of soft outlines and silvery tones. An intenser feeling for nature and a more consoling peace is in the nameless poem that bids the hill-brooks and the cool upland pastures tell the bees, when they go forth anew on their flowery way, that their old keeper fell asleep on a winter night, and will not come back with spring.[43] The lines call to mind that magnificent passage of the /Adonais/ where the thought of earth's annual resurrection calms by its glory and beauty the very sorrow which it rekindles; as those others, where, since the Malian fowler is gone, the sweet plane again offers her branches "for the holy bird to rest his swift wings,"[44] are echoed in the famous Ode where the note of the immortal bird sets the listener in the darkness at peace with Death. The dying man leaves earth with a last kind word. At rest from long wanderings, the woman, whose early memory went back to the storming of Athens by Roman legionaries, and whose later life had passed from Italy to Asia, unites the lands of her birth and adoption and decease in her farewell.[45] For all ranks and ages—the baby gone to be a flower in Persephone's crowned hair, the young scholar, dear to men and dearer to the Muses, the great sage who, from the seclusion of his Alexandrian library, has seen three kings succeed to the throne[46]— the recompense of life is peace. Peace is on the graves of the good servant, the faithful nurse, the slave who does not even in the tomb forget his master's kindness or cease to help him at need.[47] Even the pets of the household, the dog or the singing-bird, or the caged cricket shouting through the warm day, have their reward in death, their slight memorial and their lasting rest. The shrill cicala, silent and no more looked on by the sun, finds a place in the meadows whose flowers the Queen of the Dead herself keeps bright with dew.[48] The sweet-throated song-bird, the faithful watch-dog who kept the house from harm, the speckled partridge in the coppice,[49] go at the appointed time upon their silent way—/ipsas angusti terminus aevi excipit/—and come into human sympathy because their bright life is taken to its rest like man's own in so brief a term.

Before this gentler view of death grief itself becomes softened. "Fare thou well even in the house of Hades," says the friend over the grave of the friend: the words are the same as those of Achilles over Patroclus, but all the wild anguish has gone out of them.[50] Over the ashes of Theognis of Sinope, without a word of sorrow, with hardly a pang of pain, Glaucus sets a stone in memory of the companionship of many years. And in the tenderest and most placid of epitaphs on dead friends doubt vanishes with grief and acquiescence passes into hope, as the survivor of that union "which conquers Time indeed, and is eternal, separate from fears," prays Sabinus, if it be permitted, not even among the dead to let the severing water of Lethe pass his lips.[51]

Out of peace comes the fruit of blessing. The drowned sailor rests the easier in his grave that the lines written over it bid better fortune to others who adventure the sea. "Go thou upon thy business and obtain thy desire,"[52] says the dead man to the passer-by, and the kind word makes the weight of his own darkness less to bear. Amazonia of Thessalonica from her tomb bids husband and children cease their lamentations and be only glad while they remember her.[53] Such recompense is in death that the dead sailor or shepherd becomes thenceforth the genius of the shore or the hillside.[54] The sacred sleep under earth sends forth a vague and dim effluence; in a sort of trance between life and death the good still are good and do not wholly cease out of being.[55]

For the doctrine of immortality did not dawn upon the world at any single time or from any single quarter. We are accustomed, perhaps, to think of it as though it came like sunrise out of the dark, /lux sedentibus in tenebris/, giving a new sense to mankind and throwing over the whole breadth of life a vivid severance of light from shadow, putting colour and sharp form into what had till then all lain dim in the dusk, like Virgil's woodland path under the glimpses of a fitful moon. Rather it may be compared to those scattered lights that watchers from Mount Ida were said to discern moving hither and thither in the darkness, and at last slowly gathering and kindling into the clear pallor of dawn.[56] So it is that those half-formed beliefs, those hints and longings, still touch us with the freshness of our own experience. For the ages of faith, if such there be, have not yet come; still in the mysterious glimmer of a doubtful light men wait for the coming of the unrisen sun. During a brief and brilliant period the splendour of corporate life had absorbed the life of the citizen; an Athenian of the age of Pericles may have, for the moment, found Athens all-sufficient to his needs. With the decay of that glory it became plain that this single life was insufficient, that it failed in permanence and simplicity. We all dwell in a single native country, the universe, said Meleager,[57] expressing a feeling that had become the common heritage of his race. But that country, as men saw it, was but ill governed; and in nothing more so than in the rewards and punishments it gave to its citizens. To regard it as the vestibule only of another country where life should have its intricacies simplified, its injustices remedied, its evanescent beauty fixed, and its brief joy made full, became an imperious instinct that claimed satisfaction, through definite religious teaching or the dreams of philosophy or the visions of poetry. And so the last words of Greek sepulchral poetry express, through questions and doubts, in metaphor and allegory, the final belief in some blessedness beyond death. Who knows whether to live be not death, and to be dead life? so the haunting hope begins. The Master of the Portico died young; does he sleep in the quiet embrace of earth, or live in the joy of the other world?[58] "Even in life what makes each one of us to be what we are is only the soul; and when we are dead, the bodies of the dead are rightly said to be our shades or images; for the true and immortal being of each one of us, which is called the soul, goes on her way to other gods, that before them she may give an account."[59] These are the final words left to men by that superb and profound genius the dream of whose youth had ended in the flawless lines[60] whose music Shelley's own could scarcely render:

   Thou wert the Morning Star among the living
   Ere thy fair light was fled;
 Now, having died, thou art as Hesperus, giving
   New splendour to the dead.

And at last, not from the pen of Plato nor written in lines of gold, but set by a half-forgotten friend over an obscure grave,[61] comes the certitude of that long hope. Heliodorus and Diogeneia died on the same day and are buried under the same stone: but love admits no such bar to its continuance, and the tomb is as a bridal chamber for their triumphant life. ———

[1] From the inscription on the tomb of Publius Cornelius Scipio Africanus, Augur and Flamen Dialis, son of the conqueror of Hannibal.

[2] Anth. Pal. vii. 249, 251, 253; Aristides, ii. 511.

[3] Aristides, ii. 512; App. Plan. 26; Anth. Pal. vii. 258.

[4] Anth. Pal. vii. 251; Thuc. ii. 41-43.

[5] Thuc. vi. 59; Anth. Pal. vii. 509, 254, 513, 496.

[6] Marc. Aur. iv. 44.

[7] Kaibel, 576.

[8] Anth. Pal. vii. 474.

[9] iii. 33 in this selection.

[10] Anth. Pal. vii. 662.

[11] Ibid. vii. 453.

[12] Ibid. vii. 261, 466.

[13] Ibid. vii. 600; Kaibel, 204 B, 596.

[14] Anth. Pal. vii. 482, 483.

[15] Kaibel, 1 A.

[16] Anth. Pal. vii. 671.

[17] Propertius, IV. xii. 46.

[18] Anth. Pal. vii. 182, 185, 711, 712.

[19] Ibid. vi. 438, vii. 167, 163.

[20] Ibid. vii. 466, ix. 254, vii. 735.

[21] Anth. Pal. vii. 566.

[22] Ibid. xi. 8.

[23] Kaibel, 190; Anth. Pal. vii. 700, 459; C. I. G., 6261.

[24] Anth. Pal. vii. 256, 259.

[25] Ibid. vii. 477, x. 3.
[26] Ibid. vii. 225, 285.
[27] Anth. Pal. ix. 23.
[28] Anth. Pal. vii. 636, ix. 7; cf. Virgil, Georg. ii. 468-70.
[29] Ibid. vii. 284.
[30] Ibid. vii. 285, 497, 376, 651, 263.
[31] Ibid. vii. 639.
[32] Ibid. vii. 630.
[33] Anth. Pal. vii. 263, 534.
[34] Ibid. ix. 271, vii. 293.
[35] Ibid. vii. 264, 282, 675; 269, 350.
[36] Ibid. vii. 499, 502, 739.
[37] Anth. Pal. vii. 173, ix. 82, vii. 398, 660.
[38] Ibid. vii. 524.
[39] Cf. Ibid. x. 78, 85, 88, xi. 300.
[40] Anth. Pal. ix. 315.
[41] Ibid. vii. 321.
[42] Ibid. vii. 657. The spirit, and much of the language, of these epigrams is very like that of Gray's /Elegy/.
[43] Ibid. vii. 717.
[44] Ibid. vii. 171.
[45] Ibid. vii. 368.
[46] Anth. Pal. 78, 483; Diog. Laert. iv. 25.
[47] Ibid. vii. 178, 179; Kaibel, 47.
[48] Ibid. vii. 189.
[49] Ibid. vii. 199, 211, 203.
[50] Il. xxiii. 19; Anth. Pal. vii. 41.
[51] Ibid. vii. 509, 346.
[52] Kaibel, 190.
[53] Anth. Pal. vii. 667.
[54] Ibid. vii. 269, 657.
[55] Ibid. vii. 451.
[56] Lucr. v. 663.
[57] Anth. Pal. vii. 417.
[58] Infra, xi. 7.
[59] Plato, /Laws/, 959.
[60] Anth. Pal. vii. 670.
[61] Ibid. vii. 378, {agallomenoi kai taphon os thalamon}.

XV

Criticism, to be made effectively, must be made from beyond and outside the thing criticised. But as regards life itself, such an effort of abstraction is more than human. For the most part poetry looks on life from a point inside it, and the total view differs, or may even be reversed, with the position of the observer. The shifting of perspective makes things appear variously both in themselves and in their proportion to other things. What lies behind one person is before another; the less object, if nearer, may eclipse the greater; where there is no fixed standard of reference, how can it be determined what is real and what apparent, or whether there be any absolute fact at all? To some few among men it has been granted to look on life as it were from without, with vision unaffected by the limit of view and the rapid shifting of place. These, the poets who see life steadily and whole, in Matthew Arnold's celebrated phrase, are for the rest of mankind almost divine. We recognise them as such through a sort of instinct awakened by theirs and responding to it, through the inarticulate divinity of which we are all in some degree partakers.

These are the great poets; and we do not look, in any Anthology of slight and fugitive pieces, for so broad and sustained a view of life. But what we do find in the Anthology is the reflection in many epigrams of many partial criticisms from within; the expression, in the most brief and pointed form, of the total effect that life had on one man or another at certain moments, whether in the heat of blood, or the first melancholy of youth, or the graver regard of mature years. In nearly all the same sad note recurs, of the shortness of life, of the inevitableness of death. Now death is the shadow at the feast, bidding men make haste to drink before the cup is snatched from their lips with its sweetness yet undrained; again it is the bitterness within the cup itself, the lump of salt dissolving in the honeyed wine and spoiling the drink. Then comes the revolt against the cruel law of Nature in the crude thought of undisciplined minds. Sometimes this results in hard cynicism, sometimes in the relaxation of all effort; now and then the bitterness grows so deep that it almost takes the quality of a real philosophy, a nihilism, to use the barbarous term of our own day, that declares itself as a positive solution of the whole problem. "Little is the life of our rejoicing," cries Rufinus,[1] in the very words of an English ballad of the fifteenth century; "old age comes quickly, and death ends all." In many epigrams this burden is repeated. The philosophy is that of Ecclesiastes: "Go thy way, eat thy bread with joy, and drink thy wine with a merry heart, let thy garments be always white, and let thy head lack no ointment; see life with the wife whom thou lovest all the days of the life of thy vanity; for that is thy portion in life, and in thy labour which thou takest under the sun." If the irony here is unintentional it is all the bitterer; such consolation leads surely to a more profound gloom. With a selfish nature this view of life becomes degraded into cynical effrontery; under the Roman empire the lowest corruption of "good manners" took for its motto the famous words, repeated in an anonymous epigram,[2] Let us eat and drink, for to-morrow we die. In finer tempers it issues in a mood strangely mingled of weakness of will and lucidity of intelligence, like that of Omar Khayyam. Many of the stanzas of the Persian poet have a close parallel, not only in thought but in actual turn of phrase, in verses of the later epigrammatists.[3] The briefness of life when first realised makes youth feverish and self-absorbed. "Other men perhaps will be, but /I/ shall be dead and turned into black earth"—as though that were the one thing of importance.[4] Or again, the beauty of returning spring is felt in the blood as an imperious call to renew the delight in the simplest physical pleasures, food and scent of flowers and walks in the fresh country air, and to thrust away the wintry thought of dead friends who cannot share those delights now.[5] The earliest form taken by the instinct of self-preservation and the revolt against death can hardly be called by a milder name than swaggering. "I don't care," the young man cries,[6] with a sort of faltering bravado. Snatch the pleasure of the moment, such is the selfish instinct of man before his first imagination of life, and then, and then let fate do its will upon you.[7] Thereafter, as the first turbulence of youth passes, its first sadness succeeds, with the thought of all who have gone before and all who are to follow, and of the long night of silence under the ground. Touches of tenderness break in upon the reveller; thoughts of the kinship of earth, as the drinker lifts the sweet cup wrought of the same clay as he; submission to the lot of mortality; counsels to be generous while life lasts, "to give and to share"; the renunciation of gross ambitions such as wealth and power, with some likeness or shadow in it of the crowning virtue of humility.[8]

It is here that the change begins. To renounce something for the first time wittingly and spontaneously is an action of supreme importance, and its consequences reach over the whole of life. Not only is it that he who has renounced one thing has shown himself implicitly capable of renouncing all things: he has shown much more; reflection, choice, will. Thenceforth he is able to see part of life at all events from outside, the part which he has put away from himself; for the first time his criticism of life begins to be real. He has no longer a mere feeling with regard to the laws of nature, whether eager haste or sullen submission or blind revolt; behind the feeling there is now thought, the power which makes and unmakes all things.

And so in mature age Greek thought began to make criticisms on life; and of these the Anthology preserves and crystallises many brilliant fragments. Perhaps there is no thought among them which was even then original; certainly there is none which is not now more or less familiar. But the perfected expression without which thought remains obscure and ineffectual gives some of them a value as enduring as their charm. A few of them are here set side by side without comment, for no comment is needed to make their sense clear, nor to give weight to their grave and penetrating reality.[9]

"Those who have left the sweet light I mourn no longer, but those who live in perpetual expectation of death."

"What belongs to mortals is mortal, and all things pass by us; and if not, yet we pass by them."

"Now we flourish, as others did before, and others will presently, whose children we shall not see."

"I weep not for thee, dearest friend; for thou knewest much good; and likewise God dealt thee thy share of ill."

These epigrams in their clear and unimpassioned brevity are a type of the Greek temper in the age of reflection. Many others, less simple in their language, less crystalline in their structure, have the same quiet sadness in their tone. As it is said in the solemn and monumental line of Menander, sorrow and life are too surely akin.[10] The vanity of earthly labour; the deep sorrow over the passing of youth; the utter loss and annihilation of past time with all that it held of action and suffering; the bitterness of the fear of death, and the weariness of the clutch at life; such are among the thoughts of most frequent recurrence. In one view these are the commonplaces of literature; yet they are none the less the expression of the profoundest thought of mankind.

In Greek literature from first to last the view of life taken by the most serious thinkers was grave and sad. Not in one age or in one form of poetry alone, but in most that are of great import, the feeling that death was better than life is no mere caprice of melancholy, but a settled conviction. The terrible words of Zeus in the Iliad to the horses of Achilles,[11] "for there is nothing more pitiable than man, of all things that breathe and move on earth," represent the Greek criticism of life already mature and consummate. "Best of all is it for men not to be born," says Theognis in lines whose calm perfection has no trace of passion or resentment,[12] "and if born, to pass inside Hades-gates as quickly as may be." Echoing these lines of the Megarian poet, Sophocles at eighty, the most fortunate in his long and brilliant life of all his contemporaries in an age the most splendid that the world has ever witnessed, utters with the weight of a testamentory declaration the words that thrill us even now by their faultless cadence and majestic music;[13] "Not to be born excels on the whole account; and for him who has seen the light to go whence he came as soon as may be is next best by far." And in another line,[14] whose rhythm is the sighing of all the world made audible, "For there is no such pain," he says, "as length of life." So too the humane and accomplished Menander, in the most striking of all the fragments preserved from his world of comedies,[15] weighs and puts aside all the attractions that life can offer: "Him I call most happy who, having gazed without grief on these august things, the common sun, the stars, water, clouds, fire, goes quickly back whence he came." With so clear-sighted and so sombre a view of this life and with no certainty of another, it was only the inspiration of great thought and action, and the gladness of yet unexhausted youth, that sustained the ancient world so long. And this gladness of youth faded away. Throughout all the writing of the later classical period we feel one thing constantly; that life was without joy. Alike in history and poetry, alike in the Eastern and Western worlds, a settled gloom deepens into night. The one desire left is for rest. Life is brief, as men of old time said; but now there is scarcely a wish that it should be longer. "Little is thy life and afflicted," says Leonidas,[16] "and not even so is it sweet, but more bitter than loathed death." "Weeping I was born, and when I have done my weeping I die," another poet wails,[17] "and all my life is among many tears." Aesopus is in a strait betwixt two; if one might but escape from life without the horror of dying! for now it is only the revolt from death that keeps him in the anguish of life.[18] To Palladas of Alexandria the world is but a slaughter- house, and death is its blind and irresponsible lord.[19]

From the name of Palladas is inseparable the name of the famous Hypatia, and the strange history of the Neo-Platonic school. The last glimmer of light in the ancient world was from the embers of their philosophy. A few late epigrams preserve a record of their mystical doctrines, and speak in half-unintelligible language of "the one hope" that went among them, a veiled and crowned phantom, under the name of Wisdom. But, apart from those lingering relics of a faith among men half dreamers and half charlatans, patience and silence were the only two counsels left for the dying ancient world; patience, in which we imitate God himself; silence, in which all our words must soon end.[20] The Roman empire perished, it has been said, for want of men; Greek literature perished for want of anything to say; or rather, because it found nothing in the end worth saying. Its end was like that recorded of the noblest of the Roman emperors:[21] the last word uttered with its dying breath was the counsel of equanimity. Men had once been comforted for their own life and death in the thought of deathless memorials; now they had lost hope, and declared that no words and no gods could give immortality.[22] Resignation[23] was the one lesson left to ancient literature, and, this lesson once fully learned, it naturally and silently died. All know how the ages that followed were too preoccupied to think of writings its epitaph. For century after century Goth and Hun, Lombard and Frank, Bulgarian and Avar, Norman and Saracen, Catalan and Turk rolled on in a ceaseless storm of slaughter and rapine without; for century after century within raged no less fiercely the unending fury of the new theology. Filtered down through Byzantine epitomes, through Arabic translations, through every sort of strange and tortuous channel, a vague and distorted tradition of this great literature just survived long enough to kindle the imagination of the fifteenth century. The chance of history, fortunate perhaps for the whole world, swept the last Greek scholars away from Constantinople to the living soil of Italy, carrying with them the priceless relics of forgotten splendours. To some broken stones, and to the chance which saved a few hundred manuscripts from destruction, is due such knowledge as we have to-day of that Greek thought and life which still remains to us in many ways an unapproached ideal. ———

[1] Anth. Pal. v. 12; cf. the beautiful lyric with the refrain /Lytyll ioye is son done/ (Percy Society, 1847).

[2] Anth. Pal. xi. 56.

[3] Cf. Ibid. xi. 25, 43; xii. 50.

[4] Theognis, 877, Bergk.

[5] Anth. Pal. ix. 412.

[6] Ibid. xi. 23.

[7] Archestr. ap. Athenaeum, vii. 286 a; {kan apothneskein melles, arpason, . . . kata usteron eoe o ti soi pepromenon estin}.

[8] Anth. Pal. xi. 3, 43, 56.

[9] Infra, xii. 19, 31, 24, 21.

[10] Citharist. Fr. 1, {ar esti suggenes to lupe kai bios}.

[11] Il. xvii. 443-447.

[12] Theognis, 425-8, Bergk.

[13] Oed. Col. 1225-8.

[14] Fr. Scyr. 500.

[15] Hypobolimaeus, Fr. 2.

[16] Anth. Pal. vii. 472.

[17] Ibid. x. 84.

[18] Ibid. x. 123.

[19] Ibid. x. 85.

[20] Ibid. x. 94, xi. 300.

[21] /Signum/ Aequanimitatis /dedit atque ita conversus quasi dormiret spiritum reddidit./ Jul. Capitol., /Antoninus Pius/, c. xii.

[22] Anth. Pal. vii. 300, 362.

[23] {Esukhien agapan}, Ibid. x. 77.

XVI

That ancient world perished; and all the while, side by side with it, a new world was growing up with which it had so little in common that hitherto it would only have been confusing to take the latter much into account. This review of the older civilisation has, so far as may be, been kept apart from all that is implied by the introduction of Christianity; it has even spoken of the decay and death of literature, though literature and thought in another field were never more active than in the early centuries of the Church. Of the immense gain that came then to the world it is not necessary to speak; we all know it. For the latter half of the period of human history over which the Greek Anthology stretches, this new world was in truth the more important of the two. While to the ageing Greek mind life had already lost its joy, and thought begun to sicken, we hear the first notes of a new glory and passion;

{Egeire o katheudon
Kai anasta ek ton vekron
Kai epiphausei soi o KHristos}[1]—

in this broken fragment of shapeless and barbaric verse, not in the smooth and delicate couplets of contemporary poets, Polyaenus or Antiphilus, lay the germ of the music which was to charm the centuries that followed. Even through the long swoon of art which is usually thought of as following the darkness of the third century, the truth was that art was transforming itself into new shapes and learning a new language. The last words of the Neo-Platonic philosophy with its mystical wisdom were barely said when the Church of the Holy Wisdom rose in Constantinople, the most perfect work of art that has yet been known in organic beauty of design and splendour of ornament; and when Justinian by his closure of the schools of Athens marked off, as by a precise line, the end of the ancient world, in the Greek monasteries of Athos new types of beauty were being slowly wrought out which passed outward from land to land, transfiguring the face of the world as they went, kindling new life wherever they fell, miraculously transformed by the separate genius of every country from Norway to India, creating in Italy the whole of the great medieval art that stretches from Duccio and Giotto to Signorelli, and leaving to us here, as our most precious inheritances, such mere blurred and broken fragments of their glories as the cathedral churches of Salisbury and Winchester.

It is only in the growth and life of that new world that the decay and death of the old can be regarded with equanimity, or can in a certain sense be historically justified: for Greek civilisation was and still is so incomparable and so precious that its loss might otherwise fill the mind with despair, and seem to be the last irony cast by fate against the idea of human progress. But it is the law of all Nature, from her highest works to her lowest, that life only comes by death: "she replenishes one thing out of another," in the words of the Roman poet, "and does not suffer anything to be begotten before she has been recruited by the death of something else." To all things born she comes one day with her imperious message: /materies opus est ut crescant postera secla/.[2] With the infinite patience of one who has inexhaustible time and imperishable material at her absolute command, slowly, vacillatingly, not hesitating at any waste or any cruelty, Nature works out some form till it approaches perfection; then finds it flawed, finds it is not the thing she meant, and with the same strong, unscrupulous and passionless action breaks it up and begins anew. As in our own lives we sometimes feel that the slow progress of years, the structure built up cell by cell through pain and patience and weariness at lavish cost seems one day, when some great new force enters our life, to begin to crumble and fall away from us, and leave us strangers in a new world, so it is with the greater types of life, with peoples and civilisations; some secret inherent flaw was in their structure; they meet a trial for which they were not prepared, and fail; once more they must be passed into the crucible and melted down to their primitive matter. Yet Nature does not repeat herself; in some way the experience of all past generations enters into those which succeed them, and of a million of her works that have perished not one has perished wholly without account. That Greece and Rome, though they passed away, still influence us daily is indeed obvious; but it is as certain that the great races before them, of which Babylonia, Phoenicia, Egypt are only a few out of many, still live in the gradual evolution of the purpose of history. They live in us indeed as blind inherited forces, apart from our knowledge of them; yet if we can at all realise any of them to ourselves, at all enter into their spirit, our gain is great; for through time and distance they have become simple and almost abstract; only what was most living in them survives; and the loss of the vivid multiplicity and colour of a fuller knowledge makes it easier to discriminate what was important in them. Lapse of time has done for us with some portions of the past what is so difficult or even impossible for us to do for ourselves with the life actually round us, projected them upon an ideal plane: how ideal, in the case of Greek history, is obvious if we consider for a moment how nearly Homer and Herodotus are read alike by us. For Homer's world was from the first imagined, not actual; yet the actual world of the fifth century B.C. has become for us now no less an ideal, perhaps one which is even more stimulating and more fascinating. How far this may be due to any inherent excellence of its own, how far to the subtle enchantment of association, does not affect this argument. Of histories no less than of poems is it true that the best are but shadows, and that, for the highest purposes which history serves, the idea is the fact; the impression produced on us, the heightening and ennobling influence of a life, ideal or actual, akin to and yet different from ours, is the one thing which primarily matters. And so it may be questioned whether so far as this, the vital part of human culture, is concerned, modern scholarship has helped men beyond the point already reached by the more imperfect knowledge and more vivid intuitions of the fifteenth and sixteenth centuries; for if the effect produced on them, in the way of heightening and ennobling life, was more than the effect now and here produced on us, we have, so far as the Greek world is concerned, lost and not gained. Compensations indeed there are; a vast experience has enlarged our horizon and deepened our emotion, and it would be absurd to say now, as was once truly and plausibly said, that Greek means culture. Yet even now we could ill do without it; nor does there seem any reason beyond the dulness of our imagination and the imperfection of our teaching why it should not be as true and as living a help as ever in our lives.

At the present day the risk is not of Greek art and literature being too little studied, but of their being studied in too contracted and formal a spirit. Less time is spent on the corruptions of medieval texts, and on the imbecilities of the decadence; but all the more is labour wasted and insight obscured by the new pedantry; the research into unimportant origins which the Greeks themselves wisely left covered in a mist of mythology. The destruction dealt on the Athenian acropolis, under the name of scholarship, is a type of modern practice. The history of two thousand years has so far as possible been swept carelessly away in the futile attempt to lay bare an isolated picture of the age of Pericles; now archaeologists find that they cannot stop there, and fix their interest on the shapeless fragments of barbaric art beneath. But the Greek spirit and temper is perhaps less known than it once was; there appears to be a real danger that the influence upon men, the surprise of joy once given them by the work of Sophocles or Pheidias or Plato, dwindles with the accumulation of importance given to the barbarous antecedents and surroundings from which that great art sprang. The highest office of history is to preserve ideals; and where the ideal is saved its substructure may well be allowed to perish, as perish in the main it must, in spite of all that we can recover from the slight and ambiguous records which it leaves. The value of this selection of minor poetry—if one can speak of a value in poetry beyond itself—is that, however imperfectly, it draws for us in little a picture of the Greek ideal with all its virtues and its failings: it may be taken as an epitome, slightly sketched with a facile hand, of the book of Greek life. How slight the material is in which this picture is drawn becomes plain the moment we turn from these epigrams, however delicate and graceful, to the great writers. Yet the very study of the lesser and the appreciation that comes of study may quicken our understanding of the greater; and there is something more moving and pathetic in their survival, as of flowers from a strange land: white violets gathered in the morning, to recur to Meleager's exquisite metaphor, yielding still a faint and fugitive fragrance here in the never-ending afternoon. ———
———

[1] Quoted by S. Paul, Eph. v. 14.
[2] Lucr. i. 263, iii. 967.

ANTHOLOGY

TEXT AND TRANSLATIONS

CHAPTER I

LOVE

I PRELUDE POSIDIPPUS

Jar of Athens, drip the dewy juice of wine, drip, let the feast to which all bring their share be wetted as with dew; be silenced the swan, sage Zeno, and the Muse of Cleanthes, and let bitter-sweet Love be our concern.

II LAUS VENERIS ASCLEPIADES

Sweet is snow in summer for the thirsty to drink, and sweet for sailors after winter to see the garland of spring; but most sweet when one cloak shelters two lovers, and the tale of love is told by both.

III LOVE'S SWEETNESS NOSSIS

Nothing is sweeter than love, and all delicious things are second to it; yes, even honey I spit out of my mouth. Thus saith Nossis; but he whom the Cyprian loves not, knows not what roses her flowers are.

IV LOVE AND THE SCHOLAR MARCUS ARGENTARIUS

Once when turning over the Book of Hesiod in my hands, suddenly I saw Pyrrha coming in; and casting the book to the ground from my hand, I cried out, Why bring your works to me, old Hesiod?

V LOVERS' LIPS PLATO

Kissing Agathon, I had my soul upon my lips; for it rose, poor wretch, as though to cross over.

VI THE FIRST KISS STRATO

At evening, at the hour when we say good-night, Moeris kissed me, I know not whether really or in a dream; for very clearly I now have the rest in mind, all she said to me, and all that she asked me of; but whether she kissed me too, I doubt and guess; for if it is true, how, after being set in heaven, do I go to and fro upon earth?

VII THE REVELLER MELEAGER

Let the die be thrown; light up! I will on my way; see, courage!— Heavy with wine, what is thy purpose?—I will revel.—I will revel? whither wanderest, O heart?—And what is Reason to Love? light up, quick!—And where is thy old study of philosophy?—Away with the long toil of wisdom; this one thing only I know, that Love took captive even the mind of Zeus.

VIII LOVE AND WINE RUFINUS

I am armed against Love with a breastplate of Reason, neither shall he conquer me, one against one; yes, I a mortal will contend with him the immortal: but if he have Bacchus to second him, what can I do alone against the two?

IX LOVE IN THE STORM ASCLEPIADES

Snow, hail, darken, blaze, thunder, shake forth all thy glooming clouds upon the earth; for if thou slay me, then will I cease, but while thou lettest me live, though thou handle me worse than this, I will revel. For the god draws me who is thy master too, at whose persuasion, Zeus, thou didst once pierce in gold to that brazen bridal-chamber.

X A KISS WITHIN THE CUP AGATHIAS

I am no wine-bibber; but if thou wilt make me drunk, taste thou first and bring it me, and I take it. For if thou wilt touch it with thy lips, no longer is it easy to keep sober or to escape the sweet cup-bearer; for the cup ferries me over a kiss from thee, and tells me of the grace that it had.

XI LOVE'S MARTYR MELEAGER

Evermore in my ears eddies the sound of Love, and my eye silently carries sweet tears for the Desires; nor does night nor light let me rest, but already my enchanted heart bears the well-known imprint. Ah winged Loves, surely you know how to fly towards me, but have no whit of strength to fly away.

XII LOVE'S DRINK MELEAGER

The cup is glad for sweetness, and says that it touches the sweet-voiced mouth of love's darling, Zenophile. Happy! would that now, bringing up her lips to my lips, she would drink at one draught the very soul in me.

XIII LOVE THE RUNAWAY MELEAGER

I make hue and cry after wild Love; for now, even now in the morning dusk, he flew away from his bed and was gone. This boy is full of sweet tears, ever talking, swift, fearless, sly-laughing, winged on the back, and carries a quiver. But whose son he is I may not say, for Heaven denies having borne this ruffler, and so Earth and so Sea. Everywhere and by all he is hated; but look you to it lest haply even now he is laying more springes for souls. Yet—there he is, see! about his lurking-place; I see thee well, my archer, ambushed in Zenophile's eyes.

XIV LOVE'S SYMPATHY CALLIMACHUS

Our friend was wounded, and we knew it not; how bitter a sigh, mark you? he drew all up his breast. Lo, he was drinking the third time, and shedding their petals from the fellow's garlands the roses all poured to the ground. He is well in the fire, surely; no, by the gods, I guess not at random; a thief myself, I know a thief's footprints.

XV THE MAD LOVER PAULUS SILENTIARIUS

A man wounded by a rabid dog's venom sees, they say, the beast's image in all water. Surely mad Love has fixed his bitter tooth in me, and made my soul the prey of his frenzies; for both the sea and the eddies of rivers and the wine-carrying cup show me thy image, beloved.

XVI LOVE AT THE VINTAGE AGATHIAS

We, as we trod the infinite fruit of Iacchus, mingled and wound in the rhythm of the revel, and now the fathomless flood flowed down, and like boats our cups of ivy-wood swam on the sweet surges; dipping wherewith, we drank just as it lay at our hand, nor missed the warm water-nymphs overmuch. But beautiful Rhodanthe leant over the winepress, and with the splendours of her beauty lit up the welling stream; and swiftly all our hearts were fluttered, nor was there one of us but was overcome by Bacchus and the Paphian. Alas for us! he ran plenteous at our feet, but for her, hope played with us, and no more.

XVII LOVE'S GARLAND MELEAGER

I will twine the white violet and I will twine the delicate narcissus with myrtle buds, and I will twine laughing lilies, and I will twine the sweet crocus, and I will twine therewithal the crimson hyacinth, and I will twine lovers' roses, that on balsam-curled Heliodora's temples my garland may shed its petals over the lovelocks of her hair.

XVIII LOVER'S FRIGHT MELEAGER

She is carried off! What savage could do so cruel a deed? Who so high as to raise battle against very Love? Light torches, quick! and yet—a footfall; Heliodora's; go back into my breast, O my heart.

XIX LOVE IN SPRING MELEAGER

Now the white violet blooms, and blooms the moist narcissus, and bloom the mountain-wandering lilies; and now, dear to her lovers, spring flower among the flowers, Zenophile, the sweet rose of Persuasion, has burst into bloom. Meadows, why idly laugh in the brightness of your tresses? for my girl is better than garlands sweet to smell.

XX SUMMER NIGHT MELEAGER

Shrill-crying gnats, shameless suckers of the blood of men, two-winged monsters of the night, for a little, I beseech you, leave Zenophile to sleep a quiet sleep, and see, make your feast of flesh from my limbs. Yet to what end do I talk in vain? even relentless wild beasts take delight in nestling on her delicate skin. But once more now I proclaim it, O evil brood, cease your boldness or you shall know the force of jealous hands.

XXI PARTING AT DAWN MELEAGER

Farewell, Morning Star, herald of dawn, and quickly come again as the Evening Star, bringing secretly her whom thou takest away.

XXII DEARER THAN DAY PAULUS SILENTIARIUS

"Fare thou well," I would say to thee; and again I check my voice and rein it backward, and again I stay beside thee; for I shrink from the terrible separation from thee as from the bitter night of Acheron; for the light of thee is like the day. Yet that, I think, is voiceless, but thou bringest me also that murmuring talk of thine, sweeter than the Sirens', whereon all my soul's hopes are hung.

XXIII THE MORNING STAR MACEDONIUS

Morning Star, do not Love violence, neither learn, neighbour as thou art to Mars, to have a heart that pities not; but as once before, seeing Phaethon in Clymene's chamber, thou heldest not on thy fleet- foot course from the east, even so on the skirts of night, the night that so hardly has lightened on my desire, come lingering as though among the Cimmerians.

XXIV AT COCKCROWING ANTIPATER OF THESSALONICA

Grey dawn is over, Chrysilla, and ere now the morning cock clarisoning leads on the envious Lady of Morn. Be thou accursed, most envious of birds, who drivest me from my home to the endless chattering of the young men. Thou growest old, Tithonus; else why dost thou chase Dawn thy bedfellow out of her couch while yet morning is so young?

XXV DAWN'S HASTE MELEAGER

Grey dawn, why, O unloving, risest thou so swift round my bed, where but now I nestled close to dear Demo? Would God thou wouldst turn thy fleet course backward and be evening, thou shedder of the sweet light that is so bitter to me. For once before, for Zeus and his Alcmena, thou wentest contrary; thou art not unlessoned in running backward.

XXVI DAWN'S DELAY MELEAGER

Grey dawn, why, O unloving, rollest thou now so slow round the world, since another is shrouded and warm by Demo? but when I held her delicate form to my breast, swift thou wert upon us, shedding on me a light that seemed to rejoice in my grief.

XXVII WAITING PAULUS SILENTIARIUS

Cleophantis lingers long; and the third lamp now begins to give a broken glimmer as it silently wastes away. And would that the firebrand in my heart too were quenched with the lamp, and did not burn me long in wakeful desires. Ah how often she swore by the Cytherean that she would be here at evenfall; but she recks not of either men or gods.

XXVIII WAITING IN VAIN ASCLEPIADES

Nico the renowned consented to come to me at nightfall and swore by the holy Lady of Laws; and she is not come, and the watch is gone by; did she mean to forswear herself? Servants, put out the lamp.

XXIX THE SCORNED LOVER ASCLEPIADES

O Night, thee and none other I take to witness, how Nico's Pythias flouts me, traitress as she is; asked, not unasked am I come; may she yet blame thee in the selfsame plight standing by my doors!

XXX SLEEPLESS NIGHT AGATHIAS

All night long I sob; and when grey dawn rises and grants me a little grace of rest, the swallows cry around and about me, and bring me back to tears, thrusting sweet slumber away: and my unclosing eyes keep vigil, and the thought of Rhodanthe returns again in my bosom. O envious chatterers, be still; it was not I who shore away Philomela's tongue;

but weep for Itylus on the mountains, and sit wailing by the hoopoe's court, that we may sleep a little; and perchance a dream will come and clasp me round with Rhodanthe's arms.

XXXI THE LOVE LETTER RUFINUS

Rufinus to Elpis, my most sweet: well and very well be with her, if she can be well away from me. No longer can I bear, no, by thine eyes, my solitary and unmated severance from thee, but evermore blotted with tears I go to Coressus or to the temple of the great Artemis; but tomorrow my home shall receive me, and I will fly to thy face and bid thee a thousand greetings.

XXXII LOVE AND REASON PHILODEMUS

My soul forewarns me to flee the desire of Heliodora, knowing well the tears and jealousies of old. She talks; but I have no strength to flee, for, shameless that she is, she forewarns, and while she forewarns, she loves.

XXXIII ODI ET AMO MELEAGER

Take this message, Dorcas; lo again a second and a third time, Dorcas, take her all my message; run; delay no longer; fly. Wait a little, Dorcas, prithee a little; Dorcas, whither so fast before learning all I would say? And add to what I have just said—but no, I go on like a fool; say nothing at all—only that—say everything; spare not to say everything. Yet why do I send thee out, Dorcas, when myself, see, I go forth with thee?

XXXIV LOOKING AND LIKING PAULUS SILENTIARIUS

Eyes, how long are you draining the nectar of the Loves, rash drinkers of the strong unmixed wine of beauty? let us run far away, as far as we have strength to go, and in calm I will pour sober offerings to Cypris the Placable. But if haply there likewise I be caught by the sting, be you wet with chill tears and doomed for ever to bear deserved pain; since from you, alas! it was that we fell into all this labour of fire.

XXXV FORGET-ME-NOT AGATHIAS

Dost thou then also, Philinna, carry longing in thee, dost thou thyself also sicken and waste away with tearless eyes? or is thy sleep most sweet to thee, while of our care thou makest neither count nor reckoning? Thou wilt find thy fate likewise, and thy haughty cheek I shall see wetted with fast-falling tears. For the Cyprian in all else is malign, but one virtue is in her lot, hatred of proud beauties.

XXXVI AMANTIUM IRAE PAULUS SILENTIARIUS

At evening Galatea slammed-to the doors in my face, flinging at me a speech of scorn. "Scorn breaks love"; idly wanders this proverb; her scorn inflames my love-madness the more. For I swore I would stay a year away from her; out and alas! but with break of day I went to make supplication.

XXXVII INCONSTANCY MACEDONIUS

Constantia, nay verily! I heard the name and thought it beautiful, but thou art to me more bitter than death. And thou fliest him who loves thee, and him who loves thee not thou pursuest, that he may love thee and thou mayest fly him once again.

XXXVIII TIME'S REVENGE CALLIMACHUS

So mayest thou slumber, Conopion, as thou makest me sleep here in the chill doorway; so mayest thou slumber, most cruel, as thou lullest thy lover asleep; but not even in a dream hast thou known compassion. The neighbours pity me, but thou not even in a dream; but the silver hair will remind thee of all this by and by.

XXXIX FLOWN LOVE MARCUS ARGENTARIUS

Golden-horned Moon, thou seest this, and you fiery-shining Stars whom Ocean takes into his breast, how perfume-breathing Ariste has gone and left me alone, and this is the sixth day I cannot find the witch. But we will seek her notwithstanding; surely I will send the silver sleuth-hounds of the Cyprian on her track.

XL MOONLIGHT PHILODEMUS

Lady of Night, twy-horned, lover of nightlong revels, shine, O Moon, shine, darting through the latticed windows; shed thy splendour on golden Callistion; thine immortality may look down unchidden on the deeds of lovers; thou dost bless both her and me, I know, O Moon; for thy soul too was fired by Endymion.

XLI LOVE AND THE STARS PLATO

On the stars thou gazest, my Star; would I were heaven, that I might look on thee with many eyes.

XLII ROSE AUTHOR UNKNOWN

Would I were a pink rose, that fastening me with thine hands thou mightest grant me grace of thy snowy breast.

XLIII LILY THEOPHANES

Would I were a white lily, that fastening me with thine hands thou mightest satisfy me with the nearness of thy body.

XLIV LOVE AND SLEEP MELEAGER

Thou sleepest, Zenophile, dainty girl; would that I had come to thee now, a wingless sleep, upon thine eyelids, that not even he, even he who charms the eyes of Zeus, might come nigh thee, but myself had held thee, I thee alone.

XLV SLAYER AND HEALER MACEDONIUS

I have a wound of love, and from my wound flows ichor of tears, and the gash is never staunched; for I am at my wits' end for misery, and no Machaon sprinkles soothing drugs on me in my need. I am Telephus, O maiden, but be thou my true Achilles; with thy beauty allay the longing as thou didst kindle it.

XLVI LOVE THE GAMBLER MELEAGER

Still in his mother's lap, a child playing with dice in the morning,
Love played my life away.

XLVII DRIFTING MELEAGER

Bitter wave of Love, and restless gusty Jealousies and wintry sea of revellings, whither am I borne? and the rudders of my spirit are quite cast loose; shall we sight delicate Scylla once again?

XLVIII LOVE'S RELAPSES MELEAGER

Soul that weepest sore, how is Love's wound that was allayed in thee inflaming through thy heart again! nay, nay, for God's sake, nay for God's sake, O infatuate, stir not the fire that flickers low among the ashes. For soon, O oblivious of thy pains, so sure as Love catches thee in flight, again he will torture his found runaway.

XLIX LOVE THE BALL-PLAYER MELEAGER

Love who feeds on me is a ball-player, and throws to thee, Heliodora, the heart that throbs in me. Come then, take thou Love-longing for his playmate; but if thou cast me away from thee, I will not bear such wanton false play.

L LOVE'S ARROWS MELEAGER

Nay by Demo's tresses, nay by Heliodora's sandal, nay by Timarion's scent-dripping doorway, nay by great-eyed Anticleia's dainty smile, nay by Dorothea's fresh-blossomed garlands, no longer, Love, does thy quiver hide its bitter winged arrows, for thy shafts are all fixed in me.

LI LOVE'S EXCESS AUTHOR UNKNOWN

Arm thyself, Cypris, with thy bow, and go at thy leisure to some other mark; for I have not even room left for a wound.

LII MOTH AND CANDLE MELEAGER

If thou scorch so often the soul that flutters round thee, O Love, she will flee away from thee; she too, O cruel, has wings.

LIII LOVE AT AUCTION MELEAGER

Let him be sold, even while he is yet asleep on his mother's bosom, let him be sold; why should I have the rearing of this impudent thing? For it is snub-nosed and winged, and scratches with its nail-tips, and weeping laughs often between; and furthermore it is unabashed, ever-talking, sharp-glancing, wild and not gentle even to its very own mother, every way a monster; so it shall be sold; if any outward-bound merchant will buy a boy, let him come hither. And yet he beseeches, see, all in tears. I sell thee no more; be comforted; stay here and live with Zenophile.

LIV INTER MINORA SIDERA MARCUS ARGENTARIUS

Pour ten cups for Lysidice, and for beloved Euphrante, slave, give me one cup. Thou wilt say I love Lysidice more? No, by sweet Bacchus, whom I drink deep in this bowl; Euphrante for me, one against ten; for the one splendour of the moon also outshines the innumerable stars.

LV ROSA TRIPLEX MELEAGER

Pour for Heliodora as Persuasion, and as the Cyprian, and once more for her again as the sweet-speeched Grace; for she is enrolled as my one goddess, whose beloved name I will mix and drink in unmixed wine.

LVI LOVE IN ABSENCE MELEAGER

Pour, and again say, again, again, "Heliodora"; say it and mingle the sweet name with the unmixed wine; and wreath me with that garland of yesterday drenched with ointments, for remembrance of her. Lo, the lovers' rose sheds tears to see her away, and not on my bosom.

LVII LOVE'S PORTRAITURE MELEAGER

Who of my friends has imaged me sweet-voiced Zenophile? who has brought me one Grace of the three? Surely the man did a gracious deed who gave this gift, and in his grace gave Grace herself to me.

LVIII THE SEA'S WOOING MELEAGER

Fond Asclepias with her sparkling eyes as of Calm woos all to make the voyage of love.

LIX THE LIGHT OF TROY DIOSCORIDES

Athenion sang of that fatal horse to me; all Troy was in fire, and I kindled along with it, not fearing the ten years' toil of Greece; and in that single blaze Trojans and I perished together then.

LX LOVE AND MUSIC MELEAGER

Sweet is the tune, by Pan of Arcady, that thou playest on the harp, Zenophile, oversweet are the notes of the tune. Whither shall I fly from thee? on all hands the Loves encompass me, and let me not take breath for ever so little space; for either thy form shoots longing into me, or again thy music or thy graciousness, or—what shall I say? all of thee; I kindle in the fire.

LXI HONEY AND STING MELEAGER

Flower-fed bee, why touchest thou my Heliodora's skin, leaving outright the flower-bells of spring? Meanest thou that even the unendurable sting of Love, ever bitter to the heart, has a sweetness too? Yes, I think, this thou sayest; ah, fond one, go back again; we knew thy news long ago.

LXII LOVE'S MESSENGER MELEAGER

Fly for me, O gnat, a swift messenger, and touch Zenophile, and whisper lightly into her ears: "one awaits thee waking; and thou sleepest, O oblivious of thy lovers." Up, fly, yes fly, O musical one; but speak quietly, lest arousing her bedfellow too thou stir pangs of jealousy against me; and if thou bring my girl, I will adorn thee with a lion-skin, O gnat, and give thee a club to carry in thine hand.

LXIII LOVE THE SLAYER MELEAGER

I beseech thee, Love, charm asleep the wakeful longing in me for Heliodora, pitying my suppliant verse; for, by thy bow that never has learned to strike another, but always upon me pours its winged shafts, even though thou slay me I will leave letters uttering this voice, "Look, stranger, on Love's murdered man."

LXIV FORSAKEN MAECIUS

Why so woe-begone? and why, Philaenis, these reckless tearings of hair, and suffusion of sorrowful eyes? hast thou seen thy lover with another on his bosom? tell me; we know charms for grief. Thou weepest and sayest no: vainly dost thou essay to deny; the eyes are more trustworthy than the tongue.

LXV THE SLEEPLESS LOVER MELEAGER

Grasshopper, beguilement of my longings, luller asleep, grasshopper, muse of the cornfield, shrill-winged, natural mimic of the lyre, harp to me some tune of longing, striking thy vocal wings with thy dear feet, that so thou mayest rescue me from the all-wakeful trouble of my pains, grasshopper, as thou makest thy love-luring voice tremble on the string; and I will give thee gifts at dawn, ever-fresh groundsel and dewy drops sprayed from the mouths of the watering-can.

LXVI REST AT NOON MELEAGER

Voiceful cricket, drunken with drops of dew thou playest thy rustic music that murmurs in the solitude, and perched on the leaf-edges shrillest thy lyre-tune with serrated legs and swart skin. But my dear, utter a new song for the tree-nymphs' delight, and make thy harp-notes echo to Pan's, that escaping Love I may seek out sleep at noon here lying under the shady plane.

LXVII THE BURDEN OF YOUTH ASCLEPIADES

I am not two and twenty yet, and I am weary of living; O Loves, why misuse me so? why set me on fire; for when I am gone, what will you do? Doubtless, O Loves, as before you will play with your dice, unheeding.

LXVIII BROKEN VOWS MELEAGER

Holy night, and thou, O lamp, you and none other we took to witness of our vows; and we swore, he that he would love me, and I that I would never leave him, and you kept witness between us. And now he says that these vows are written in running water, O lamp, and thou seest him on the bosom of another.

LXIX DOUBTFUL DAWN MELEAGER

O night, O wakeful longing in me for Heliodora, and eyes that sting with tears in the creeping grey of dawn, do some remnants of affection yet remain mine, and is her memorial kiss warm upon my cold picture? has she tears for bedfellows, and does she clasp to her bosom and kiss a deluding dream of me? or has she some other new love, a new plaything? Never, O lamp, look thou on that, but be guardian of her whom I gave to thy keeping.

LXX THE DEW OF TEARS ASCLEPIADES

Stay there, my garlands, hanging by these doors, nor hastily scattering your petals, you whom I have wetted with tears (for lovers' eyes are rainy); but when you see him as the door opens, drip my rain over his head, that so at least that golden hair may drink my tears.

LXXI LOVE'S GRAVE MELEAGER

When I am gone, Cleobulus—for what avails? cast among the fire of young loves, I lie a brand in the ashes—I pray thee make the burial- urn drunk with wine ere thou lay it under earth, and write thereon, "Love's gift to Death."

LXXII LOVE'S MASTERDOM MELEAGER

Terrible is Love, terrible; and what avails it if again I say and again, with many a moan, Terrible is Love? for surely the boy laughs at this, and is pleased with manifold reproaches; and if I say bitter things, they are meat and drink to him. And I wonder how thou, O Cyprian, who didst arise through the green waves, out of water hast borne a fire.

LXXIII LOVE THE CONQUEROR MELEAGER

I am down: tread with thy foot on my neck, cruel divinity; I know thee, by the gods, heavy as thou art to bear: I know too thy fiery arrows: but hurling thy brands at my soul thou wilt no longer kindle it, for it is all ashes.

LXXIV LOVE'S PRISONER MELEAGER

Did I not cry aloud to thee, O soul, "Yes, by the Cyprian, thou wilt be caught, poor lover, if thou flutterest so often near the lime- twigs"? did I not cry aloud? and the snare has taken thee. Why dost thou gasp vainly in the toils? Love himself has bound thy wings and set thee on the fire, and sprinkled thee to swooning with perfumes, and given thee in thy thirst hot tears to drink.

LXXV FROST AND FIRE MELEAGER

Ah suffering soul, now thou burnest in the fire, and now thou revivest, and fetchest breath again: why weepest thou? when thou didst feed pitiless Love in thy bosom, knewest thou not that he was being fed for thy woe? knewest thou not? Know now his repayment, a fair foster-hire! take it, fire and cold snow together. Thou wouldst have it so; bear the pain; thou sufferest the wages of thy work, scorched with his burning honey.

LXXVI THE SCULPTOR OF SOULS MELEAGER

Within my heart Love himself has moulded Heliodora with her lovely voice, the soul of my soul.

LXXVII LOVE'S IMMORTALITY STRATO

Who may know if a loved one passes the prime, while ever with him and never left alone? who may not satisfy to-day who satisfied yesterday? and if he did satisfy, what should befall him not to satisfy to-morrow?

CHAPTER II

PRAYERS AND DEDICATIONS

I TO ZEUS OF SCHERIA JULIUS POLYAENUS

Though the terror of those who pray, and the thanks of those who have prayed, ever fill thine ears with myriad voice, O Zeus, who abidest in the holy plain of Scheria, yet hearken to us also, and bow down with a promise that lies not, that my exile now may have an end, and I may live in my native land at rest from labour of long journeys.

II TO THE GOD OF THE SEA CRINAGORAS

Holy Spirit of the great Shaker of Earth, be thou gracious to others also who ply across the Aegean brine; since even to me, chased by the Thracian hurricane, thou didst open out the calm haven of my desire.

III TO THE GODS OF HARBOUR AND HEADLAND ANTIPHILUS

Harbour-god, do thou, O blessed one, send with a gentle breeze the outward-bound sail of Archelaus down smooth water even to the sea; and thou who hast the point of the shore in ward, keep the convoy that is bound for the Pythian shrine; and thenceforward, if all we singers are in Phoebus' care, I will sail cheerily on with a fair-flowing west wind.

IV TO POSEIDON OF AEGAE ALPHEUS

Thou who holdest sovereignty of swift-sailing ships, steed-loving god, and the great overhanging cliff of Euboea, give to thy worshippers a favourable voyage even to the City of Ares, who loosed moorings from Syria.

V TO THE LORD OF SEA AND LAND MACEDONIUS

This ship to thee, O king of sea and sovereign of land, I Crantas dedicate, this ship wet no longer, a feather tossed by the wandering winds, whereon many a time I deemed in my terror that I drove to death; now renouncing all, fear and hope, sea and storms, I have planted my foot securely upon earth.

VI TO THE GODS OF SEA AND WEATHER PHILODEMUS

O Melicerta son of Ino, and thou, sea-green Leucothea, mistress of Ocean, deity that shieldest from harm, and choirs of the Nereïds, and waves, and thou Poseidon, and Thracian Zephyrus, gentlest of the winds, carry me propitiously, sped through the broad wave, safe to the sweet shore of the Peiraeus.

VII TO POSEIDON, BY A FISHERMAN MACEDONIUS

Old Amyntichus tied his plummeted fishing-net round his fish-spear, ceasing from his sea-toil, and spake towards Poseidon and the salt surge of the sea, letting a tear fall from his eyelids; Thou knowest, blessed one, I am weary; and in an evil old age clinging Poverty keeps her youth and wastes my limbs: give sustenance to a poor old man while he yet draws breath, but from the land as he desires, O ruler of both earth and sea.

VIII TO PALAEMON AND INO ANTIPATER OF SIDON

This shattered fragment of a sea-wandering scolopendra, lying on the sandy shore, twice four fathom long, all befouled with froth, much torn under the sea-washed rock, Hermonax chanced upon when he was hauling a draught of fishes out of the sea as he plied his fisher's craft; and having found it, he hung it up to the boy Palaemon and Ino, giving the sea-marvel to the sea-deities.

IX TO ARTEMIS OF THE FISHING-NETS APOLLONIDES

A red mullet and a hake from the embers to thee, Artemis of the Haven, I Menis, the caster of nets, offer, and a brimming cup of wine mixed strong, and a broken crust of dry bread, a poor man's sacrifice; in recompence whereof give thou nets ever filled with prey; to thee, O blessed one, all meshes have been given.

X TO PRIAPUS OF THE SHORE MAECIUS

Priapus of the seashore, the trawlers lay before thee these gifts by the grace of thine aid from the promontory, having imprisoned a tunny shoal in their nets of spun hemp in the green sea-entrances: a beechen cup and a rude stool of heath and a glass cup holding wine, that thou mayest rest thy foot weary and cramped with dancing while thou chasest away the dry thirst.

XI TO APOLLO OF LEUCAS PHILIPPUS

Phoebus who holdest the sheer steep of Leucas, far seen of mariners and washed by the Ionian sea, receive of sailors this mess of hand- kneaded barley bread and a libation mingled in a little cup, and the gleam of a brief-shining lamp that drinks with half-saturate mouth from a sparing oil-flask; in recompence whereof be gracious, and send on their sails a favourable wind to run with them to the harbours of Actium.

XII TO ARTEMIS OF THE WAYS ANTIPHILUS

Thou of the Ways, to thee Antiphilus dedicates this hat from his own head, a voucher of his wayfaring; for thou wast gracious to his prayers, wast favouring to his paths; and his thank-offering is small indeed but sacred. Let not any greedy traveller's hand snatch our gift; sacrilege is not safe even in little things.

XIII TO THE TWIN BRETHREN CALLIMACHUS

He who set me here, Euaenetus, says (for of myself I know not) that I am dedicated in recompence of his single-handed victory, I the cock of brass, to the Twin Brethren; I believe the son of Phaedrus the Philoxenid.

XIV TO THE DELPHIAN APOLLO PAULUS SILENTIARIUS

Eunomus the Locrian hangs up this brazen grasshopper to the Lycorean god, a memorial of the contest for the crown. The strife was of the Lyre, and Parthis stood up against me: but when the Locrian shell sounded under the plectrum, a lyre-string rang and snapped jarringly; but ere ever the tune halted in its fair harmonies, a delicate- trilling grasshopper seated itself on the lyre and took up the note of the lost string, and turned the rustic sound that till then was vocal in the groves to the strain of our touch upon the lyre; and therefore, blessed son of Leto, he does honour to thy grasshopper, seating the singer in brass upon his harp.

XV TO ARTEMIS THE HEALER PHILIPPUS

Huntress and archer, maiden daughter of Zeus and Leto, Artemis to whom are given the recesses of the mountains, this very day send away beyond the North Wind this hateful sickness from the best of kings; for so above thine altars will Philippus offer vapour of frankincense, doing goodly sacrifice of a hill-pasturing boar.

XVI TO ASCLEPIUS THEOCRITUS

Even to Miletus came the son of the Healer to succour the physician of diseases Nicias, who ever day by day draws near him with offerings, and had this image carved of fragrant cedar, promising high recompence to Eetion for his cunning of hand; and he put all his art into the work.

XVII TO THE NYMPHS OF ANIGRUS MOERO

Nymphs of Anigrus, maidens of the river, who evermore tread with rosy feet these divine depths, hail and save Cleonymus who set these fair images to you, goddesses, beneath the pines.

XVIII TO PAN PAEAN AUTHOR UNKNOWN

This for thee, O pipe-player, minstrel, gracious god, holy lord of the Naiads who pour their urns, Hyginus made as a gift, whom thou, O king, didst draw nigh and make whole of his hard sickness; for among all my children thou didst stand by me visibly, not in a dream of night, but about the mid-circle of the day.

XIX TO HERACLES OF OETA DIONYSIUS

Heracles who goest on stony Trachis and on Oeta and the deep brow of tree-clad Pholoe, to thee Dionysius offers this green staff of wild olive, cut off by him with his billhook.

XX TO APOLLO AND THE MUSES THEOCRITUS

These dewy roses and yonder close-curled wild thyme are laid before the maidens of Helicon, and the dark-leaved laurels before thee, Pythian Healer, since the Delphic rock made this thine ornament; and this white-horned he-goat shall stain your altar, who nibbles the tip of the terebinth shoot.

XXI TO APHRODITE OF THE GOLDEN HOUSE MOERO

Thou liest in the golden portico of Aphrodite, O grape-cluster filled full of Dionysus' juice, nor ever more shall thy mother twine round thee her lovely tendril or above thine head put forth her honeyed leaf.

XXII TO APHRODITE, BY CALLISTION POSIDIPPUS

Thou who inhabitest Cyprus and Cythera and Miletus and the fair plain of horse-trampled Syria, come graciously to Callistion, who never thrust her lover away from her house's doors.

XXIII TO APHRODITE, BY LAÏS PLATO

I Laïs who laughed exultant over Greece, I who held that swarm of young lovers in my porches, give my mirror to the Paphian; since such as I am I will not see myself, and such as I was I cannot.

XXIV TO APHRODITE, WITH A TALISMAN AUTHOR UNKNOWN

Nico's wryneck, that knows how to draw a man even from overseas, and girls out of their wedding-chambers, chased with gold, carven out of translucent amethyst, lies before thee, Cyprian, for thine own possession, tied across the middle with a soft lock of purple lamb's wool, the gift of the sorceress of Larissa.

XXV TO APHRODITE EUPLOIA GAETULICUS

Guardian of the seabeach, to thee I send these cakes, and the gifts of a scanty sacrifice; for to-morrow I shall cross the broad wave of the Ionian sea, hastening to our Eidothea's arms. But shine thou favourably on my love as on my mast, O Cyprian, mistress of the bride-chamber and the beach.

XXVI TO THE GOD OF CANOPUS CALLIMACHUS

To the god of Canopus Callistion, wife of Critias, dedicated me, a lamp enriched with twenty wicks, when her prayer for her child Apellis was heard; and regarding my splendours thou wilt say, How art thou fallen, O Evening Star!

XXVII TO HERACLES, WITH A SHIELD HEGESIPPUS

Receive me, O Heracles, the consecrated shield of Archestratus, that leaning against thy polished portico, I may grow old in hearing of dances and hymns; let the War-God's hateful strife be satisfied.

XXVIII TO THE MILESIAN ARTEMIS NICIAS

So I was destined, I also, once to abandon the hateful strife of Ares and hear the maiden choirs around Artemis' temple, where Epixenus placed me when white old age began to waste his limbs.

XXIX TO ATHENE ERGANE ANTIPATER OF SIDON

The shuttle that sang at morning with the earliest swallows' cry, kingfisher of Pallas in the loom, and the heavy-headed twirling spindle, light-running spinner of the twisted yarn, and the bobbins, and this basket, friend to the distaff, keeper of the spun warp-thread and the reel, Telesilla, the industrious daughter of good Diocles, dedicates to the Maiden, mistress of wool-dressers.

XXX TO THE ORCHARD GOD AUTHOR UNKNOWN

This fresh-cloven pomegranate and fresh-downed quince, and the wrinkled navel-like fig, and the purple grape-bunch spirting wine, thick-clustered, and the nut fresh-stripped of its green husk, to this rustic staked Priapus the keeper of the fruit dedicates, an offering from his orchard trees.

XXXI TO DEMETER AND THE SEASONS ZONAS

To Demeter of the winnowing-fan and the Seasons whose feet are in the furrows Heronax lays here from the poverty of a small tilth their share of ears from the threshing-floor, and these mixed seeds of pulse on a slabbed table, the least of a little; for no great inheritance is this he has gotten him, here on the barren hill.

XXXII TO THE CORN GODDESS PHILIPPUS

Those handfuls of corn from the furrows of a tiny field, Demeter lover of wheat, Sosicles the tiller dedicates to thee, having reaped now an abundant harvest; but again likewise may he carry back his sickle blunted from shearing of the straw.

XXXIII TO THE GODS OF THE FARM AUTHOR UNKNOWN

To Pan of the goats and fruitful Dionysus and Demeter Lady of Earth I dedicate a common offering, and beseech of them fair fleeces and fair wine and fair fruit of the corn-ears in my reaping.

XXXIV TO THE WEST WIND BACCHYLIDES

Eudemus dedicates this shrine in the fields to Zephyrus, most bountiful of the winds, who came to aid him at his prayer, that he might right quickly winnow the grain from the ripe ears.

XXXV TO PAN OF THE FOUNTAIN AUTHOR UNKNOWN

We supplicate Pan, the goer on the cliffs, twy-horned leader of the Nymphs, who abides in this house of rock, to be gracious to us, whosoever come to this spring of ever-flowing drink to rid us of our thirst.

XXXVI TO PAN AND THE NYMPHS ANYTE

To Pan the bristly-haired, and the Nymphs of the farm-yard, Theodotus the shepherd laid this gift under the crag, because they stayed him when very weary under the parching summer, stretching out to him honey-sweet water in their hands.

XXXVII TO THE SHEPHERD-GOD THEOCRITUS

White-skinned Daphnis, the player of pastoral hymns on his fair pipe, offers these to Pan, the pierced reeds, the stick for throwing at hares, a sharp javelin and a fawn-skin, and the scrip wherein once he carried apples.

XXXVIII TO PAN, BY A HUNTER, A FOWLER, AND A FISHER ARCHIAS

To thee, Pan of the cliff, three brethren dedicate these various gifts of their threefold ensnaring; Damis toils for wild beasts, and Pigres springes for birds, and Cleitor nets that swim in the sea; whereof do thou yet again make the one fortunate in the air, and the one in the sea and the one among the oakwoods.

XXXIX TO ARTEMIS OF THE OAKWOOD MNASALCAS

This to thee, Artemis the bright, this statue Cleonymus set up; do thou overshadow this oakwood rich in game, where thou goest afoot, our lady, over the mountain tossing with foliage as thou hastest with thy terrible and eager hounds.

XL TO THE GODS OF THE CHASE CRINAGORAS

Fountained caverns of the Nymphs that drip so much water down this jagged headland, and echoing hut of pine-coronalled Pan, wherein he dwells under the feet of the rock of Bassae, and stumps of aged juniper sacred among hunters, and stone-heaped seat of

Hermes, be gracious and receive the spoils of the swift stag-chase from Sosander prosperous in hunting.

XLI TO ARCADIAN ARTEMIS ANTIPATER OF SIDON

This deer that fed about Ladon and the Erymanthian water and the ridges of Pholoe haunted by wild beasts, Lycormas son of Thearidas of Lasion got, striking her with the diamond-shaped butt of his spear, and, drawing off the skin and the double-pointed antlers on her forehead, laid them before the Maiden of the country.

XLII TO APOLLO, WITH A HUNTER'S BOW PAULUS SILENTIARIUS

Androclus, O Apollo, gives this bow to thee, wherewith in the chase striking many a beast he had luck in his aim: since never did the arrow leap wandering from the curved horn or speed vainly from his hand; for as often as the inevitable bowstring rang, so often he brought down his prey in air or thicket; wherefore to thee, O Phoebus, he brings this Lyctian weapon as an offering, having wound it round with rings of gold.

XLIII TO PAN OF THE SHEPHERDS AUTHOR UNKNOWN

O Pan, utter thy holy voice to the feeding flocks, running thy curved lip over the golden reeds, that so they may often bring gifts of white milk in heavy udders to Clymenus' home, and for thee the lord of the she-goats, standing fairly by thy altars, may spirt the red blood from his shaggy breast.

XLIV TO THE GOD OF ARCADY AGATHIAS

These unsown domains, O Pan of the hill, Stratonicus the ploughman dedicated to thee in return of thy good deeds, saying, Feed in joy thine own flocks and look on thine own land, never more to be shorn with brass; thou wilt find the resting-place a gracious one; for even here charmed Echo will fulfil her marriage with thee.

CHAPTER III

EPITAPHS

I OF THE ATHENIAN DEAD AT PLATAEA SIMONIDES

If to die nobly is the chief part of excellence, to us out of all men
Fortune gave this lot; for hastening to set a crown of freedom on
Greece we lie possessed of praise that grows not old.

II ON THE LACEDAEMONIAN DEAD AT PLATAEA SIMONIDES

These men having set a crown of imperishable glory on their own land were folded in the dark cloud of death; yet being dead they have not died, since from on high their excellence raises them gloriously out of the house of Hades.

III ON THE SPARTANS AT THERMOPYLAE PARMENIO

Him, who over changed paths of earth and sea sailed on the mainland and went afoot upon the deep, Spartan valour held back on three hundred spears; be ashamed, O mountains and seas.

IV ON THE SAME SIMONIDES

O passer by, tell the Lacedaemonians that we lie here obeying their orders.

V ON THE DEAD IN AN UNKNOWN BATTLE MNASALCAS

These men, in saving their native land that lay with tearful fetters on her neck, clad themselves in the dust of darkness; and they win great praise of excellence; but looking on them let a citizen dare to die for his country.

VI ON THE DEAD IN A BATTLE IN BOEOTIA AUTHOR UNKNOWN

O Time, all-surveying deity of the manifold things wrought among mortals, carry to all men the message of our fate, that striving to save the holy soil of Greece we die on the renowned Boeotian plains.

VII ON A SLAIN WARRIOR ANACREON

Valiant in war was Timocritus, whose monument this is; but Ares spares the bad, not the good.

VIII ON THE SLAIN IN A BATTLE IN THESSALY AESCHYLUS

These men also, the steadfast among spears, dark Fate destroyed as they defended their native land rich in sheep; but they being dead their glory is alive, who woefully clad their limbs in the dust of Ossa.

IX ON THE ATHENIAN DEAD AT THE BATTLE OF CHALCIS SIMONIDES

We fell under the fold of Dirphys, and a memorial is reared over us by our country near the Euripus, not unjustly; for we lost lovely youth facing the rough cloud of war.

X ON THE ERETRIAN EXILES IN PERSIA PLATO

We who of old left the booming surge of the Aegean lie here in the mid-plain of Ecbatana: fare thou well, renowned Eretria once our country, farewell Athens nigh to Euboea, farewell dear sea.

XI ON THE SAME PLATO

We are Eretrians of Euboea by blood, but we lie near Susa, alas! how far from our own land.

XII ON AESCHYLUS AESCHYLUS

Aeschylus son of Euphorion the Athenian this monument hides, who died in wheat-bearing Gela; but of his approved valour the Marathonian grove may tell, and the deep-haired Mede who knew it.

XIII ON AN EMPTY TOMB IN TRACHIS EUPHORION

Not rocky Trachis covers over thy white bones, nor this stone with her dark-blue lettering; but them the Icarian wave dashes about the shingle of Doliche and steep Dracanon; and I, this empty earth, for old friendship with Polymedes, am heaped among the thirsty herbage of Dryopis.

XIV ON THE GRAVE OF AN ATHENIAN AT MEROË AUTHOR UNKNOWN

Straight is the descent to Hades, whether thou wert to go from Athens or takest thy journey from Meroë; let it not vex thee to have died so far away from home; from all lands the wind that blows to Hades is but one.

XV ON THE GRAVE OF AN ATHENIAN WOMAN AT CYZICUS ERYCIUS

I am an Athenian woman; for that was my city; but from Athens the wasting war-god of the Italians plundered me long ago and made a Roman citizen; and now that I am dead, seagirt Cyzicus wraps my bones. Fare thou well, O land that nurturedst me, and thou that thereafter didst hold me, and thou that at last hast taken me to thy breast.

XVI ON A SHIPWRECKED SAILOR PLATO

I am the tomb of one shipwrecked; and that opposite me, of a husbandman; for a common Hades lies beneath sea and earth.

XVII ON THE SAME PLATO

Well be with you, O mariners, both at sea and on land; but know that you pass by the grave of a shipwrecked man.

XVIII ON THE SAME THEODORIDES

I am the tomb of one shipwrecked; but sail thou; for when we were perishing, the other ships sailed on over the sea.

XIX ON THE SAME LEONIDAS OF TARENTUM

May the seafarer have a prosperous voyage; but if, like me, the gale drive him into the harbour of Hades, let him blame not the inhospitable sea-gulf, but his own foolhardiness that loosed moorings from our tomb.

XX ON THE SAME AUTHOR UNKNOWN

Mariner, ask not whose tomb I am here, but be thine own fortune a kinder sea.

XXI ON THE SAME CALLIMACHUS

What stranger, O shipwrecked man? Leontichus found me here a corpse on the shore, and heaped this tomb over me, with tears for his own calamitous life: for neither is he at peace, but flits like a gull over the sea.

XXII ON THE EMPTY TOMB OF ONE LOST AT SEA GLAUCUS

Not dust nor the light weight of a stone, but all this sea that thou beholdest is the tomb of Erasippus; for he perished with his ship, and in some unknown place his bones moulder, and the sea-gulls alone know them to tell.

XXIII ON THE SAME SIMONIDES

Cloudcapt Geraneia, cruel steep, would thou hadst looked on far Ister and long Scythian Tanaïs, and not lain nigh the surge of the Scironian sea by the ravines of the snowy Meluriad rock: but now he is a chill corpse in ocean, and the empty tomb here cries aloud of his heavy voyage.

XXIV ON THE SAME DAMAGETUS

Thymodes also, weeping over unlooked-for woes, reared this empty tomb to Lycus his son; for not even in a strange land did he get a grave, but some Thynian beach or Pontic island holds him, where, forlorn of all funeral rites, his shining bones lie naked on an inhospitable shore.

XXV ON A SAILOR DROWNED IN HARBOUR ANTIPATER OF SIDON

Everywhere the sea is the sea; why idly blame we the Cyclades or the narrow wave of Helle and the Needles? in vain have they their fame; or why when I had escaped them did the harbour of Scarphe cover me? Pray whoso will for a fair passage home; that the sea's way is the sea, Aristagoras knows who is buried here.

XXVI ON ARISTON OF CYRENE, LOST AT SEA THEAETETUS

O sailing mariners, Ariston of Cyrene prays you all for the sake of Zeus the Protector, to tell his father Meno that he lies by the Icarian rocks, having given up the ghost in the Aegean sea.

XXVII ON BITON OF AMPHIPOLIS, LOST AT SEA NICAENETUS

I am the grave of Biton, O wayfarer; and if leaving Torone thou goest even to Amphipolis, tell Nicagoras that Strymonias at the setting of the Kids lost him his only son.

XXVIII ON POLYANTHUS OF TORONE, LOST AT SEA PHAEDIMUS

I bewail Polyanthus, O thou who passest by, whom Aristagore his wife laid newly-wedded in the grave, having received dust and bones (but him the ill-blown Aegean wave cast away off Sciathus), when at early dawn the fishermen drew his luckless corpse, O stranger, into the harbour of Torone.

XXIX ON A WAYSIDE TOMB NICIAS

Sit beneath the poplars here, traveller, when thou art weary, and drawing nigh drink of our spring; and even far away remember the fountain that Simus sets by the side of Gillus his dead child.

XXX ON THE CHILDREN OF NICANDER AND LYSIDICE AUTHOR UNKNOWN

This is the single tomb of Nicander's children; the light of a single morning ended the sacred offspring of Lysidice.

XXXI ON A BABY AUTHOR UNKNOWN

Me a baby that was just tasting life heaven snatched away, I know not whether for good or for evil; insatiable Death, why hast thou snatched me cruelly in infancy? why hurriest thou? Are we not all thine in the end?

XXXII ON A CHILD OF FIVE LUCIAN

Me Callimachus, a five-years-old child whose spirit knew not grief, pitiless Death snatched away; but weep thou not for me; for little was my share in life, and little in life's ills.

XXXIII ON A CHILD OF SEVEN AUTHOR UNKNOWN

Hermes messenger of Persephone, whom usherest thou thus to the laughterless abyss of Death? what hard fate snatched Ariston from the fresh air at seven years old? and the child stands between his parents. Pluto delighting in tears, are not all mortal spirits allotted to thee? why gatherest thou the unripe grapes of youth?

XXXIV ON A BOY OF TWELVE CALLIMACHUS

Philip the father laid here the twelve-years-old child, his high hope,
Nicoteles.

XXXV ON CLEOETES AUTHOR UNKNOWN

Looking on the monument of a dead boy, Cleoetes son of Menesaechmus, pity him who was beautiful and died.

XXXVI ON A BEAUTIFUL BOY AUTHOR UNKNOWN

Not death is bitter, since that is the fate of all, but to die ere the time and before our parents: I having seen not marriage nor wedding- chant nor bridal bed, lie here the love of many, and to be the love of more.

XXXVII ON A BOY OF NINETEEN AUTHOR UNKNOWN

Bidding hail to me, Diogenes beneath the earth, go about thy business and obtain thy desire; for at nineteen years old I was laid low by cruel sickness and leave the sweet sun.

XXXVIII ON A SON, BY HIS MOTHER DIOTIMUS

What profits it to labour in childbirth? what to bear children? let not her bear who must see her child's death: for to stripling Bianor his mother reared the tomb; but it was fitting that the mother should obtain this service of the son.

XXXIX ON A GIRL CALLIMACHUS

The daughters of the Samians often require Crethis the teller of tales, who knew pretty games, sweetest of workfellows, ever talking; but she sleeps here the sleep to which they all must come.

XL ON A BETROTHED GIRL ERINNA

I am of Baucis the bride; and passing by my oft-wept pillar thou mayest say this to Death that dwells under ground, "Thou art envious, O Death"; and the coloured monument tells to him who sees it the most bitter fortune of Bauco, how her father-in-law burned the girl on the funeral pyre with those torches by whose light the marriage train was to be led home; and thou, O Hymenaeus, didst change the tuneable bridal song into a voice of wailing dirges.

XLI ON THE SAME ANTIPATER OF THESSALONICA

Ausonian earth holds me a woman of Libya, and I lie a maiden here by the sea-sand near Rome; and Pompeia, who nurtured me like a daughter, wept over me and laid me in a free tomb, while hastening on that other torch-fire for me; but this one came first, and contrary to our prayers Persephone lit the lamp.

XLII ON A SINGING-GIRL AUTHOR UNKNOWN

Blue-eyed Musa, the sweet-voiced nightingale, suddenly this little grave holds voiceless, and she lies like a stone who was so accomplished and so famous; fair Musa, be this dust light over thee.

XLIII ON CLAUDIA HOMONOEA AUTHOR UNKNOWN

I Homonoea, who was far clearer-voiced than the Sirens, I who was more golden than the Cyprian herself at revellings and feasts, I the chattering bright swallow lie here, leaving tears to Atimetus, to whom I was dear from girlhood; but unforeseen fate scattered all that great affection.

XLIV ON PAULA OF TARENTUM DIODORUS OF SARDIS

Bear witness this my stone house of night that has hidden me, and the wail-circled water of Cocytus, my husband did not, as men say, kill me, looking eagerly to marriage with another; why should Rufinius have an ill name idly? but my predestined Fates lead me away; not surely is Paula of Tarentum the only one who has died before her day.

XLV ON A MOTHER, DEAD IN CHILDBIRTH DIODORUS OF SARDIS

These woeful letters of Diodorus' wisdom tell that I was engraven for one early dead in child-birth, since she perished in bearing a boy; and I weep to hold Athenaïs the comely daughter of Melo, who left grief to the women of Lesbos and her father Jason; but thou, O Artemis, wert busy with thy beast-slaying hounds.

XLVI ON A MOTHER OF EIGHTEEN, AND HER BABY AUTHOR UNKNOWN

Name me Polyxena wife of Archelaus, child of Theodectes and hapless Demarete, and a mother as far as the birth-pangs; but fate overtook the child before full twenty suns, and myself died at eighteen years, just a mother and just a bride, so brief was all my day.

XLVII ON A YOUNG WIFE AUTHOR UNKNOWN

To his wife Paulina, holy of life and blameless, who died at nineteen years, Andronicus the physician paying memorial placed this witness the last of all.

XLVIII ON ATTHIS OF CNIDOS AUTHOR UNKNOWN

Atthis who didst live for me and breathe thy last toward me, source of joyfulness formerly as now of tears, holy, much lamented, how sleepest thou the mournful sleep, thou whose head was never laid away from thy husband's breast, leaving Theius alone as one who is no more; for with thee the hopes of our life went to darkness.

XLIX ON PREXO, WIFE OF THEOCRITUS OF SAMOS LEONIDAS OF TARENTUM

Who and of whom art thou, O woman, that liest under the Parian column? Prexo, daughter of Calliteles. And of what country? Of Samos. And also who buried thee? Theocritus, to whom my parents gave me in marriage. And of what diedst thou? Of child-birth. How old? Two-and-twenty. And childless? Nay, but I left a three-year-old Calliteles. May he live at least and come to great old age. And to thee, O stranger, may Fortune give all prosperity.

L ON AMAZONIA OF THESSALONICA AUTHOR UNKNOWN

Why idly bemoaning linger you by my tomb? nothing worthy of lamentation is mine among the dead. Cease from plaints and be at rest,

O husband, and you my children fare well, and keep the memory of Amazonia.

LI ON A LACEDAEMONIAN NURSE AUTHOR UNKNOWN

Here earth holds the Peloponnesian woman who was the most faithful nurse of the children of Diogeitus.

LII ON A LYDIAN SLAVE DIOSCORIDES

A Lydian am I, yes a Lydian, but in a free tomb, O my master, thou didst lay thy fosterer Timanthes; prosperously mayest thou lengthen out an unharmed life, and if under the hand of old age thou shalt come to me, I am thine, O master, even in the grave.

LIII ON A PERSIAN SLAVE AUTHOR UNKNOWN

Even now beneath the earth I abide faithful to thee, yes my master, as before, forgetting not thy kindness, in that then thou broughtest me thrice out of sickness to safe foothold, and now didst lay me here beneath sufficient shelter, calling me by name, Manes the Persian; and for thy good deeds to me thou shalt have servants readier at need.

LIV ON A FAVOURITE DOG AUTHOR UNKNOWN

Thou who passest on the path, if haply thou dost mark this monument, laugh not, I pray thee, though it is a dog's grave; tears fell for me, and the dust was heaped above me by a master's hands, who likewise engraved these words on my tomb.

LV ON A MALTESE WATCH-DOG TYMNES

Here the stone says it holds the white dog from Melita, the most faithful guardian of Eumelus; Bull they called him while he was yet alive; but now his voice is prisoned in the silent pathways of night.

LVI ON A TAME PARTRIDGE AGATHIAS

No longer, poor partridge migrated from the rocks, does thy woven house hold thee in its thin withies, nor under the sparkle of fresh-faced Dawn dost thou ruffle up the edges of thy basking wings; the cat bit off thy head, but the rest of thee I snatched away, and she did not fill her greedy jaw; and now may the earth cover thee not lightly but heavily, lest she drag out thy remains.

LVII ON A THESSALIAN HOUND SIMONIDES

Surely even as thou liest dead in this tomb I deem the wild beasts yet fear thy white bones, huntress Lycas; and thy valour great Pelion knows, and splendid Ossa and the lonely peaks of Cithaeron.

LVIII ON CHARIDAS OF CYRENE CALLIMACHUS

Does Charidas in truth sleep beneath thee? If thou meanest the son of Arimmas of Cyrene, beneath me. O Charidas, what of the under world? Great darkness. And what of the resurrection? A lie. And Pluto? A fable; we perish utterly. This my tale to you is true; but if thou wilt have the pleasant one of the Samian, I am a large ox in Hades.

LIX ON THEOGNIS OF SINOPE SIMONIDES

I am the monument of Theognis of Sinope, over whom Glaucus set me in guerdon of their long fellowship.

LX ON A DEAD FRIEND AUTHOR UNKNOWN

This little stone, good Sabinus, is the record of our great friendship; ever will I require thee; and thou, if it is permitted, drink not among the dead of the water of Lethe for me.

LXI ON AN UNHAPPY MAN AUTHOR UNKNOWN

I Dionysius of Tarsus lie here at sixty, having never married; and would that my father had not.

LXII ON A CRETAN MERCHANT SIMONIDES

I Brotachus of Gortyna, a Cretan, lie here, not having come hither for this, but for traffic.

LXIII ON SAON OF ACANTHUS CALLIMACHUS

Here Saon, son of Dicon of Acanthus, rests in a holy sleep; say not that the good die.

CHAPTER IV

LITERATURE AND ART

I THE GROVE OF THE MUSES AUTHOR UNKNOWN

Say thou that this grave is consecrate to the Muses, pointing to the books by the plane-trees, and that we guard it; and if a true lover of ours come hither, we crown him with our ivy.

II THE VOICE OF THE WORLD ANTIPATER OF SIDON

The herald of the prowess of heroes and the interpreter of the immortals, a second sun on the life of Greece, Homer, the light of the Muses, the ageless mouth of all the world, lies hid, O stranger, under the sea-washed sand.

III THE TALE OF TROY ALPHEUS

Still we hear the wail of Andromache, still we see all Troy toppling from her foundations, and the battling of Ajax, and Hector, bound to the horses, dragged under the city's crown of towers, through the Muse of Maeonides, the poet with whom no one country adorns herself as her own, but the zones of both worlds.

IV ORPHEUS ANTIPATER OF SIDON

No longer, Orpheus, wilt thou lead the charmed oaks, no longer the rocks nor the lordless herds of the wild beasts; no longer wilt thou lull the roaring of the winds, nor hail and sweep of snowstorms nor dashing sea; for thou perishedst; and the daughters of Mnemosyne wept sore for thee, and thy mother Calliope above all. Why do we mourn over dead sons, when not even gods avail to ward off Hades from their children?

V SAPPHO POSIDIPPUS

Doricha, long ago thy bones are dust, and the ribbon of thy hair and the raiment scented with unguents, wherein once wrapping lovely Charaxus round thou didst cling to him carousing into dawn; but the white leaves of the dear ode of Sappho remain yet and shall remain speaking thy blessed name, which Naucratis shall keep here so long as a sea-going ship shall come to the lagoons of Nile.

VI ERINNA (1) AUTHOR UNKNOWN

Thee, as thou wert just giving birth to a springtide of honeyed songs and just finding thy swan-voice, Fate, mistress of the threaded spindle, drove to Acheron across the wide water of the dead; but the fair labour of thy verses, Erinna, cries that thou art not perished, but keepest mingled choir with the Maidens of Pieria.

VII ERINNA (2) LEONIDAS OF TARENTUM

The young maiden singer Erinna, the bee among poets, who sipped the flowers of the Muses, Hades snatched away to be his bride; truly indeed said the girl in her wisdom, "Thou art envious, O Death."

VIII ANACREON'S GRAVE (1) AUTHOR UNKNOWN

O stranger who passest this the tomb of Anacreon, pour libation over me in going by; for I am a drinker of wine.

IX ANACREON'S GRAVE (2) ANTIPATER OF SIDON

O stranger who passest by the humble tomb of Anacreon, if thou hast had aught of good from my books pour libation on my ashes, pour libation of the jocund grape, that my bones may rejoice wetted with wine; so I, who was ever deep in the wine-steeped revels of Dionysus, I who was bred among drinking tunes, shall not even when dead endure without Bacchus this place to which the generation of mortals must come.

X PINDAR ANTIPATER OF SIDON

As high as the trumpet's blast outsounds the thin flute, so high above all others did thy lyre ring; nor idly did the tawny swarm mould their waxen-celled honey, O Pindar, about thy tender lips: witness the horned god of Maenalus when he sang thy hymn and forgot his own pastoral reeds.

XI THESPIS DIOSCORIDES

I am Thespis who first shaped the strain of tragedy, making new partition of fresh graces among the masquers when Bacchus would lead home the wine-stained chorus, for whom a goat and a basket of Attic figs was as yet the prize in contests. A younger race reshape all this; and infinite time will make many more inventions yet; but mine are mine.

XII SOPHOCLES SIMMIAS

Gently over the tomb of Sophocles, gently creep, O ivy, flinging forth thy pale tresses, and all about let the rose-petal blow, and the clustered vine shed her soft tendrils round, for the sake of the wise- hearted eloquence mingled of the Muses and Graces that lived on his honeyed tongue.

XIII ARISTOPHANES PLATO

The Graces, seeking to take a sanctuary that will not fall, found the soul of Aristophanes.

XIV RHINTHO NOSSIS

With a ringing laugh, and a friendly word over me do thou pass by; I am Rhintho of Syracuse, a small nightingale of the Muses; but from our tragical mirth we plucked an ivy of our own.

XV MELEAGER (1) MELEAGER

Tread softly, O stranger; for here an old man sleeps among the holy dead, lulled in the slumber due to all, Meleager son of Eucrates, who united Love of the sweet tears and the Muses with the joyous Graces; whom God-begotten Tyre brought to manhood, and the sacred land of Gadara, but lovely Cos nursed in old age among the Meropes. But if thou art a Syrian, say /Salam/, and if a Phoenician, /Naidios/, and if a Greek, Hail; they are the same.

XVI MELEAGER (2) MELEAGER

Island Tyre was my nurse; and the Attic land that lies in Syrian Gadara is the country of my birth; and I sprang of Eucrates, I Meleager, the companion of the Muses, first of all who have run side by side with the Graces of Menippus. And if I am a Syrian, what wonder? We all dwell in one country, O stranger, the world; one Chaos brought all mortals to birth. And when stricken in years, I inscribed this on my tablets before burial, since old age is death's near neighbour; but do thou, bidding hail to me, the aged talker, thyself reach a talking old age.

XVII PYLADES THE HARP-PLAYER ALCAEUS OF MESSENE

All Greece bewails thee departed, Pylades, and cuts short her undone hair; even Phoebus himself laid aside the laurels from his unshorn tresses, honouring his own minstrel as was meet, and the Muses wept, and Asopus stayed his stream, hearing the cry from their wailing lips; and Dionysus' halls ceased from dancing when thou didst pass down the iron path of Death.

XVIII THE DEATH OF MUSIC LEONTIUS

When Orpheus was gone, a Muse was yet haply left, but when thou didst perish, Plato, the harp likewise ceased; for till then there yet lived some little fragment of the old melodies, saved in thy soul and hands.

XIX APOLLO AND MARSYAS (1) ALCAEUS OF MESSENE

No more through pine-clad Phrygia, as of old, shalt thou make melody, uttering thy notes through the pierced reeds, nor in thy hands as before shall the workmanship of Tritonian Athena flower forth, nymph-born Satyr; for thy hands are bound tight in gyves, since being mortal thou didst join immortal strife with Phoebus; and the flutes, that cried as honey-sweet as his harp, gained thee from the contest no crown but death.

XX APOLLO AND MARSYAS (2) ARCHIAS

Thou hangest high where the winds lash thy wild body, O wretched one, swinging from a shaggy pine; thou hangest high, for thou didst stand up to strife against Phoebus, O Satyr, dweller on the cliff of Celaenae; and we nymphs shall no longer as before hear the honey- sounding cry of thy flute on the Phrygian hills.

XXI GLAPHYRUS THE FLUTE-PLAYER ANTIPATER OF THESSALONICA

Phoebus said over clear-voiced Glaphyrus as he breathed desire through the pierced lotus-pipes, "O Marsyas, thou didst tell false of thy discovery, for this is he who carried off Athena's flutes out of Phrygia; and if thou hadst blown then in such as his, Hyagnis would not have wept that disastrous flute-strife by Maeander."

XXII VIOL AND FLUTE THEOCRITUS

Wilt thou for the Muses' sake play me somewhat of sweet on thy twin flutes? and I lifting the harp will begin to make music on the strings; and Daphnis the neatherd will mingle enchantment with tuneable breath of the wax-bound pipe; and thus standing nigh within the fringed cavern mouth, let us rob sleep from Pan the lord of the goats.

XXIII POPULAR SONGS LUCILIUS

Eutychides, the writer of songs, is dead; flee, O you under earth! Eutychides is coming with his odes; he left instructions to burn along with him twelve lyres and twenty-five boxes of airs. Now Charon has come upon you; whither may one retreat in future, since Eutychides fills Hades too?

XXIV GRAMMAR, MUSIC, RHETORIC LUCILIUS

Pluto turns away the dead rhetorician Marcus, saying, "Let the dog Cerberus suffice us here; yet if thou needs must, declaim to Ixion and Melito the song-writer, and Tityus; for I have no worse evil than thee, till Rufus the critic comes to murder the language here."

XXV CALAMUS AUTHOR UNKNOWN

I the reed was a useless plant; for out of me grew not figs nor apple nor grape-cluster; but man consecrated me a daughter of Helicon, piercing my delicate lips and making me the channel of a narrow stream; and thenceforth, whenever I sip black drink, like one inspired I speak all words with this voiceless mouth.

XXVI IN THE CLASSROOM CALLIMACHUS

Simus son of Miccus, giving me to the Muses, asked for himself learning, and they, like Glaucus, gave a great gift for a little one; and I lean gaping up against this double letter of the Samian, a tragic Dionysus, listening to the little boys; and they repeat /Holy is the hair/, telling me my own dream.

XXVII THE POOR SCHOLAR ARISTON

O mice, if you are come after bread, go to another cupboard (for we live in a tiny cottage) where you will feed daintily on rich cheese and dried raisins, and make an abundant supper off the scraps; but if you sharpen your teeth again on my books and come in with your graceless rioting, you shall howl for it.

XXVIII THE HIGHER METAPHYSIC AGATHIAS

That second Aristotle, Nicostratus, Plato's peer, splitter of the straws of the sublimest philosophy, was asked about the soul as follows: How may one rightly describe the soul, as mortal, or, on the contrary, immortal? and should we speak of it as a body or incorporeal? and is it to be placed among intelligible or sensible objects, or compounded of both? So he read through the treatises of the transcendentalists, and Aristotle's /de Anima/, and explored the Platonic heights of the /Phaedo/, and wove into a single fabric the whole exact truth on all its sides. Then wrapping his threadbare cloak about him, and stroking down the end of his beard, he proffered the solution:—If there exists at all a nature of the soul—for of this I am not sure—it is certainly either mortal or immortal, of solid nature or immaterial; however, when you cross Acheron, there you shall know the certainty like Plato. And if you will, imitate young Cleombrotus of Ambracia, and let your body drop from the roof; and you may at once recognise your self apart from the body by merely getting rid of the subject of your inquiry.

XXIX THE PHAEDO OF PLATO AUTHOR UNKNOWN

If Plato did not write me, there were two Platos; I carry in me all the flowers of Socratic talk. But Panaetius concluded me to be spurious; yes, he who concluded that the soul was mortal, would conclude me spurious as well.

XXX CLEOMBROTUS OF AMBRACIA CALLIMACHUS

Saying, "Farewell, O Sun," Cleombrotus of Ambracia leaped off a high wall to Hades, having seen no evil worthy of death, but only having read that one writing of Plato's on the soul.

XXXI THE DEAD SCHOLAR CALLIMACHUS

One told me of thy fate, Heraclitus, and wrung me to tears, and I remembered how often both of us let the sun sink as we talked; but thou, methinks, O friend from Halicarnassus, art ashes long and long ago; yet thy nightingale-notes live, whereon Hades the ravisher of all things shall not lay his hand.

XXXII ALEXANDRIANISM CALLIMACHUS

I hate the cyclic poem, nor do I delight in a road that carries many hither and thither; I detest, too, one who ever goes girt with lovers, and I drink not from the fountain; I loathe everything popular.

XXXIII SPECIES AETERNITATIS PTOLEMAEUS

I know that I am mortal, and ephemeral; but when I scan the multitudinous circling spirals of the stars, no longer do I touch earth with my feet, but sit with Zeus himself, and take my fill of the ambrosial food of gods.

XXXIV THE PASTORAL POETS ARTEMIDORUS

The pastoral Muses, once scattered, now are all a single flock in a single fold.

XXXV ON A RELIEF OF EROS AND ANTEROS AUTHOR UNKNOWN

Nemesis fashioned a winged Love contrary to winged Love, warding off bow with bow, that he may be done by as he did; and, bold and fearless before, he sheds tears, having tasted of the bitter arrows, and spits thrice into his low-girt bosom. Ah, most wonderful! one will burn with fire: Love has set Love aflame.

XXXVI ON A LOVE BREAKING THE THUNDERBOLT AUTHOR UNKNOWN

Lo, how winged Love breaks the winged thunderbolt, showing that he is a fire more potent than fire.

XXXVII ON A LOVE PLOUGHING MOSCHUS

Laying down his torch and bow, soft Love took the rod of an ox-driver, and wore a wallet over his shoulder; and coupling patient-necked bulls under his yoke, sowed the wheat-bearing furrow of Demeter; and spoke, looking up, to Zeus himself, "Fill thou the corn-lands, lest I put thee, bull of Europa, under my plough."

XXXVIII ON A PAN PIPING ARABIUS

One might surely have clearly heard Pan piping, so did the sculptor mingle breath with the form; but in despair at the sight of flying, unstaying Echo, he renounced the pipe's unavailing sound.

XXXIX ON A STATUE OF THE ARMED VENUS AUTHOR UNKNOWN

Pallas said, seeing Cytherea armed, "O Cyprian, wilt thou that we go so to judgment?" and she, laughing softly, "why should I lift a shield in contest? if I conquer when naked, how will it be when I take arms?"

XL ON THE CNIDIAN VENUS OF PRAXITELES AUTHOR UNKNOWN

The Cyprian said when she saw the Cyprian of Cnidus, "Alas where did Praxiteles see me naked?"

XLI ON A SLEEPING ARIADNE AUTHOR UNKNOWN

Strangers, touch not the marble Ariadne, lest she even start up on the quest of Theseus.

XLII ON A NIOBE BY PRAXITELES AUTHOR UNKNOWN

From life the gods made me a stone; and from stone again Praxiteles wrought me into life.

XLIII ON A PICTURE OF A FAUN AGATHIAS

Untouched, O young Satyr, does thy reed utter a sound, or why leaning sideways dost thou put thine ear to the pipe? He laughs and is silent; yet haply had he spoken a word, but was held in forgetfulness by delight? for the wax did not hinder, but of his own will he welcomed silence, with his whole mind turned intent on the pipe.

XLIV ON THE HEIFER OF MYRON AUTHOR UNKNOWN

Ah thou wert not quick enough, Myron, in thy casting; but the bronze grew solid before thou hadst cast in a soul.

XLV ON A SLEEPING SATYR PLATO

This Satyr Diodorus engraved not, but laid to rest; your touch will wake him; the silver is asleep.

XLVI THE LIMIT OF ART PARRHASIUS

Even though incredible to the hearer, I say this; for I affirm that the clear limits of this art have been found under my hand, and the mark is fixed fast that cannot be exceeded. But nothing among mortals is faultless.

CHAPTER V

RELIGION

I WORSHIP IN SPRING (1) THEAETETUS

Now at her fruitful birth-tide the fair green field flowers out in blowing roses; now on the boughs of the colonnaded cypresses the cicala, mad with music, lulls the binder of sheaves; and the careful mother-swallow, having fashioned houses under the eaves, gives harbourage to her brood in the mud-plastered cells: and the sea slumbers, with zephyr-wooing calm spread clear over the broad ship-tracks, not breaking in squalls on the stern-posts, not vomiting foam upon the beaches. O sailor, burn by the altars the glittering round of a mullet or a cuttle-fish, or a vocal scarus, to Priapus, ruler of ocean and giver of anchorage; and so go fearlessly on thy seafaring to the bounds of the Ionian Sea.

II WORSHIP IN SPRING (2) AGATHIAS

Ocean lies purple in calm; for no gale whitens the fretted waves with its ruffling breath, and no longer is the sea shattered round the rocks and sucked back again down towards the deep. West winds breathe, and the swallow titters over the straw-glued chamber that she has built. Be of good cheer, O skilled in seafaring, whether thou sail to the Syrtis or the Sicilian shingle: only by the altars of Priapus of the Anchorage burn a scarus or ruddy wrasse.

III ZEUS OF THE FAIR WIND AUTHOR UNKNOWN

Let one call from the stern on Zeus the Fair Wind for guide on his road, shaking out sail against the forestays; whether he runs to the Dark Eddies, where Poseidon rolls his curling wave along the sands, or whether he searches the backward passage down the Aegean sea-plain, let him lay honey-cakes by this image, and so go his way; here Philon, son of Antipater, set up the ever-gracious god for pledge of fair and fortunate voyaging.

IV THE SACRED CITY MACEDONIUS

Beneath flowering Tmolus, by the stream of Maeonian Hermus, am I, Sardis, capital city of the Lydians. I was the first who bore witness for Zeus; for I would not betray the hidden child of our Rhea. I too was nurse of Bromius, and saw him amid the thunder-flash shining with broader radiance; and first on our slopes the golden-haired god pressed the harvest of wine out of the breasts of the grape. All grace has been given me, and many a time has many an age found me envied by the happiest cities.

V HERMES OF THE WAYS AUTHOR UNKNOWN

Go and rest your limbs here for a little under the juniper, O wayfarers, by Hermes, Guardian of the Way, not in crowds, but those of you whose knees are tired with heavy toil and thirst after traversing a long road; for there a breeze and a shady seat and the fountain under the rock will lull your toil-wearied limbs; and having so escaped the midday breath of the autumnal dogstar, as is right, honour Hermes of the Ways.

VI BELOW CYLLENE NICIAS

I who inherit the tossing mountain-forests of steep Cyllene, stand here guarding the pleasant playing fields, Hermes, to whom boys often offer marjoram and hyacinth and fresh garlands of violets.

VII PAN OF THE SEA-CLIFF ARCHIAS

Me, Pan, the fishermen placed upon this holy cliff, Pan of the seashore, the watcher here over the fair anchorages of the harbour; and I take care now of the baskets and again of the trawlers off this shore. But sail thou by, O stranger, and in requital of this good service of theirs I will send behind thee a gentle south wind.

VIII THE SPIRIT OF THE SEA ARCHIAS

Small to see, I, Priapus, inhabit this spit of shore, not much bigger than a sea-gull, sharp-headed, footless, such an one as upon lonely beaches might be carved by the sons of toiling fishermen. But if any basket-finder or angler call me to succour, I rush fleeter than the blast: likewise I see the creatures that run under water; and truly the form of godhead is known from deeds, not from shape.

IX THE GUARDIAN OF THE CHASE SATYRUS

Whether thou goest on the hill with lime smeared over thy fowler's reed, or whether thou killest hares, call on Pan; Pan shows the dog the prints of the furry foot, Pan raises the stiff-jointed lime-twigs.

X THE HUNTER GOD LEONIDAS OF TARENTUM

Fair fall thy chase, O hunter of hares, and thou fowler who comest pursuing the winged people beneath this double hill; and cry thou to me, Pan, the guardian of the wood from my cliff; I join the chase with both dogs and reeds.

XI FORTUNA PARVULORUM PERSES

Even me the little god of small things if thou call upon in due season thou shalt find; but ask not for great things; since whatsoever a god of the commons can give to a labouring man, of this I, Tycho, have control.

XII THE PRAYERS OF THE SAINTS ADDAEUS

If thou pass by the hero (and he is called Philopregmon) who lies by the cross-roads in front of Potidaea, tell him to what work thou leadest thy feet; straightway will he, being by thee, make thy business easy.

XIII SAVED BY FAITH LEONIDAS OF TARENTUM

They call me the little one, and say I cannot go straight and fearless on a prosperous voyage like ships that sail out to sea; and I deny it not; I am a little boat, but to the sea all is equal; fortune, not size, makes the difference. Let another have the advantage in rudders; for some put their confidence in this and some in that, but may my salvation be of God.

XIV THE SERVICE OF GOD AUTHOR UNKNOWN

Me Chelidon, priestess of Zeus, who knew well in old age how to make offering on the altars of the immortals, happy in my children, free from grief, the tomb holds; for with no shadow in their eyes the gods saw my piety.

XV BEATI MUNDO CORDE AUTHOR UNKNOWN

He who enters the incense-filled temple must be holy; and holiness is to have a pure mind.

XVI THE WATER OF PURITY AUTHOR UNKNOWN

Hallowed in soul, O stranger, come even into the precinct of a pure god, touching thyself with the virgin water; for the good a few drops are set; but a wicked man the whole ocean cannot wash in its waters.

XVII THE GREAT MYSTERIES CRINAGORAS

Though thy life be fixed in one seat, and thou sailest not the sea nor treadest the roads on dry land, yet by all means go to Attica that thou mayest see those great nights of the worship of Demeter; whereby thou shalt possess thy soul without care among the living, and lighter when thou must go to the place that awaiteth all.

CHAPTER VI

NATURE

I THE GARDEN GOD AUTHOR UNKNOWN

Call me not him who comes from Libanus, O stranger, who delights in the talk of young men love-making by night; I am small and a rustic, born of a neighbour nymph, and all my business is labour of the garden; whence four garlands at the hands of the four Seasons crown me from the beloved fruitful threshing-floor.

II PAN'S PIPING ALCAEUS OF MESSENE

Breathe music, O Pan that goest on the mountains, with thy sweet lips, breathe delight into thy pastoral reed, pouring song from the musical pipe, and make the melody sound in tune with the choral words; and about thee to the pulse of the rhythm let the inspired foot of these water-nymphs keep falling free.

III THE ROADSIDE POOL LEONIDAS OF TARENTUM

Drink not here, traveller, from this warm pool in the brook, full of mud stirred by the sheep at pasture; but go a very little way over the ridge where the heifers are grazing; for there by yonder pastoral stone-pine thou wilt find bubbling through the fountained rock a spring colder than northern snow.

IV THE MEADOW AT NOON AUTHOR UNKNOWN

Here fling thyself down on the grassy meadow, O traveller, and rest thy relaxed limbs from painful weariness; since here also, as thou listenest to the cicalas' tune, the stone-pine trembling in the wafts of west wind will lull thee, and the shepherd on the mountains piping at noon nigh the spring under a copse of leafy plane: so escaping the ardours of the autumnal dogstar thou wilt cross the height to-morrow; trust this good counsel that Pan gives thee.

V BENEATH THE PINE PLATO

Sit down by this high-foliaged voiceful pine that rustles her branches beneath the western breezes, and beside my chattering waters Pan's pipe shall bring drowsiness down on thy enchanted eyelids.

VI WOOD-MUSIC AUTHOR UNKNOWN

Come and sit under my stone-pine that murmurs so honey-sweet as it bends to the soft western breeze; and lo this honey-dropping fountain, where I bring sweet sleep playing on my lonely reeds.

VII THE PLANE-TREE ON HYMETTUS HERMOCREON

Sit down, stranger, as thou passest by, under this shady plane, whose leaves flutter in the soft breath of the west wind, where Nicagoras consecrated me, the renowned Hermes son of Maia, protector of his orchard-close and cattle.

VIII THE GARDEN OF PAN PLATO

Let the shaggy cliff of the Dryads be silent, and the springs welling from the rock, and the many-mingled bleating of the ewes; for Pan himself makes music on his melodious pipe, running his supple lip over the jointed reeds; and around him stand up to dance with glad feet the water-nymphs and the nymphs of the oakwood.

IX THE FOUNTAIN OF LOVE MARIANUS

Here beneath the plane-trees, overborne by soft sleep, Love slumbered, giving his torch to the Nymphs' keeping; and the Nymphs said one to another, "Why do we delay? and would that with this we might have quenched the fire in the heart of mortals." But now, the torch having kindled even the waters, the amorous Nymphs pour hot water thence into the bathing pool.

X ON THE LAWN COMETAS

Dear Pan, abide here, drawing the pipe over thy lips, for thou wilt find Echo on these sunny greens.

XI THE SINGING STONE AUTHOR UNKNOWN

Remember me the singing stone, thou who passest by Nisaea; for when Alcathous was building his bastions, then Phoebus lifted on his shoulder a stone for the house, and laid down on me his Delphic harp; thenceforth I am lyre-voiced; strike me lightly with a little pebble, and carry away witness of my boast.

XII THE WOODLAND WELL AUTHOR UNKNOWN

I the ever-flowing Clear Fount gush forth for by-passing wayfarers from the neighbouring dell; and everywhere I am bordered well with planes and soft-bloomed laurels, and make coolness and shade to lie in. Therefore pass me not by in summer; rest by me in quiet, ridding thee of thirst and weariness.

XIII ASLEEP IN THE WOOD THEOCRITUS

Thou sleepest on the leaf-strewn floor, Daphnis, resting thy weary body; and the hunting-snakes are freshly set on the hills; and Pan pursues thee, and Priapus who binds the yellow ivy on his lovely head, passing side by side into the cave; but flee thou, flee, shaking off the dropping drowsiness of slumber.

XIV THE ORCHARD-CORNER ANYTE

I, Hermes, stand here by the windy orchard in the cross-ways nigh the grey sea-shore, giving rest on the way to wearied men; and the fountain wells forth cold stainless water.

XV PASTORAL SOLITUDE SATYRUS

Tongueless Echo along this pastoral slope makes answering music to the birds with repeating voice.

XVI TO A BLACKBIRD SINGING MARCUS ARGENTARIUS

No longer now warble on the oak, no longer sing, O blackbird, sitting on the topmost spray; this tree is thine enemy; hasten where the vine rises in clustering shade of silvered leaves; on her bough rest the sole of thy foot, around her sing and pour the shrill music of thy mouth; for the oak carries mistletoe baleful to birds, and she the grape-cluster; and the Wine-god cherishes singers.

XVII UNDER THE OAK ANTIPHILUS

Lofty-hung boughs of the tall oak, a shadowy height over men that take shelter from the fierce heat, fair-foliaged, closer-roofing than tiles, houses of wood-pigeons, houses of crickets, O noontide branches, protect me likewise who lie beneath your tresses, fleeing from the sun's rays.

XVIII THE RELEASE OF THE OX ADDAEUS

The labouring ox, outworn with old age and labour of the furrow, Alcon did not lead to the butchering knife, reverencing it for its works; and astray in the deep meadow grass it rejoices with lowings over freedom from the plough.

XIX THE SWALLOW AND THE GRASSHOPPER EVENUS

Attic maid, honey-fed, chatterer, snatchest thou and bearest the chattering cricket for feast to thy unfledged young, thou chatterer the chatterer, thou winged the winged, thou summer guest the summer guest, and wilt not quickly throw it away? for it is not right nor just that singers should perish by singers' mouths.

XX THE COMPLAINT OF THE CICALA AUTHOR UNKNOWN

Why in merciless chase, shepherds, do you tear me the solitude-haunting cricket from the dewy sprays, me the roadside nightingale of the Nymphs, who at midday talk shrilly in the hills and the shady dells? Lo, here is the thrust and the blackbird, lo here such flocks of starlings, plunderers of the cornfield's riches; it is allowed to seize the ravagers of your fruits: destroy them: why grudge me my leaves and fresh dew?

XXI THE LAMENT OF THE SWALLOW PAMPHILUS

Why all day long, hapless maiden daughter of Pandion, soundest thou wailingly through thy twittering mouth? has longing come on thee for thy maidenhead, that Tereus of Thrace ravished from thee by dreadful violence?

XXII THE SHEPHERD OF THE NYMPHS MYRINUS

Thyrsis the reveller, the shepherd of the Nymphs' sheep, Thyrsis who pipes on the reed like Pan, having drunk at noon, sleeps under the shady pine, and Love himself has taken his crook and watches the flocks.

XXIII THE SHRINE BY THE SEA (1) MNASALCAS

Let us stand by the low shore of the spray-scattering deep, looking on the precinct of Cypris of the Sea, and the fountain overshadowed with poplars, from which the shrill kingfishers draw water with their bills.

XXIV THE SHRINE BY THE SEA (2) ANYTE

This is the Cyprians ground, since it was her pleasure ever to look from land on the shining sea, that she may give fulfilment of their voyage to sailors; and around the deep trembles, gazing on her bright image.

XXV THE LIGHTHOUSE AUTHOR UNKNOWN

No longer dreading the rayless night-mist, sail towards me confidently, O seafarers; for all wanderers I light my far-shining torch, memorial of the labours of the Asclepiadae.

XXVI SPRING ON THE COAST (1) LEONIDAS OF TARENTUM

Now is the season of sailing; for already the chattering swallow is come, and the gracious west wind; the meadows flower, and the sea, tossed up with waves and rough blasts, has sunk to silence. Weigh thine anchors and unloose thine hawsers, O mariner, and sail with all thy canvas set: this I Priapus of the harbour bid thee, O man, that thou mayest sail forth to all thy trafficking.

XXVII SPRING ON THE COAST (2) ANTIPATER OF SIDON

Now is the season for a ship to run through the gurgling water, and no longer does the sea gloom, fretted with gusty squalls, and now the swallow plasters her round houses under the eaves, and the soft leafage laughs in the meadows. Therefore wind up your soaked cables, O sailors, and weight your hidden anchors from the harbours, and stretch the forestays to carry your well-woven sails. This I the son of Bromius bid you, Priapus of the anchorage.

XXVIII GREEN SUMMER NICAENETUS

I do not wish to feast down in the city, Philotherus, but in the country, delighting myself with the breath of the west wind; sufficient couch for me is a strewing of boughs under my side, for at hand is a bed of native willow and osier, the ancient garland of the Carians; but let wine be brought, and the delightful lyre of the Muses, that drinking at our will we may sing the renowned bride of Zeus, lady of our island.

XXIX PALACE GARDENS ARABIUS

I am filled with waters and gardens and groves and vineyards, and the joyousness of the bordering sea; and fisherman and farmer from different sides stretch forth to me the pleasant gifts of sea and land: and them who abide in me either a bird singing or the sweet cry of the ferrymen lulls to rest.

CHAPTER VII

THE FAMILY

I THE HOUSE OF THE RIGHTEOUS MACEDONIUS

Righteousness has raised this house from the first foundation even to the lofty roof; for Macedonius fashioned not his wealth by heaping up from the possessions of others with plundering sword, nor has any poor man here wept over his vain and profitless toil, being robbed of his most just hire; and as rest from labour is kept inviolate by the just man, so let the works of pious mortals endure.

II THE GIRL'S CUP PAULUS SILENTIARIUS

Aniceteia wets her golden lip in me; but may I give her also the draught of bridal.

III THE FLOWER UNBLOWN PHILODEMUS

Not yet is thy summer unfolded from the bud, nor does the purple come upon thy grape that throws out the first shoots of its maiden graces; but already the young Loves are whetting their fleet arrows, Lysidice, and the hidden fire is smouldering. Flee we, wretched lovers, ere yet the shaft is on the string; I prophesy a mighty burning soon.

IV A ROSE IN WINTER CRINAGORAS

Roses were now bloomed in spring, but now in midwinter we have opened our crimson cups, smiling in delight on this thy birthday morning, that brings thee so nigh the bridal bed: better for us to be wreathed on the brows of so fair a woman than wait for the spring sun.

V GOODBYE TO CHILDHOOD AUTHOR UNKNOWN

Her tambourines and pretty ball, and the net that confined her hair, and her dolls and dolls' dresses, Timareta dedicates before her marriage to Artemis of Limnae, a maiden to a maiden, as is fit; do thou, daughter of Leto, laying thine hand over the girl Timareta, preserve her purely in her purity.

VI THE WIFE'S PRAYER ANTIPATER OF THESSALONICA

Cythera of Bithynia dedicated me, the marble image of thy form, O Cyprian, having vowed it: but do thou impart in return thy great grace for this little one, as is thy wont; and concord with her husband satisfies her.

VII BRIDEGROOM AND BRIDE JOANNES BARBUCALLUS

To Persuasion and the Paphian, Hermophiles the neatherd, bridegroom of flower-chapleted Eurynome, dedicates a cream-cheese and combs from his hives; but accept for her the cheese, for me the honey.

VIII THE BRIDE'S VIGIL AGATHIAS

Never grow mould, O lamp, nor call up the rain, lest thou stop my bridegroom in his coming; always thou art jealous of the Cyprian; yes and when she betrothed Hero to Leander—O my heart, leave the rest alone. Thou art the Fire-God's, and I believe that by vexing the Cyprian thou flatterest thy master's pangs.

IX HEAVEN ON EARTH THEOCRITUS

This is not the common Cyprian; revere the goddess, and name her the Heavenly, the dedication of holy Chrysogone in the house of Amphicles, with whom she had children and life together; and ever it was better with them year by year, who began with thy worship, O mistress; for mortals who serve the gods are the better off themselves.

X WEARY PARTING MELEAGER

Fair-freighted sea-faring ships that sail the Strait of Helle, taking the good north wind in your sails, if haply on the island shores of Cos you see Phanion gazing on the sparkling sea, carry this message: Fair bride, thy desire beings me, not a sailor but a wayfarer on my feet. For if you say this, carrying good news, straitway will Zeus of the Fair Weather likewise breathe into your canvas.

XI MOTHERHOOD CALLIMACHUS

Again, O Ilithyia, come thou at Lycaenis' call, Lady of Birth, even thus with happy issue of travail; whose offering now this is for a girl; but afterwards may thy fragrant temple hold another for a boy.

XII PAST PERIL CALLIMACHUS

Thou knowest, Asclepius, that thou hast received payment of the debt that Aceson owed, having vowed it for his wife Demodice; yet if it be forgotten, and thou demand thy wages, this tablet says it will give testimony.

XIII FATHER AND MOTHER PHAEDIMUS

Artemis, to thee the son of Cichesias dedicates his shoes, and Themostodice the strait folds of her gown, because thou didst graciously hold thy two hands over her in childbed, coming, O our Lady, without thy bow. And do thou, O Artemis, grant yet to Leon to see his infant child a sturdy-limbed boy.

XIV HOUSEHOLD HAPPINESS AGATHIAS

Callirhoë dedicates to the Paphian garlands, to Pallas a tress of hair, to Artemis her girdle; for she found a wooer to her heart, and was given a stainless prime, and bore male children.

XV GRACIOUS CHILDREN THEAETETUS

Be happy, children; whose family are you? and what gracious name is given to so pretty things as you?—I am Nicanor, and my father is Aepioretus, and my mother Hegeso, and I am a Macedonian born.—And I am Phila, and this is my brother; and we both stand here fulfilling a vow of our parents.

XVI THE UNBROKEN HOME AUTHOR UNKNOWN

Androtion built me, a burying-place for himself and his children and wife, but as yet I am the tomb of no one; so likewise may I remain for a long time; and if it must be, let me take to myself the eldest first.

XVII THE BROKEN HOME BIANOR

I wept the doom of my Theionoë, but borne up by hopes of her child I wailed in lighter grief; and now a jealous fate has bereft me of the child also; alas, babe, I am cozened even of thee, all that was left me. Persephone, hear thou this at a father's lamentation; lay the babe on the bosom of its mother who is gone.

XVIII SUNDERING ANTIPATER OF SIDON

Surely, methinks, when thou hadst set thy footprint, Aretemias, from the boat upon Cocytus' shore, carrying in thy young hand thy baby just dead, the fair Dorian women had compassion in Hades, inquiring of thy fate; and thou, fretting thy cheeks with tears, didst utter that woful word: O friends, having travailed of two children, I left one for my husband Euphron, and the other I bring to the dead.

XIX NUNC DIMITTIS JOANNES BARBUCALLUS

Gazing upon my husband as my last thread was spun, I praised the gods of death, and I praised the gods of marriage, those that I left my husband alive, and these that he was even such an one; but may he remain, a father for our children.

XX LEFT ALONE AUTHOR UNKNOWN

Marathonis laid Nicopolis in this stone, wetting the marble coffin with tears, but all to no avail; for what is there more than sorrow for a man alone upon earth when his wife is gone?

XXI EARTH'S FELICITY CARPHYLLIDES

Find no fault as thou passest by my monument, O wayfarer; not even in death have I aught worthy of lamentation. I have left children's children; I had joy of one wife, who grew old along with me; I made marriage for three sons whose sons I often lulled asleep on my breast, and never moaned over the sickness or the death of any: who, shedding tears without sorrow over me, sent me to slumber the sweet sleep in the country of the holy.

CHAPTER VIII

BEAUTY

I SUMMER NOON MELEAGER

I saw Alexis at noon walking on the way, when summer was just cutting the tresses of the cornfields; and double rays burned me; these of Love from the boy's eyes, and those from the sun. But those night allayed again, while these in dreams the phantom of a form kindled yet higher; and Sleep, the releaser of toil for others, brought toil upon me, fashioning the image of beauty in my soul, a breathing fire.

II IN THE FIELD-PATH RHIANUS

Surely, O Cleonicus, the lovely Graces met thee going along the narrow field-path, and clasped thee close with their rose-like hands, O boy, and thou wert made all grace. Hail to thee from afar; but it is not safe, O my dear, for the dry asphodel stalk to move too near the fire.

III THE NEW LOVE MELEAGER

The Cyprian denies that she bore Love, seeing Antiochus among the youths, another Desire; but O you who are young, cherish the new Longing; for assuredly this boy is found a Love stronger than Love.

IV CONTRA MUNDUM CALLIMACHUS

Pour in and say again, "Diocles"; nor does Acheloüs touch the cups consecrated to him; fair is the boy, O Acheloüs, exceeding fair; and if any one says no, let me be alone in my judgment of beauty.

V THE FLOWER OF COS MELEAGER

Praxiteles the sculptor made a Parian image of Love, moulding the Cyprian's son; but now Love, the most beautiful of all the gods, imaging himself, has fashioned a breathing statue, Praxiteles, that the one among mortals and the other in heaven may have all love-charms in control, and at once on earth and among the immortals they may bear the sceptres of Desire. Most happy the sacred city of the Meropes, which nurtured as prince of her youth the god-born new Love.

VI THE SUN OF TYRE MELEAGER

Delicate, so help me Love, are the fosterlings of Tyre; but Myïscus blazes out and quenches them all as the sun the stars.

VII THE LOADSTAR MELEAGER

On thee, Myïscus, the cables of my life are fastened; in thee is the very breath of my soul, what is left of it; for by thine eyes, O boy, that speak even to the deaf, and by thy shining brow, if thou ever dost cast a clouded glance on me, I gaze on winter, and if thou lookest joyously, sweet spring bursts into bloom.

VIII LAUREL AND HYACINTH MELEAGER

O pastoral pipes, no longer sing of Daphnis on the mountains, to pleasure Pan the lord of the goats; neither do you, O lyre interpretess of Phoebus, any more chant Hyacinthus chapleted with maiden laurel; for time was when Daphnis was delightful to the mountain-nymphs, and Hyacinthus to thee; but now let Dion hold the sceptre of Desire.

IX THE QUEST OF PAN GLAUCUS

Nymphs, tell me true when I inquire if Daphnis passing by rested his white kids here.—Yes, yes, piping Pan, and carved in the bark of yonder poplar a letter to say to thee, "Pan, Pan, come to Malea, to the Psophidian mount; I will be there."—Farewell, Nymphs, I go.

X THE AUTUMN BOWER MNASALCAS

Vine, that hastenest so to drop thy leaves to earth, fearest thou then the evening setting of the Pleiad? abide for sweet sleep to fall on Antileon beneath thee, giving all grace to beauty till then.

XI AN ASH IN THE FIRE MELEAGER

Now grey dawn is sweet; but sleepless in the doorway Damis swoons out all that is left of his breath, unhappy, having but seen Heraclitus; for he stood under the beams of his eyes as wax cast among the embers: but arise, I pray thee, luckless Damis; even myself I wear Love's wound and shed tears over thy tears.

CHAPTER IX

FATE AND CHANGE

I THE FLOWER OF YOUTH MARCUS ARGENTARIUS

Sweet-breathed Isias, though thy sleep be tenfold spice, awake and take this garland in thy dear hands, which, blooming now, thou wilt see withering at daybreak, the likeness of a maiden's prime.

II THE MAIDEN'S POSY RUFINUS

I send thee, Rhodocleia, this garland, which myself have twined of fair flowers beneath my hands; here is lily and rose-chalice and moist anemone, and soft narcissus and dark-glowing violet; garlanding thyself with these, cease to be high-minded; even as the garland thou also dost flower and fall.

III WITHERED BLOSSOMS STRATO

If thou boast in thy beauty, know that the rose too blooms, but quickly being withered, is cast on the dunghill; for blossom and beauty have the same time allotted to them, and both together envious time withers away.

IV ROSE AND THORN AUTHOR UNKNOWN

The rose is at her prime a little while; which once past, thou wilt find when thou seekest no rose, but a thorn.

V THE BIRD OF TIME THYMOCLES

Thou remembered haply, thou rememberest when I said to thee that holy word, "Opportunity is the fairest, opportunity the lightest-footed of things; opportunity may not be overtaken by the swiftest bird in air." Now lo! all thy flowers are shed on the ground.

VI THE END OF DESIRE SECUNDUS

I who once was Laïs, an arrow in all men's hearts, no longer Laïs, am plainly to all the Nemesis of years. Ay, by the Cyprian (and what is the Cyprian now to me but an oath to swear by?) not Laïs herself knows Laïs now.

VII HOARDED BEAUTY STRATO

If beauty grows old, impart thou of it before it be gone; and if it abides, why fear to give away what thou dost keep?

VIII DUST AND ASHES ASCLEPIADES

Thou hoardest thy maidenhood; and to what profit? for when thou art gone to Hades thou wilt not find a lover, O girl. Among the living are the Cyprian's pleasures; but in Acheron, O maiden, we shall lie bones and dust.

IX TO-MORROW MACEDONIUS

"To-morrow I will look on thee"—but that never comes for us, while the accustomed putting-off ever grows and grows. This is all thy grace to my longing; and to others thou bearest other gifts, despising my faithful service. "I will see thee at evening." And what is the evening of a woman's life? old age, full of a million wrinkles.

X THE CASKET OF PANDORA MACEDONIUS

I laugh as I look on the jar of Pandora, nor do I blame the woman, but the wings of the Blessings themselves; for they flutter through the sky over the abodes of all the earth, while they ought to have descended on the ground. But the woman behind the lid, with cheeks grown pallid, has lost the splendour of the beauties that she had, and now our life has missed both ways, because she grows old in it, and the jar is empty.

XI COMING WINTER ANTIPATER OF SIDON

Now is autumn, Epicles, and out of the belt of Bootes the clear splendour of Arcturus has risen; now the grape-clusters take thought of the sickle, and men thatch their cottages against winter; but thou hast neither warm fleecy cloak nor garment indoors, and thou wilt be shrivelled up with cold and curse the star.

XII NEMESIS MELEAGER

Thou saidst, by the Cyprian, what not even a god might, O greatly- daring spirit; Theron did not appear fair to thee; to thee Theron did not appear fair; nay, thou wouldst have it so: and thou wilt not quake even before the flaming thunderbolt of Zeus. Wherefore lo! indignant Nemesis hath set thee forth to see, who wert once so voluble, for an example of rashness of tongue.

XIII THE BLOODY WELL APOLLONIDES

I the Clear Fount (for the Nymphs gave this surname to me beyond all other springs) since a robber slew men who were resting beside me and washed his bloodstained hand in my holy waters, have turned that sweet flow backward, and no longer gush out for wayfarers; for who any more will call me the Clear?

XIV A STORY OF THE SEA ANTIPATER OF THESSALONICA

Once on a time when a ship was shattered at sea, two men fell at strife fighting for one plank. Antagoras struck away Pisistratus; one could not blame him, for it was for his life; but Justice took cognisance. The other swam ashore; but him a dog-fish seized; surely the Avenger of the Fates rests not even in the watery deep.

XV EMPTY HANDS CALLIMACHUS

I know that my hands are empty of wealth; but by the Graces, O Menippus, tell me not my own dream; it hurts me to hear evermore this bitter word: yes, my dear, this is the most unloving thing of all I have borne from thee.

XVI LIGHT LOVE MARCUS ARGENTARIUS

Thou wert loved when rich, Sosicrates, but being poor thou art loved no longer; what magic has hunger! And she who before called thee spice and darling Adonis, Menophila, now inquires thy name. Who and whence of men art thou? where is thy city? Surely thou art dull in learning this saying, that none is friend to him who has nothing.

XVII FORTUNE'S PLAYTHING AUTHOR UNKNOWN

Not of good-will has Fortune advanced thee; but that she may show her omnipotence, even down to thee.

XVIII TIME THE CONQUEROR PLATO

Time carries all things; length of days knows how to change name and shape and nature and fortune.

XIX MEMNON AND ACHILLES ASCLEPIODOTUS

Know, O Thetis of the sea, that Memnon yet lives and cries aloud, warmed by his mother's torch, in Egypt beneath Libyan brows, where the running Nile severs fairportalled Thebes; but Achilles, the insatiate of battle, utters no voice either on the Trojan plain or in Thessaly.

XX CORINTH ANTIPATER OF SIDON

Where is thine admired beauty, Dorian Corinth, where thy crown of towers? where thy treasures of old, where the temples of the immortals, where the halls and where the wives of the Sisyphids, and the tens of thousands of thy people that were? for not even a trace, O most distressful one, is left of thee, and war has swept up together and clean devoured all; only we, the unravaged sea-nymphs, maidens of Ocean, abide, halcyons wailing for thy woes.

XXI DELOS ANTIPATER OF THESSALONICA

Would I were yet blown about by ever-shifting gales, rather than fixed for wandering Leto's childbed; I had not so bemoaned my desolation. Ah miserable me, how many Greek ships sail by me, desert Delos, once so worshipful: late, but terrible, is Hera's vengeance laid on me thus for Leto's sake.

XXII TROY AGATHIAS

If thou art a Spartan born, O stranger, deride me not, for not to me only has Fortune accomplished this; and if of Asia, mourn not, for every city has bowed to the Dardanian sceptre of the Aeneadae. And though the jealous sword of enemies has emptied out Gods' precincts and walls and inhabitants, I am queen again; but do thou, O my child, fearless Rome, lay the yoke of thy law over Greece.

XXIII MYCENAE (1) ALPHEUS

Few of the native places of the heroes are in our eyes, and those yet left rise little above the plain; and such art thou, O hapless Mycenae, as I marked thee in passing by, more desolate than any hill- pasture, a thing that goatherds point at; and an old man said, "Here stood the Cyclopean city rich in gold."

XXIV MYCENAE (2) POMPEIUS

Though I am but drifted desolate dust where once was Mycenae, though I am more obscure to see than any chance rock, he who looks on the famed city of Ilus, whose walls I trod down and emptied all the house of Priam, will know thence how great my former strength was; and if old age has done me outrage, I am content with Homer's testimony.

XXV AMPHIPOLIS ANTIPATER OF THESSALONICA

City built upon Strymon and the broad Hellespont, grave of Edonian Phyllis, Amphipolis, yet there remain left to thee the traces of the temple of her of Aethopion and Brauron, and the water of the river so often fought around; but thee, once the high strife of the sons of Aegeus, we see like a torn rag of sea-purple on either shore.

XXVI SPARTA AUTHOR UNKNOWN

O Lacedaemon, once unsubdued and untrodden, thou seest shadeless the smoke of Olenian camp-fires on the Eurotas, and the birds building their nests on the ground wail for thee, and the wolves to do not hear any sheep.

XXVII BERYTUS AUTHOR UNKNOWN

Formerly the dead left their city living; but we living hold the city's funeral.

XXVIII SED TERRAE GRAVIORA LEONIDAS OF TARENTUM

Me, a hull that had measured such spaces of sea, fire consumed on the land that cut her pines to make me. Ocean brought me safe to shore; but I found her who bore me more treacherous than the sea.

XXIX YOUTH AND RICHES AUTHOR UNKNOWN

I was young, but poor; now in old age I am rich, alas, alone of all men pitiable in both, who then could enjoy when I had nothing, and now have when I cannot enjoy.

XXX THE VINE'S REVENGE EVENUS

Though thou devour me down to the root, yet still will I bear so much fruit as will serve to pour libation on thee, O goat, when thou art sacrificed.

XXXI REVERSAL PLATO

A man finding gold left a halter; but he who had left the gold, not finding it, knotted the halter he found.

XXXII TENANTS AT WILL AUTHOR UNKNOWN

I was once the field of Achaemenides, now I am Menippus', and again I shall pass from another to another; for the former thought once that he owned me, and the latter thinks so now in his turn; and I belong to no man at all, but to Fortune.

XXXIII PARTING COMPANY AUTHOR UNKNOWN

Hope, and thou Fortune, a long farewell; I have found the haven; there is nothing more between me and you; make your sport of those who come after me.

XXXIV FORTUNE'S MASTER PALLADAS

No more is Hope or Fortune my concern, nor for what remains do I reck of your deceit; I have reached harbour. I am a poor man, but living in Freedom's company I turn my face away from wealth the scorner of poverty.

XXXV BREAK OF DAY JULIUS POLYAENUS

Hope evermore steals away life's period, till the last morning cuts short all those many businesses.

CHAPTER X

THE HUMAN COMEDY

I PROLOGUE STRATO

Seek not on my pages Priam at the altars nor Medea's and Niobe's woes, nor Itys in the hidden chambers, and the nightingales among the leaves; for of all these things former poets wrote abundantly; but mingling with the blithe Graces, sweet Love and the Wine-god; and grave looks become not them.

II FLOWER O' THE ROSE DIONYSIUS

You with the roses, you are fair as a rose; but what sell you? yourself, or your roses, or both together?

III LOST DRINK NICARCHUS

At the Hermaea, Aphrodisius, while lifting six gallons of wine for us, stumbled and dealt us great woe. "From wine also perished the Centaur," and ah that we had too! but now it perished from us.

IV THE VINTAGE-REVEL LEONIDAS OF TARENTUM

To the must-drinking Satyrs and to Bacchus, planter of the vine, Heronax consecrated the first handfuls of his plantation, these three casks from three vineyards, filled with the first flow of the wine; from which we, having poured such libation as is meet to crimson Bacchus and the Satyrs, will drink deeper than they.

V SNOW IN SUMMER SIMONIDES

With this once the sharp North Wind rushing from Thrace covered the flanks of Olympus, and nipped the spirits of thinly-clad men; then it was buried alive, clad in Pierian earth. Let a share of it be mingled for me; for it is not seemly to bear a tepid draught to a friend.

VI A JUG OF WINE AUTHOR UNKNOWN

Round-bellied, deftly-turned, one eared, long-throated, straight- necked, bubbling in thy narrow mouth, blithe handmaiden of Bacchus and the Muses and Cytherea, sweet of laughter, delightful ministress of social banquets, why when I am sober art thou in liquor, and when I am drunk, art sober again? Thou wrongest the good-fellowship of drinking.

VII THE EMPTY JAR ERATOSTHENES

Xenophon the wine-bibber dedicates an empty jar to thee, Bacchus; receive it graciously, for it is all he has.

VIII ANGELORUM CHORI MARCUS ARGENTARIUS

I hold revel, regarding the golden choir of the stars at evening, nor do I spurn the dances of others; but garlanding my hair with flowers that drop their petals over me, I waken the melodious harp into passion with musical hands; and doing thus I lead a well-ordered life, for the order of the heavens too has its Lyre and Crown.

IX SUMMER SAILING ANTIPHILUS

Mine be a mattress on the poop, and the awnings over it surrounding with the blows of the spray, and the fire forcing its way out of the hearth-stones, and a pot upon them with empty turmoil of bubbles; and let me see the boy dressing the meat, and my table be a ship's plank covered with a cloth; and a game of pitch and toss, and the boatswain's whistle: the other day I had such fortune, for I love common life.

X L'ALLEGRO JULIANUS AEGYPTIUS

All the ways of life are pleasant; in the market-place are goodly companionships, and at home griefs are hidden; the country brings pleasure, seafaring wealth, foreign lands knowledge. Marriages make a united house, and the unmarried life is never anxious; a child is a bulwark to his father; the childless are far from fears; youth knows the gift of courage, white hairs of wisdom: therefore, taking courage, live, and beget a family.

XI DUM VIVIMUS VIVAMUS AUTHOR UNKNOWN

Six hours fit labour best: and those that follow, shown forth in letters, say to mortals, "Live."

XII HOPE AND EXPERIENCE AUTHOR UNKNOWN

Whoso has married once and again seeks a second wedding, is a shipwrecked man who sails twice through a difficult gulf.

XIII THE MARRIED MAN PALLADAS

If you boast high that you are not obedient to your wife's commands, you talk idly, for you are not sprung of oak or rock, as the saying is; and, as is the hard case with most or all of us, you too are in woman's rule. But if you say, "I am not struck with a slipper, nor my wife being unchaste have I to bear it and shut my eyes." I reply that your bondage is lighter, in that you have sold yourself to a reasonable and not to too hard a mistress.

XIV AN UNGROUNDED SCANDAL LUCILIUS

Some say, Nicylla, that you dye your hair; which is as black as can be bought in the market.

XV THE POPULAR SINGER NICARCHUS

The night-raven's song is deadly; but when Demophilus sings, the very night-raven dies.

XVI THE FAULTLESS DANCER PALLADAS

Snub-nosed Memphis danced Daphnis and Niobe; Daphne like a stock,
Niobe like a stone.

XVII THE FORTUNATE PAINTER LUCILIUS

Eutychus the portrait-painter got twenty sons, and never got one likeness, even among his children.

XVIII SLOW AND SURE NICARCHUS

Charmus ran for the three miles in Arcadia with five others; surprising to say, he actually came in seventh. When there were only six, perhaps you will say, how seventh? A friend of his went along in his great-coat crying, "Keep it up, Charmus!" and so he arrives seventh; and if only he had had five more friends, Zoïlus, he would have come in twelfth.

XIX MARCUS THE RUNNER LUCILIUS

Marcus once saw midnight out in the armed men's race, so that the race-course was all locked up, as the police all thought that he was one of the stone men in armour who stand there in honour of victors. Very well, it was opened next day, and then Marcus turned up, still short of the goal by the whole course.

XX HERMOGENES LUCILIUS

Little Hermogenes, when he lets anything fall on the ground, has to drag it down to him with a hook at the end of a pole.

XXI PHANTASMS OF THE LIVING LUCILIUS

Lean Gaius yesterday breathed his very last breath, and left nothing at all for burial, but having passed down into Hades just as he was in life, flutters there the thinnest of the anatomies under earth; and his kinsfolk lifted an empty bier on their shoulders, inscribing above it, "This is Gaius' funeral."

XXII A LABOUR OF HERCULES LUCILIUS

Tiny Macron was found asleep one summer day by a mouse, who pulled him by his tiny foot into its hole; but in the hole he strangled the mouse with his naked hands and cried, "Father Zeus, thou hast a second Heracles."

XXIII EROTION LUCILIUS

Small Erotion while playing was carried aloft by a gnat, and cried,
"What can I do, Father Zeus, if thou dost claim me?"

XXIV ARTEMIDORA LUCILIUS

Fanning thin Artemidora in her sleep, Demetrius blew her clean out of the house.

XXV THE ATOMIC THEORY LUCILIUS

Epicurus wrote that the whole universe consisted of atoms, thinking, Alcimus, that the atom was the least of things. But if Diophantus had lived then, he would have written, "consisted of Diophantus," who is much more minute than even the atoms, or would have written that all other things indeed consist of atoms, but the atoms themselves of him.

XXVI CHAEREMON LUCILIUS

Borne up by a slight breeze, Chaeremon floated through the clear air, far lighter than chaff, and probably would have gone spinning off through ether, but that he caught his feet in a spider's web, and dangled there on his back; there he hung five nights and days, and on the sixth came down by a strand of the web.

XXVII GOD AND THE DOCTOR NICARCHUS

Marcus the doctor called yesterday on the marble Zeus; though marble, and though Zeus, his funeral is to-day.

XXVIII THE PHYSICIAN AND THE ASTROLOGER NICARCHUS

Diophantus the asrologer said that Hermogenes the physician had only nine months to live; and he laughing replied, "what Cronus may do in nine months, do you consider; but

I can make short work with you." He spoke, and reaching out, just touched him, and Diophantus, while forbidding another to hope, gasped out his own life.

XXIX A DEADLY DREAM LUCILIUS

Diophantus, having seen Hermogenes the physician in sleep, never awoke again, though he wore an amulet.

XXX SIMON THE OCULIST NICARCHUS

If you have an enemy, Dionysius, call not down upon him Isis nor Harpocrates, nor whatever god strikes men blind, but Simon; and you will know what God and what Simon can do.

XXXI SCIENTIFIC SURGERY NICARCHUS

Agclaus killed Acestorides while operating; for, "Poor man," he said, "he would have been lame for life."

XXXII THE WISE PROPHET LUCILIUS

All the astrologers as from one mouth prophesied to my father that his brother would reach a great old age; Hermocleides alone said he was fated to die early; and he said so, when we were mourning over his corpse in-doors.

XXXIII SOOTHSAYING NICARCHUS

Some one came inquiring of the prophet Olympicus whether he should sail to Rhodes, and how he should have a safe voyage; and the prophet replied, "First have a new ship, and set sail not in winter but in summer; for if you do this you will travel there and back safely, unless a pirate captures you at sea."

XXXIV THE ASTROLOGER'S FORECAST AGATHIAS

Calligenes the farmer, when he had cast his seed into the land, came to the house of Aristophenes the astrologer, and asked him to tell whether he would have a prosperous summer and abundant plenty of corn. And he, taking the counters and ranging them closely on the board, and crooking his fingers, uttered his reply to Calligenes: "If the cornfield gets sufficient rain, and does not breed a crop of flowering weeds, and frost does not crack the furrows, nor hail flay the heads of the springing blades, and the pricket does not devour the crop, and it sees no other injury of weather or soil, I prophesy you a capital summer, and you will cut the ears successfully: only fear the locusts."

XXXV A SCHOOL OF RHETORIC AUTHOR UNKNOWN

All hail, seven pupils of Aristides the rhetorician, four walls and three benches.

XXXVI CROSS PURPOSES NICARCHUS

A deaf man went to law with a deaf man, and the judge was a long way deafer than both. The one claimed that the other owed him five months' rent; and he replied that he had ground his corn by night; then the judge, looking down on them, said, "Why quarrel? she is your mother; keep her between you."

XXXVII THE PATENT STOVE NICARCHUS

You have bought a brass hot-water urn, Heliodorus, that is chillier than the north wind about Thrace; do not blow, do not labour, you but raise smoke in vain; it is a brass wine-cooler you have bought against summer.

XXXVIII THE WOODEN HORSE LUCILIUS

You have a Thessalian horse, Erasistratus, but the drugs of all Thessaly cannot make him go; the real wooden horse, that if Trojans and Greeks had all pulled together, would never have entered at the Scaean gate; set it up as an offering to some god, if you take my advice, and make gruel for your little children with its barley.

XXXIX A MYSTERIOUS DISAPPEARANCE LUCILIUS

Antiochus once set eyes on Lysimachus' cushion, and Lysimachus never set eyes on his cushion again.

XL CINYRAS THE CILICIAN DEMODOCUS

All Cilicians are bad men; among the Cilicians there is one good man, Cinyras, and Cinyras is a Cilician.

XLI A GENERATION OF VIPERS AUTHOR UNKNOWN

Keep clear of a cobra, a toad, a viper, and the Laodiceans; also of a mad dog, and of the Laodiceans once again.

XLII THE LIFEBOAT NICARCHUS

Philo had a boat, the Salvation, but not Zeus himself, I believe, can be safe in her; for she was salvation in name only, and those who got on board her used either to go aground or to go underground.

XLIII THE MISER AND THE MOUSE LUCILIUS

Asclepiades the miser saw a mouse in his house, and said, "What do you want with me, my very dear mouse?" and the mouse, smiling sweetly, replied, "Do not be afraid, my friend; we do not ask board from you, only lodging."

XLIV THE FRUITS OF PHILOSOPHY LUCIAN

We saw at dinner the great wisdom of that sturdy beggar the Cynic with the long beard; for at first he abstained from lupines and radishes, saying that Virtue ought not to be a slave to the belly; but when he saw a snowy womb dressed with sharp sauce before his eyes, which at once stole away his sagacious intellect, he unexpectedly asked for it, and ate of it heartily, observing that an entrée could not harm Virtue.

XLV VEGETARIANISM AUTHOR UNKNOWN

You were not alone in keeping your hands off live things; we do so too; who touches live food, Pythagoras? but we eat what has been boiled and roasted and pickled, and there is no life in it then.

XLVI NICON'S NOSE NICARCHUS

I see Nicon's hooked nose, Menippus; it is evident he is not far off now; oh, he will be here, let us just wait; for at the most his nose is not, I fancy, five stadia off him. Nay, here it is, you see, stepping forward; if we stand on a high mound we shall catch sight of him in person.

XLVII WHO SO PALE AND WAN, FOND LOVER ASCLEPIADES

Drink, Asclepiades; why these tears? what ails thee? not of thee only has the cruel Cyprian made her prey, nor for thee only bitter Love whetted the arrows of his bow; why while yet alive liest thou in the dust?

XLVIII THE WORLD'S REVENGE LUCIAN

In a company where all were drunk, Acindynus must needs be sober; and so he seemed himself the one drunk man there.

XLIX EPILOGUE PHILODEMUS

I was in love once; who has not been? I have revelled; who is uninitiated in revels? nay, I was mad; at whose prompting but a god's? Let them go; for now the silver hair is fast replacing the black, a messenger of wisdom that comes with age. We too played when the time of playing was; and now that it is no longer, we will turn to worthier thoughts.

CHAPTER XI

DEATH

I THE SPAN OF LIFE MACEDONIUS

Earth and Birth-Goddess, thou who didst bear me and thou who coverest, farewell; I have accomplished the course between you, and I go, not discerning whither I shall travel; for I know not either whose or who I am, or whence I came to you.

II DUSTY DEATH AUTHOR UNKNOWN

Pay no offering of ointments or garlands on my stony tomb, nor make the fire blaze up; the expense is in vain. While I live be kind to me if thou wilt; but drenching my ashes with wine thou wilt make mire, and the dead man will not drink.

III A CITIZEN OF THE REPUBLIC LEONIDAS OF TARENTUM

A little dust of earth suffices me; let another lie richly, weighed down by his extravagant tombstone, that grim weight over the dead, who will know me here in death as Alcander son of Calliteles.

IV BENE MERENTI AUTHOR UNKNOWN

Dear Earth, take old Amyntichus to thy bosom, remembering his many labours on thee; for ever he planted in thee the olive-stock, and often made thee fair with vine-cuttings, and filled thee full of corn, and, drawing channels of water along, made thee rich with herbs and plenteous in fruit: do thou in return lie softly over his grey temples and flower into tresses of spring herbage.

V PEACE IN THE END DIONYSIUS

A gentler old age and no dulling disease quenched thee, and thou didst fall asleep in the slumber to which all must come, O Eratosthenes, after pondering over high matters; nor did Cyrene where thou sawest the light receive thee within the tomb of thy fathers, O son of Aglaus; yet dear even in a foreign land art thou buried here, by the edge of the beach of Proteus.

VI THE WITHERED VINE LEONIDAS OF TARENTUM

Even as a vine on her dry pole I support myself now on a staff, and death calls me to Hades. Be not obstinately deaf, O Gorgus; what is it the sweeter for thee if for three or four summers yet thou shalt warm thyself beneath the sun? So saying the aged man quietly put his life aside, and removed his house to the greater company.

VII ACCOMPLISHMENT THEAETETUS

Crantor was delightful to men and yet more delightful to the Muses, and did not live far into age: O earth, didst thou enfold the sacred man in death, or does he still live in gladness there?

VIII LOCA PASTORUM DESERTA AUTHOR UNKNOWN

Naiads and chill cattle-pastures, tell to the bees when they come on their springtide way, that old Leucippus perished on a winter's night, setting snares for scampering hares, and no longer is the tending of the hives dear to him; but the pastoral dells mourn sore for him who dwelt with the mountain peak for neighbour.

IX THE OLD SHEPHERD LEONIDAS OF TARENTUM

Shepherds who pass over this ridge of hill pasturing your goats and fleecy sheep, pay to Clitagoras, in Earth's name, a small but kindly grace, for the sake of Persephone under ground; let sheep bleat by me, and the shepherd on an unhewn stone pipe softly to them as they feed, and in early spring let the countryman pluck the meadow flower to engarland my tomb with a garland, and let one make milk drip from a fruitful ewe, holding up her milking-udder, to wet the base of my tomb: there are returns for favours to dead men, there are, even among the departed.

X THE DEAD FOWLER MNASALCAS

Even here shall the holy bird rest his swift wing, sitting on this murmuring plane, since Poemander the Malian is dead and comes no more with birdlime smeared on his fowling reeds.

XI THE ANT BY THE THRESHING FLOOR ANTIPATER OF SIDON

Here to thee by the threshing floor, O toiling worker ant, I rear a memorial to thee of a thirsty clod, that even in death the ear- nurturing furrow of Demeter may lull thee as thou liest in thy rustic cell.

XII THE TAME PARTRIDGE SIMMIAS

No more along the shady woodland copse, O hunter partridge, dost thou send thy clear cry from thy mouth as thou decoyest thy speckled kinsfolk in their forest feeding-ground; for thou art gone on the final road of Acheron.

XIII THE SILENT SINGING-BIRD TYMNES

O bird beloved of the Graces, O rivalling the halcyons in likeness of thy note, thou art snatched away, dear warbler, and thy ways and thy sweet breath are held in the silent paths of night.

XIV THE FIELDS OF PERSEPHONE ARISTODICUS

No longer in the wealthy house of Alcis, O shrill grasshopper, shall the sun behold thee singing; for now thou art flown to the meadows of Clymenus and the dewy flowers of golden Persephone.

XV THE DISCONSOLATE SHEPHERD THEOCRITUS

Ah thou poor Thyrsis, what profit is it if thou shalt waste away the apples of thy two eyes with tears in thy mourning? the kid is gone, the pretty young thing, is gone to Hades; for a savage wolf crunched her in his jaws; and the dogs bay; what profit is it, when of that lost one not a bone nor a cinder is left?

XVI LAMPO THE HOUND ANTIPATER OF SIDON

Thirst slew hunter Lampo, Midas' dog, though he toiled hard for his life; for he dug with his paws in the moist flat, but the slow water made no haste out of her blind spring, and he fell in despair; then the water gushed out. Ah surely, Nymphs, you laid on Lampo your wrath for the slain deer.

XVII STORM ON THE HILLS DIOTIMUS

Unherded at evenfall the oxen came to the farmyard from the hill, snowed on with heavy snow; alas, and Therimachus sleeps the long sleep beside an oak, stretched there by fire from heaven.

XVIII A WET NIGHT ANTIPATER OF SIDON

I know not whether I shall complain of Dionysus or blame the rain of Zeus, but both are treacherous for feet. For the tomb holds Polyxenus, who returning once to the country from a feast, tumbled over the slippery slopes, and lies far from Aeolic Smyrna: but let one full of wine fear a rainy footpath in the dark.

XIX FAR FROM HOME TYMNES

Let not this be of too much moment to thee, O Philaenis, that thou hast not found thine allotted earth by the Nile, but this tomb holds thee in Eleutherne; for to comers from all places there is an equal way to Hades.

XX DEATH AT SEA SIMONIDES

Strange dust covers thy body, and the lot of death took thee, O Cleisthenes, wandering in the Euxine sea; and thou didst fail of sweet and dear home-coming, nor ever didst reach sea-girt Chios.

XXI AT THE WORLD'S END CRINAGORAS

Alas, why wander we, trusting in vain hopes and forgetting baneful death? this Seleucus was perfect in his words and ways, but, having enjoyed his youth but a little, among the utmost Iberians, so far away from Lesbos, he lies a stranger on unmapped shores.

XXII IN LIMINE PORTUS ANTIPHILUS

Already almost in touch of my native land, "To-morrow," I said, "the wind that has set so long against me will abate"; not yet had the speech died on my lip, and the sea was even as Hades, and that light word broke me down. Beware of every speech with to-morrow in it; not even small things escape the Nemesis that avenges the tongue.

XXIII DROWNED IN HARBOUR ANTIPATER OF THESSALONICA

Not even when at anchor trust the baleful sea, O sailor, nor even if dry land hold thy cables; for Ion fell into the harbour, and at the plunge wine tied his quick sailor's hands. Beware of revelling on ship-board; the sea is enemy to Iacchus; this law the Tyrrhenians ordained.

XXIV IN SOUND OF THE SEA ANTIPATER OF THESSALONICA

Even in death shall the implacable sea vex me, Lysis hidden beneath a lonely rock, ever sounding harshly by my ear and alongside of my deaf tomb. Why, O fellow-men, have you made my dwelling by this that reft me of breath, me whom not trading in my merchant-ship but sailing in a little rowing-boat, it brought to shipwreck? and I who sought my living out of the sea, out of the sea likewise drew my death.

XXV THE EMPTY HOUSE ANTIPATER OF THESSALONICA

Hapless Nicanor, doomed by the grey sea, thou liest then naked on a strange beach, or haply by the rocks, and those wealthy halls are perished from thee, and lost is the hope of all Tyre; nor did aught of thy treasures save thee; alas, pitiable one! thou didst perish, and all thy labour was for the fishes and the sea.

XXVI THE SINKING OF THE PLEIAD AUTOMEDON

O man, be sparing of life, neither go on sea-faring beyond the time; even so the life of man is not long. Miserable Cleonicus, yet thou didst hasten to come to fair Thasos, a merchantman out of hollow Syria, O merchant Cleonicus; but hard on the sinking of the Pleiad as thou journeyedst over the sea, as the Pleiad sank, so didst thou.

XXVII A RESTLESS GRAVE ARCHIAS

Not even in death shall I Theris, tossed shipwrecked upon land by the waves, forget the sleepless shores; for beneath the spray-beaten reefs, nigh the disastrous main, I found a grave at the hands of strangers, and for ever do I wretchedly hear roaring even among the dead the hated thunder of the sea.

XXVIII TELLURIS AMOR CRINAGORAS

O happy shepherd, would that even I had shepherded on the mountain along this white grassy hill, making the bleating folk move after the leader rams, rather than have dipped a ship's steering-rudders in the bitter brine: so I sank under the depths, and the east wind that swallowed me down cast me up again on this shore.

XXIX A GRAVE BY THE SEA ASCLEPIADES

Keep eight cubits away from me, O rough sea, and billow and roar with all thy might; but if thou pullest down the grave of Eumares, thou wilt find nothing of value, but only bones and dust.

XXX AN EMPTY TOMB CALLIMACHUS

Would that swift ships had never been, for we should not have bewailed Sopolis son of Diocleides; but now somewhere in the sea he drifts dead, and instead of him we pass by a name on an empty tomb.

XXXI THE DAYS OF THE HALCYONS APOLLONIDES

And when shall thy swirling passage be free from fear, say, O sea, if even in the days of the halcyons we must weep, of the halcyons for whom Ocean evermore stills his windless wave, that one might think dry land less trustworthy? but even when thou callest thyself a gentle nurse and harmless to women in labour, thou didst drown Aristomenes with his freight.

XXXII A WINTER VOYAGE AUTHOR UNKNOWN

Thee too, son of Cleanor, desire after thy native land destroyed, trusting to the wintry gust of the South; for the unsecured season entangled thee, and the wet waves washed away thy lovely youth.

XXXIII THE DEAD CHILD AUTHOR UNKNOWN

Not yet were thy tresses cut, nor had the monthly courses of the moon driven a three years' space, O poor Cleodicus, when thy mother Nicasis, clasping thy coffin, wailed long over thy lamented grave, and thy father Pericleitus; but an unknown Acheron thou shalt flower out the youth that never, never returns.

XXXIV THE LITTLE SISTER LEONIDAS OF TARENTUM

This girl passed to Hades untimely, in her seventh year, before her many playmates, poor thing, pining for her baby brother, who at twenty months old tasted of loveless Death. Alas, ill-fated Peristeris, how near at hand God has set the sorest griefs to men.

XXXV PERSEPHONE'S PLAYTHING AUTHOR UNKNOWN

Hades inexorable and inflexible, why hast thou thus reft infant Callaeschrus of life? Surely the child will be a plaything in the palace of Persephone, but at home he has left bitter sorrows.

XXXVI CHILDLESS AMONG WOMEN LEONIDAS OF TARENTUM

Ah wretched Anticles, and wretched I who have laid on the pyre in the flower of youth my only son, thee, child, who didst perish at eighteen years; and I weep, bewailing an orphaned old age: fain would I go to the shadowy house of Hades; neither is morn sweet to me, nor the beam of the swift sun. Ah wretched Anticles, struck down by fate, be thou healer of my sorrow, taking me with thee out of life.

XXXVII FATE'S PERSISTENCY PHILIPPUS

I Philaenion who gave birth but for the pyre, I the woeful mother, I who had seen the threefold grave of my children, anchored my trust on another's pangs; for I surely hoped that he at least would live, whom I had not borne. So I, who once had fair children, brought up an adopted son; but God would not let me have even a second mother's grace; for being called ours he perished, and now I am become a woe to the rest of mothers too.

XXXVIII ANTE DIEM BIANOR

Ever insatiate Charon, why hast thou wantonly taken young Attalus? was he not thine, even if he had died old?

XXXIX UNFORGOTTEN SIMONIDES

Protomachus said, as his father held him in his hands when he was breathing away his lovely youth, "O son of Timenor, thou wilt never forget thy dear son, nor cease to long for his valour and his wisdom."

XL THE BRIDECHAMBER ANTIPATER OF SIDON

Already the saffron-strewn bride-bed was spread within the golden wedding-chamber for the bride of Pitane, Cleinareta, and her guardians Demo and Nicippus hoped to light the torch-flame held at stretch of arm and lifted in both hands, when sickness snatched her away yet a maiden, and drew her to the sea of Lethe; and her sorrowing companions knocked not on the bridal doors, but on their own smitten breasts in the clamour of death.

XLI BRIDEGROOM DEATH MELEAGER

Not marriage but Death for bridegroom did Clearista receive when she loosed the knot of her maidenhood: for but now at even the flutes sounded at the bride's portal, and the doors of the wedding-chamber were clashed; and at morn they cried the wail, and Hymenaeus put to silence changed into a voice of lamentation; and the same pine-brands flashed their torchlight before the bride-bed, and lit the dead on her downward way.

XLII THE YOUNG WIFE JULIANUS AEGYTPIUS

In season the bride-chamber held thee, out of season the grave took thee, O Anastasia, flower of the blithe Graces; for thee a father, for thee a husband pours bitter tears; for thee haply even the ferryman of the dead weeps; for not a whole year didst thou accomplish beside thine husband, but at sixteen years old, alas! the tomb holds thee.

XLIII SANCTISSIMA CONIUNX CRINAGORAS

Unhappy, by what first word, by what second shall I name thee? unhappy! this word is true in every ill. Thou art gone, O gracious wife, who didst carry off the palm in bloom of beauty and in bearing of soul; Prote wert thou truly called, for all else comes second to those inimitable graces of thine.

XLIV SUNDERED HANDS DAMAGETUS

This last word, O famous city of Phocaea, Theano spoke as she went down into the unharvested night: "Woe's me unhappy; Apellichus, husband, what length, what length of sea dost thou cross on thine own ship! but nigh me stands my doom; would God I had but died with my hand clasped in thy dear hand."

XLV UNDIVIDED APOLLONIDES

Heliodorus went first, and Diogeneia the wife, not an hour's space after, followed her dear husband; and both, even as they dwelt together, are buried under this slab, rejoicing in their common tomb even as in a bride-chamber.

XLVI FIRST LOVE MELEAGER

Tears I give to thee even below with earth between us, Heliodora, such relic of love as may pass to Hades, tears sorely wept; and on thy much-wailed tomb I pour the libation of my longing, the memorial of my affection. Piteously, piteously, I Meleager make lamentation for thee, my dear, even among the dead, an idle gift to Acheron. Woe's me, where is my cherished flower? Hades plucked her, plucked her and marred the freshly-blown blossom with his dust. But I beseech thee, Earth, that nurturest all, gently to clasp her, the all-lamented, O mother, to thy breast.

XLVII FIRST FRIENDSHIP AUTHOR UNKNOWN

Ah blessed one, dearest companion of the immortal Muses, fare thou well even in the house of Hades, Callimachus.

XLVIII STREWINGS FOR GRAVES AUTHOR UNKNOWN

May flowers grow thick on thy newly-built tomb, not the dry bramble, not the evil weed, but violets and margerain and wet narcissus, Vibius, and around thee may all be roses.

XLIX DIMITTE MORTUOS PAULUS SILENTIARIUS

My name—Why this?—and my country—And to what end this?—and I am of illustrious race—Yea, if thou hadst been of the obscurest?—Having lived nobly I left life—If ignobly?—and I lie here now—Who art thou that sayest this, and to whom?

L MORS IMMORTALIS AUTHOR UNKNOWN

I died, but I await thee; and thou too shalt await some one else: one Death receives all mortals alike.

LI THE LIGHT OF THE DEAD PLATO

Morning Star that once didst shine among the living, now deceased thou shinest the Evening Star among the dead.

CHAPTER XII

LIFE

I THE JOY OF YOUTH RUFINUS

Let us bathe, Prodice, and garland ourselves, and drain unmixed wine, lifting larger cups; little is our life of gladness, then old age will stop the rest, and death is the end.

II THE USE OF LIFE NICARCHUS

Must I not die? what matters it to me whether I depart to Hades gouty or fleet of foot? for many will carry me; let me become lame, for hardly on their account need I ever cease from revelling.

III VAIN RICHES ANTIPHANES

Thou reckonest, poor wretch; but advancing time breeds white old age even as it does interest; and neither having drunk, nor bound a flower on thy brows, nor ever known myrrh nor a delicate darling, thou shalt be dead, leaving thy great treasury in its wealth, out of those many coins carrying with thee but the one.

IV MINIMUM CREDULA POSTERO PALLADAS

All human must pay the debt of death, nor is there any mortal who knows whether he shall be alive to-morrow; learning this clearly, O man, make thee merry, keeping the wine-god close by thee for oblivion of death, and take thy pleasure with the Paphian while thou drawest thy ephemeral life; but all else give to Fortune's control.

V DONEC HODIE AUTHOR UNKNOWN

Drink and be merry; for what is to-morrow or what the future? no man knows. Run not, labour not; as thou canst, give, share, consume, be mortal-minded; to be alive and not to be alive are no way at all apart. All life is such, only the turn of the scale; if thou art beforehand, it is thine; and if thou diest, all is another's, and thou hast nothing.

VI REQUIESCE ANIMA MIMNERMUS

Be young, dear my soul: soon will others be men, and I being dead shall be dark earth.

VII ONE EVENT MARCUS ARGENTARIUS

Five feet shalt thou possess as thou liest dead, nor shalt see the pleasant things of life nor the beams of the sun; then joyfully lift and drain the unmixed cup of wine, O Cincius, holding a lovely wife in thine arms; and if philosophy say that thy mind is immortal, know that Cleanthes and Zeno went down to deep Hades.

VIII THE PASSING OF YOUTH APOLLONIDES

Thou slumberest, O comrade; but the cup itself cries to thee, "Awake; do not make thy pleasure in the rehearsal of death." Spare not, Diodorus, slipping greedily into wine, drink deep, even to the tottering of the knee. Time shall be when we shall not drink, long and long; nay come, make haste; prudence already lays her hand on our temples.

IX THE HIGHWAY TO DEATH ANTIPATER OF SIDON

Men skilled in the stars call me brief-fated; I am, but I care not, O Seleucus. There is one descent for all to Hades; and if ours comes quicker, the sooner shall we look on Minos. Let us drink; for surely wine is a horse for the high-road, when foot-passengers take a by-path to Death.

X BEFORE THE DELUGE STRATO

Drink now and love, Damocrates, since not for ever shall we drink nor for ever hold fast our delight; let us crown our heads with garlands and perfume ourselves, before others bring these offerings to our graves. Now rather let my bones drink wine inside me; when they are dead, let Deucalion's deluge sweep them away.

XI FLEETING DAWN ASCLEPIADES

Let us drink an unmixed draught of wine; dawn is an hand-breadth; are we waiting to see the bed-time lamp once again? Let us drink merrily; after no long time yet, O luckless one, we shall sleep through the long night.

XII OUTRE-TOMBE JULIANUS AEGYPTUS

Often I sang this, and even out of the grave will I cry it: "Drink, before you put on this raiment of dust."

XIII EARTH TO EARTH ZONAS

Give me the sweet cup wrought of the earth from which I was born, and under which I shall lie dead.

XIV THE COFFIN-MAKER AUTHOR UNKNOWN

I would have liked to be rich as Croesus of old was rich, and to be king of great Asia; but when I look on Nicanor the coffin-maker, and know for what he is making these flute-cases of his, sprinkling my flour and wetting it with my jug of wine, I sell all Asia for ointments and garlands.

XV RETURNING SPRING PHILODEMUS

Now is rose-time and peas are in season, and the heads of early cabbage, O Sosylus, and the milky maena, and fresh-curdled cheese, and the soft-springing leaves of curled lettuces; and do we neither pace the foreland nor climb to the outlook, as always, O Sosylus, we did before? for Antagoras and Bacchius too frolicked yesterday, and now to-day we bear them forth for burial.

XVI A LIFE'S WANDERING AUTHOR UNKNOWN

Know ye the flowery fields of the Cappadocian nation? thence I was born of good parents: since I left them I have wandered to the sunset and the dawn; my name was Glaphyrus, and like my mind. I lived out my sixtieth year in perfect freedom; I know both the favour of Fortune and the bitterness of life.

XVII ECCE MYSTERIUM BIANOR

This man, inconsiderable, mean, yes, a slave, this man is loved, and is lord of another's soul.

XVIII THE SHADOW OF LIFE THEOGNIS

Fools and children are mankind to weep the dead, and not the flower of youth perishing.

XIX THE SHADOW OF DEATH AUTHOR UNKNOWN

Those who have left the sweet light I bewail no longer, but those who live ever in expectation of death.

XX PARTA QUIES PALLADAS

Expectation of death is woful grief, and this is the gain of a mortal when he perishes; weep not then for him who departs from life, for after death there is no other accident.

XXI THE CLOSED ACCOUNT PHILETAS

I weep not for thee, O dearest of friends; for thou knewest many fair things; and again God dealt thee thy lot of ill.

XXII THE VOYAGE OF LIFE PALLADAS

Life is a dangerous voyage; for tempest-tossed in it we often strike rocks more pitiably than shipwrecked men; and having Chance as pilot of life, we sail doubtfully as on the sea, some on a fair voyage, and others contrariwise; yet all alike we put into the one anchorage under earth.

XXIII DAILY BIRTH PALLADAS

Day by day we are born as night retires, no more possessing aught of our former life, estranged from our course of yesterday, and beginning to-day the life that remains. Do not then call thyself, old man, abundant in years; for to-day thou hast no share in what is gone.

XXIV THE LIMIT OF VISION AUTHOR UNKNOWN

Now we flourish as before others did, and soon others will, whose children we shall never see.

XXV THE BREATH OF LIFE PALLADAS

Breathing thin air into our nostrils we live and look on the torch of the sun, all we who live what is called life; and are as organs, receiving our spirits from quickening airs. If one then chokes that little breath with his hand, he robs us of life, and brings us down to Hades. Thus being nothing we wax high in hardihood, feeding on air from a little breath.

XXVI TWO ETERNITIES LEONIDAS OF TARENTUM

Infinite, O man, was the foretime until thou camest to thy dawn, and what remains is infinite on through Hades: what share is left for life but the bigness of a pinprick, and tinier than a pinprick if such there be? Little is thy life and afflicted; for not even so it is sweet, but more loathed than hateful death.

XXVII THE LORD OF LANDS AMMIANUS

Though thou pass beyond thy landmarks even to the pillars of Heracles, the share of earth that is equal to all men awaits thee, and thou shalt lie even as Irus, having nothing more than thine obolus, mouldering into a land that at last is not thine.

XXVIII THE PRICE OF RICHES PALLADAS

Thou art rich, and what of it in the end? as thou departest, dost thou drag thy riches with thee, pulling them into the coffin? Thou gatherest riches at expense of time, and thou canst not heap up more exceeding measures of life.

XXIX THE DARKNESS OF DAWN AMMIANUS

Morning by morning passes; then, while we heed not, suddenly the Dark One will be come, and, some by decaying, and some by parching, and some by swelling, will lead us all to the one pit.

XXX NIL EXPEDIT PALLADAS

Naked I came on earth, and naked I depart under earth, and why do I vainly labour, seeing the naked end?

XXXI THE WAY OF THE WORLD LUCIAN

Mortal is what belongs to mortals, and all things pass by us; and if not, yet we pass by them.

XXXII THE SUM OF KNOWLEDGE AUTHOR UNKNOWN

I was not, I came to be; I was, I am not: that is all; and who shall say more, will lie: I shall not be.

XXXIII NIHILISM GLYCON

All is laughter, and all is dust, and all is nothing; for out of unreason is all that is.

XXXIV NEPENTHE AUTHOR UNKNOWN

How was I born? whence am I? why did I come? to go again: how can I learn anything, knowing nothing? Being nothing, I was born; again I shall be as I was before; nothing and nothing-worth is the human race. But come, serve to me the joyous fountain of Bacchus; for this is the drug counter-charming ills.

XXXV THE SLAUGHTER-HOUSE PALLADAS

We all are watched and fed for Death as a herd of swine butchered wantonly.

XXXVI LACRIMAE RERUM PALLADAS

Weeping I was born and having wept I die, and I found all my living amid many tears. O tearful, weak, pitiable race of men, dragged under earth and mouldering away!

XXXVII THE WORLD'S WORTH AESOPUS

How might one escape thee, O life, without dying? for thy sorrows are numberless, and neither escape nor endurance is easy. For sweet indeed are thy beautiful things of nature, earth, sea, stars, the orbs of moon and sun; but all else is fears and pains, and though one have a good thing befal him, there succeeds it an answering Nemesis.

XXXVIII PIS-ALLER THEOGNIS

Of all things not to be born into the world is best, nor to see the beams of the keen sun; but being born, as swiftly as may be to pass the gates of Hades, and lie under a heavy heap of earth.

XXXIX THE SORROW OF LIFE POSIDIPPUS

What path of life may one hold? In the market-place are strifes and hard dealings, in the house cares; in the country labour enough, and at sea terror; and abroad, if thou hast aught, fear, and if thou art in poverty, vexation. Art married? thou wilt not be without anxieties; unmarried? thy life is yet lonelier. Children are troubles; a childless life is a crippled one. Youth is foolish, and grey hairs again feeble. In the end then the choice is of one of these two, either never to be born, or, as soon as born, to die.

XL THE JOY OF LIFE METRODORUS

Hold every path of life. In the market-place are honours and prudent dealings, in the house rest; in the country the charm of nature, and at sea gain; and abroad, if thou hast aught, glory, and if thou art in poverty, thou alone knowest it. Art married? so will thine household be best; unmarried? thy life is yet lighter. Children are darlings; a childless life is an unanxious one: youth is strong, and grey hairs again reverend. The choice is not then of one of the two, either never to be born or to die; for all things are good in life.

XLI QUIETISM PALLADAS

Why vainly, O man, dost thou labour and disturb everything when thou art slave to the lot of thy birth? Yield thyself to it, strive not with Heaven, and, accepting thy fortune, be content with rest.

XLII EQUANIMITY PALLADAS

If that which bears all things bears thee, bear thou and be borne; and if thou art indignant and vexest thyself, even so that which bears all things bears thee.

XLIII THE RULES OF THE GAME PALLADAS

All life is a stage and a game: either learn to play it, laying by seriousness, or bear its pains.

XLIV THE ONE HOPE PAULUS SILENTIARIUS

It is not living that has essential delight, but throwing away out of the breast cares that silver the temples. I would have wealth sufficient for me, and the excess of maddening care for gold ever eats away the spirit; thus among men thou wilt find often death better than life, as poverty than wealth. Knowing this, do thou make straight the paths of thine heart, looking to our one hope, Wisdom.

XLV AMOR MYSTICUS MARIANUS

Where is that backward-bent bow of thine, and the reeds that leap from thy hand and stick fast in mid-heart? where are thy wings? where they grievous torch? and why carriest thou three crowns in thy hands, and wearest another on thy head? I spring not from the common Cyprian, O stranger, I am not from earth, the offspring of wild joy; but I light the torch of learning in pure human minds, and lead the soul upwards into heaven. And I twine crowns of the four virtues; whereof carrying these, one from each, I crown myself with the first, the crown of Wisdom.

XLVI THE LAST WORD PALLADAS

Thou talkest much, O man, and thou art laid in earth after a little: keep silence, and while thou yet livest, meditate on death.

BIOGRAPHICAL INDEX OF EPIGRAMMATISTS

Greek literature from its earliest historical beginnings to its final extinction in the Middle Ages falls naturally under five periods. These are:—(1) Greece before the Persian warbs; (2) the ascendancy of Athens; (3) the Alexandrian monarchies; (4) Greece under Rome; (5) the Byzantine empire of the East. The authors of epigrams included in this selection are spread over all these periods through a space of about fifteen centuries.

I. Period of the lyric poets and of the complete political development of Greece, from the earliest time to the repulse of the Persian invasion, B.C. 480.

MIMNERMUS of Smyrna fl. B.C. 634-600, and was the contemporary of Solon. He is spoken of as the "inventor of elegy", and was apparently the first to employ the elegiac metre in threnes and love-poems. Only a few fragments, about eighty lines in all, of his poetry survive.

ERINNA of Rhodes, the contemporary of Sappho according to ancient tradition, fl. 600 B.C., and died very young. There are three epigrams in the Palatine Anthology under her name, probably genuine: see Bergk, /Lyr. Gr./ iii. p. 141. Besides the fragments given by Bergk, detached phrases of hers are probably preserved in /Anth. Pal./ vii. 12 and 13, and in the description by Christodorus of her statue in the gymnasium at Constantinople, /Anth. Pal./ ii. 108-110. She was included in the /Garland/ of Meleager, who speaks, l. 12, of the "sweet maiden-fleshed crocus of Erinna."

THEOGNIS of Megara, the celebrated elegiac and gnomic poet, fl. B.C. 548, and was still alive at the beginning of the Persian wars. The fragments we possess are from an Anthology of his works, and amount to about 1400 lines in all. He employed elegiac verse as a vehicle for every kind of political and social poetry; some of the poems were sung to the flute at banquets and are more akin to lyric poetry; others, described as {gnomai di elegeias}, elegiac sentences, can hardly be distinguished in essence from "hortatory" epigrams, and two of them have accordingly been included as epigrams of Life in this selection.

ANACREON of Teos in Ionia, B.C. 563-478, migrated with his countrymen to Abdera on the capture of Teos by the Persians, B.C. 540. He then lived for some years at the court of Polycrates of Samos (who died B.C. 522), and afterwards, like Simonides, at that of Hipparchus of Athens, finally returning to Teos, where he died at the age of eighty-five. Of his genuine poetry only a few inconsiderable fragments are left; and his wide fame rests chiefly on the /pseudo-Anacreontea/, a collection of songs chiefly of a convivial and amatory nature, written at different times but all of a late date, which have come down to us in the form of an appendix to the Palatine MS. of the Anthology, and from being used as a school-book have obtained a circulation far beyond their intrinsic merit. The /Garland/ of Meleager, l. 35, speaks of "the unsown honey-suckle of Anacreon," including both lyrical poetry ({melisma}) and epigrams ({elegoi}) as distinct from one another. The Palatine Anthology contains twenty-one epigrams under his name, a group of twelve together (vi. 134-145) transferred bodily, it would seem, from some collection of his works, and the rest scattered; and there is one other in Planudes. Most are plainly spurious, and none certainly authentic; but one of the two given here (iii. 7) has the note of style of this period, and is probably genuine. The other (xi. 32) is obviously of Alexandrian date, and is probably by Leonidas of Tarentum.

SIMONIDES of Ceos, B.C. 556-467, the most eminent of the lyric poets, lived for some years at the court of Hipparchus of Athens (B.C. 528- 514), afterwards among the feudal nobility of Thessaly, and was again living at Athens during the Persian wars. The later years of his life were spent with Pindar and Aeschylus at the court of Hiero of Syracuse. He was included in the /Garland/ of Meleager (l. 8, "the fresh shoot of the vine-blossom of Simonides"); fifty-nine epigrams are under his name in the Palatine MS., and eighteen more in Planudes, besides nine others doubtfully ascribed to him. Several of his epigrams are quoted by Herodotus; others are preserved by Strabo, Plutarch, Athenaeus, etc. In all, according to Bergk, we have ninety authentic epigrams from his hand. There were two later poets of the same name, Simonides of Magnesia, who lived under Antiochus the Great about 200 B.C., and Simonides of Carystus, of whom nothing definite is known; some of the spurious epigrams may be by one or other of them.

Beyond the point to which Simonides brought it the epigram never rose. In him there is complete ease of workmanship and mastery of form together with the noble and severe simplicity which later poetry lost. His dedications retain something of the antique stiffness; but his magnificent epitaphs are among our most precious inheritances from the greatest thought and art of Greece.

BACCHYLIDES of Iulis in Ceos flourished B.C. 470. He was the nephew of Simonides, and lived with him at the court of Hiero. There are only two epigrams in the Anthology under his name. The /Garland/ of Meleager, l. 34, speaks of "the yellow ears from the blade of Bacchylides." This phrase may contain an allusion to his dedicatory epigram to the West Wind, ii. 34 in this selection.

Finally, forming the transition between this and the great Athenian period, comes AESCHYLUS, B.C. 525-456. That Aeschylus wrote elegiac verse, including a poem on the dead at Marathon, is certain; fragments are preserved by Plutarch and Theophrastus, and there is a well- supported tradition that he competed with Simonides on that occasion. As to the authorship of the two epigrams extant under his name there is much difference of opinion. Bergk does not come to any definite conclusion. Perhaps all that can be said is that they do not seem unworthy of him, and that they certainly have the style and tone of the best period. It was not till the decline of literature that the epoch of forgeries began. It is, however, suspicious that a poet of his great eminence should not be mentioned in the /Garland/ of Meleager; for we can hardly suppose these epigrams, if genuine, either unknown to Meleager or intentionally omitted by him.

II. Period of the ascendancy of Athens, and of the great dramatists and historians; from the repulse of the Persian invasion to the extinction of Greek freedom at the battle of Chaeronea, B.C. 480- 338.

In this period the epigram almost disappears, overwhelmed apparently by the greater forms of poetry which were then in their perfection. Between Simonides and Plato there is not a single name on our list; and it is not till the period of the transition, the first half of the fourth century B.C., that the epigram begins to reappear. About 400 B.C. a new grace and delicacy is added to it by PLATO (B.C. 428-347; the tradition, in itself probable, is that he wrote poetry when a very young man). Thirty-two epigrams in the Anthology are ascribed, some doubtfully, to one Plato or another; a few of obviously late date to a somewhat mythical PLATO JUNIOR ({o Neoteros}), and one to PLATO THE COMEDIAN (fl. 428-389), the contemporary and rival of Aristophanes. In a note to i. 5 in this selection something is said as to the authenticity of the epigrams ascribed to the great Plato [omitted in this text—JB.] He was included in the /Garland/ of Meleager, who speaks, ll. 47-8, of "the golden bough of the ever- divine Plato, shining everywhere in excellence"—one of the finest criticisms ever made by a single phrase, and the more remarkable that it anticipates, and may even in some degree have suggested, the mystical golden bough of Virgil.

To the same period belongs PARRHASIUS of Ephesus, who fl. 400 B.C., the most eminent painter of his time, in whose work the rendering of the ideal human form was considered to have reached its highest perfection. Two epigrams and part of a third ascribed to him are preserved in Athenaeus.

DEMODOCUS of Leros, a small island in the Sporades, is probably to be placed here. Nothing is known as to his life, nor as to his date beyond the one fact that an epigram of his is quoted by Aristotle, /Eth. N./ vii. 9. Four epigrams of his, all couplets containing a sarcastic point of the same kind, are preserved in the Palatine Anthology.

III. Period of the great Alexandrian monarchies; from the accession of Alexander the Great to the annexation of Syria by the Roman Republic, B.C. 336-65.

Throughout these three centuries epigrammatists flourished in great abundance, so much so that the epigram ranked as one of the important forms of poetry. After the first fifty years of the period there is no appreciable change in the manner and style of the epigram; and so, in many cases where direct evidence fails, dates can only be ascribed vaguely. The history of the Alexandrian epigram begins with two groups of poets, none of them quite of the first importance, but all of great literary interest, who lived just before what is known as the Alexandrian style became pronounced; the first group continuing the tradition of pure Greece, the second founding the new style. After them the most important names, in chronological order, are Callimachus of Alexandria, Leonidas of Tarentum, Theocritus of Syracuse, Antipater of Sidon, and Meleager of Gadara. These names show how Greek literature had now become diffused with Greek civilisation through the countries bordering the eastern half of the Mediterranean.

The period may then be conveniently subdivided under five heads—
  (1) Poets of Greece Proper and Macedonia, continuing the purely Greek tradition in literature.
  (2) Founds of the Alexandrian School.
  (3) The earlier Alexandrians of the third century B.C.
  (4) The later Alexandrians of the second century B.C.
  (5) Just on the edge of this period, Meleager and his contemporaries: transition to the Roman period.

(1) ADAEUS or ADDAEUS, called "the Macedonian" in the title of one of his epigrams, was a contemporary of Alexander the Great. Among his epigrams are epitaphs on Alexander and on Philip; his date is further fixed by the mention of Potidaea in another epigram, as Cassander, who died B.C. 296, changed the name of the city into Cassandrea. Eleven epigrams are extant under his name, but one is headed "Adaeus of Mitylene" and may be by a different hand, as Adaeus was a common Macedonian name. They are chiefly poems of country life, prayers to Demeter and Artemis, and hunting scenes, full of fresh air and simplicity out of doors, with a serious sense of religion and something of Macedonian gravity. The picture they give of the simple and refined life of the Greek country gentleman, like Xenophon in his old age at Scillus, is one of the most charming and intimate glimpses we have of the ancient world, carried on quietly among the drums and tramplings of Alexander's conquests, of which we are faintly reminded by another epigram on an engraved Indian beryl.

ANYTE of Tegea is one of the foremost names among the epigrammatists, and it is somewhat surprising that we know all but nothing of her from external sources. "The lilies of Anyte" stand at the head of the list of poets in the /Garland/ of Meleager; and Antipater of Thessalonica in a catalogue of poetesses (/Anth. Pal./ ix. 26) speaks of {Anutes stoma thelun Omeron}. The only epigram which gives any clue to her date is one on the death of three Milesian girls in a Gaulish invasion, probably that of B.C. 279; but this is headed "Anyte of Mitylene," and is very possibly by another hand. A late tradition says that her statue was made by the sculptors Cephisodotus and Euthycrates, whose date is about 300 B.C., but we are not told whether they were her contemporaries. Twenty-four epigrams are ascribed to her, twenty of which seem genuine. They are so fine that some critics have wished to place her in the great lyric period; but their deep and most refined feeling for nature rather belongs to this age. They are principally dedications and epitaphs, written with great simplicity of description and much of the grand style of the older poets, and showing (if the common theory as to her date be true) a deep and sympathetic study of Simonides.

Probably to this group belong also the following poets:

HEGESIPPUS, the author of eight epigrams in the Palatine Anthology, three dedications and five epitaphs, in a simple and severe style. The reference in the /Garland/ of Meleager, l. 25, to "the maenad grape- cluster of Hegesippus" is so wholly inapplicable to these that we must suppose it to refer to a body of epigrams now lost, unless this be the same Hegesippus with the poet of the New Comedy who flourished at Athens about 300 B.C., and the reference be to him as a comedian rather than an epigrammatist.

PERSES, called "the Theban" in the heading of one epigram, "the Macedonian" in that of another (no difference of style can be traced between them), a poet of the same type as Addaeus, with equal simplicity and good taste, but inferior power. The /Garland/ of Meleager, l. 26, speaks of "the scented reed of Perses." There are nine epigrams of his in the Palatine Anthology, including some beautiful epitaphs.

PHAEDIMUS of Bisanthe in Macedonia, author of an epic called the /Heracleia/ according to Athenaeus. "The yellow iris of Phaedimus" is mentioned in the /Garland/ of Meleager, l. 51. Two of the four epigrams under his name, a beautiful dedication, and a very noble epitaph, are in this selection; the other two, which are in the appendix of epigrams in mixed metres at the end of the Palatine Anthology (Section xiii.) are very inferior and seem to be by another hand.

(2) Under this head is a group of three distinguished poets and critics:

PHILETAS of Cos, a contemporary of Alexander, and tutor to the children of Ptolemy I. He was chiefly distinguished as an elegiac poet. Theocritus (vii. 39) names him along with Asclepiades as his master in style, and Propertius repeatedly couples him in the same way with Callimachus. If one may judge from the few fragments extant, chiefly in Stobaeus, his poetry was simpler and more dignified than that of the Alexandrian school, of which he may be called the founder. He was also one of the earliest commentators on Homer, the celebrated Zenodotus being his pupil.

SIMMIAS of Rhodes, who fl. rather before 300 B.C., and was the author of four books of miscellaneous poems including an epic history of Apollo. "The tall wild-pear of Simmias" is in the /Garland/ of Meleager, l. 30. Two of the seven epigrams under his name in the Palatine Anthology are headed "Simmias of Thebes." This would be the disciple of Socrates, best known as one of the interlocutors in the /Phaedo/. But these epigrams are undoubtedly of the Alexandrian type, and quite in the same style as the rest; and the title is probably a mistake. Simmias is also the reputed author of several of the {griphoi} or pattern-poems at the end of the Palatine MS.

ASCLEPIADES, son of Sicelides of Samos, who flourished B.C. 290, one of the most brilliant authors of the period. Theocritus (l.c. supra) couples him with Philetas as a model of excellence in poetry. This passage fixes his date towards the end of the reign of Ptolemy I., to whose wife Berenice and daughter Cleopatra there are references in his epigrams. There are forty-three epigrams of his in the Anthology; nearly all of them amatory, with much wider range and finer feeling that most of the erotic epigrams, and all with the firm clear touch of the best period. There are also one or two fine epitaphs. The reference in the /Garland/ of Meleager, l. 46, to "the wind-flower of the son of Sicelides" is another of Meleager's exquisite criticisms.

(3) LEONIDAS OF TARENTUM is the reputed author of one hundred and eleven epigrams in the Anthology, chiefly dedicatory and sepulchural. In the case of some of these, however, there is confusion between him and his namesake, Leonidas of Alexandria, the author of about forty epigrams in the Anthology who flourished in the reign of Nero. In two epigrams Leonidas speaks of himself as a poor man, and in another, an epitaph written for himself, says that he led a wandering life and died far from his native Tarentum. His date is most nearly fixed by the inscription (/Anth. Pal./ vi. 130, attributed to him on the authority of Planudes) for a dedication by Pyrrhus of Epirus after a victory over Antigonus and his Gaulish mercenaries, probably that recorded under B.C. 274. Tarentum, with the other cities of Magna Graecia, was about this time in the last straits of the struggle against the Italian confederacy; this or private reasons may account for the tone of melancholy in the poetry of Leonidas. He invented a particular style of dedicatory epigram, in which the implements of some trade or profession are enumerated in ingenious circumlocutions; these have been singled out for special praise by Sainte-Beuve, but will hardly be interesting to many readers. The /Garland/ of Meleager, l. 15, mentions "the rich ivy-clusters of Leonidas," and the phrase well describes the diffuseness and slight want of firmness and colour in his otherwise graceful style.

NOSSIS of Locri, in Magna Graecia, is the contemporary of Leonidas; her date being approximately fixed by an epitaph on Rhinthon of Syracuse, who flourished 300 B.C. We know a good many details about her from her eleven epigrams in the Anthology, some of which are only inferior to those of Anyte. The /Garland/ of Meleager, l. 10, speaks of "the scented fair-flowering iris of Nissus, on whose tablets Love himself melted the wax"; and, like Anyte, she is mentioned, with the characteristic epithet "woman-tongued," by Antipater of Thessalonica in his list of poetesses. She herself claims (/Anth. Pal./ vii. 718) to be a rival of Sappho.

THEOCRITUS of Syracuse lived for some time at Alexandria under Ptolemy II., about 280 B.C., and afterwards at Syracuse under Hiero II. From some allusions to the latter in the Idyls, it seems that he lived into the first Punic war, which broke out B.C. 264.

Twenty-nine epigrams are ascribed to him on some authority or other in the Anthology; of these Ahrens allows only nine as genuine.

NICIAS of Miletus, physician, scholar, and poet, was the contemporary and close friend of Theocritus. Idyl xi. is addressed to him, and the scholiast says he wrote an idyl in reply to it; idyl xxii was sent with the gift of an ivory spindle to his wife, Theugenis; and one of Theocritus' epigrams (/Anth. Pal./ vi. 337) was written for him as a dedication. There are eight epigrams of his in the Anthology (/Anth. Pal./ xi. 398 is wrongly attributed to him, and should be referred to Nicarchus), chiefly dedications and inscriptions for rural places in the idyllic manner. "The green mint of Nicias" is mentioned, probably with an allusion to his profession, in the /Garland/ of Meleager, l. 19.

CALLIMACHUS of Alexandria, the most celebrated and the most wide in his influence of Alexandrian scholars and poets, was descended from the noble family of the Battiadae of Cyrene. He studied at Alexandria, and was appointed principal keeper of the Alexandrian library by Ptolemy II., about the year 260 B.C. This position he held till his death, about B.C. 240. He was a prolific author in both prose and verse. Sixty-three epigrams of his are preserved in the Palatine Anthology, and two more by Strabo and Athenaeus; five others in the Anthology are ascribed to him on more or less doubtful authority. He brought to the epigram the utmost finish of which it is capable. Many of his epigrams are spoiled by over-elaboration and affected daintiness of style; but when he writes simply his execution is incomparable. The /Garland/ of Meleager, l. 21, speaks of "the sweet myrtle-berry of Callimachus, ever full of acid honey"; and there is in all his work a pungent flavour which is sometimes bitter and sometimes exquisite.

POSIDIPPUS, the author of twenty-five extant epigrams, of which twenty are in the Anthology, is more than once referred to as "the epigrammatist," and so is probably a different person from the comedian, the last distinguished name of the New Comedy, who began to exhibit after the death of Menander in B.C. 291. He probably lived somewhat later; the /Garland/ of Meleager, l. 45, couples "the wild corn-flowers of Posidippus and Hedylus," and Hedylus was the contemporary of Callimachus. One of his epigrams refers to the Stoic Cleanthes, who became head of the school B.C. 263 and died about B.C. 220, as though already an old master.

With Posidippus may be placed METRODORUS, the author of an epigram in reply to one by Posidippus (xii. 39, 40 in this selection). Whether this be contemporary or not, it can hardly be by the same Metrodorus as the forty arithmetical problems which are given in an appendix to the Palatine Anthology (Section xiv.), or the epigram on a Byzantine lawyer, /Anth. Pal./ ix. 712. These may be all by a geometrician of the name who is mentioned as having lived in the age of Constantine.

MOERO or MYRO of Byzantium, daughter of the tragedian Homerus, flourished towards the end of the reign of Ptolemy II., about 250 B.C. She wrote epic and lyric poetry as well as epigrams; a fragment of her epic called /Mnemosyne/ is preserved in Athenaeus. Antipater of Thessalonica mentions her in his list of famous poetesses. Of the "many martagon-lilies of Moero" in the Anthology of Meleager (/Garland/, l. 5) only two are extant, both dedications.

NICAENETUS of Samos flourished about the same time. There are four epigrams of his in the Anthology, and another is quoted by Athenaeus, who, in connexion with a Samian custom, adduces him as "a poet of the country." He also wrote epic poems. The /Garland/ of Meleager, l. 29, speaks of "the myrrh-twigs of Nicaenetus."

EUPHORION of Chalcis in Euboea, grammarian and poet, was born B.C. 274, and in later life was chief librarian at the court of Antiochus the Great, who reigned B.C. 224-187. His most famous work was his five books of {KHiliades}, translated into Latin by

C. Cornelius Gallus (Virgil, /Ecl./ vi. 64-73) and of immense reputation. His influence on Latin poetry provoked the well-known sneer of Cicero (/Tusc./ iii. 19) at the /cantores Euphorionis/; cf. also Cic. /de Div./ ii. 64, and Suetonius, /Tiberius/, c. 70. Only two epigrams of his are extant in the Palatine Anthology. The /Garland/ of Meleager, l. 23, speaks of "the rose-campion of Euphorion."

RHIANUS of Crete flourished about 200 B.C., and was chiefly celebrated as an epic poet. Besides mythological epics, he wrote metrical histories of Thessaly, Elis, Achaea, and Messene; Pausinias quotes verses from the last of these, /Messen./ i. 6, xvii. 11. Seutonius, /Tiberius/, c. 70, mentions him along with Euphorion as having been greatly admired by Tiberius. There are nine epigrams by him, erotic and dedicatory, in the Palatine Anthology, and another is quoted by Athenaeus. The /Garland/ of Meleager, l. 11, couples him with the marjoram-blossom.

THEODORIDES of Syracuse, the author of nineteen epigrams in the Anthology, flourished towards the close of the third century B.C., one of his epigrams being an epitaph on Euphorion. He also wrote lyric poetry; Athenaeus mentions a dithyrambic poem of his called the /Centaurs/, and a /Hymn to Love/. The /Garland/ of Meleager, l. 53, speaks of "the fresh-blooming festal wild-thyme of Theodorides."

A little earlier in date is MNASALCAS of Plataeae, near Sicyon, on whom Theodorides wrote an epitaph (/Anth. Pal./ xiii. 21), which speaks of him as imitating Simonides, and criticises his style as turgid. This criticism is not born out by his eighteen extant epigrams in the Palatine Anthology, which are in the best manner, with something of the simplicity of his great model, and even a slight austerity of style which takes us back to Greece Proper. The /Garland/ of Meleager seizes this quality when it speaks, l. 16, of "the tresses of the sharp pine of Mnasalcas."

MOSCHUS of Syracuse, the last of the pastoral poets, flourished towards the end of the third century B.C., perhaps as late as B.C. 200 if he was the friend of the grammarian Aristarchus. A single epigram of his is extant in Planudes. The Palatine Anthology includes his idyll of /Love the Runaway/ (ix. 440), and the lovely hexameter fragment by Cyrus (ix. 136), which has without authority been attributed to him and is generally included among his poems.

To this period may belong DIOTIMUS, whose name is at the head of eleven epigrams in the Anthology. One of these is headed "Diotimus of Athens," one "Diotimus of Miletus," the rest have the name simply. Nothing is known from other sources of any one of them. An Athenion Diotimus was one of the orators surrendered to Antipater B.C. 322, and some of the epigrams might be of that period. A grammarian Diotimus of Adramyttium is mentioned in an epigram by Aratus of Soli (who fl. 270 B.C.); perhaps he was the poet of the /Garland/ of Meleager, who speaks, l. 27, of "the quince from the boughs of Diotimus."

AUTOMEDON of Aetolia is the author of an epigram in the Palatine Anthology, of which the first two lines are in Planudes under the name of Theocritus; it is in his manner, and in the best style of this period. There are twelve other epigrams by an Automedon of the Roman period in the Anthology, one of them headed "Automedon of Cyzicus." From internal evidence these belong to the reign of Nerva or Trajan. An Automedon was probably one of the poets in the Anthology of Philippus (/Garland/, l. 11), but is most probably different from both of these, as that collection cannot well be put later than the reign of Nero, and purports to include only poets subsequent to Meleager: cf. supra p. 17.

THEAETETUS is only known as the author of three epigrams in the Palatine Anthology (a fourth usually ascribed to him, /Anth. Pal./ vii. 444, should be referred to Theaetetus Scholasticus, a Byzantine epigrammatist of the period of Justinian) and two more in Diogenes Laërtius. One of these last is an epitaph on the philosopher Crantor, who flourished about 300 B.C., but is not necessarily contemporaneous.

(4) ALCAEUS of Messene, who flourished 200 B.C., represents the literary and political energy still surviving in Greece under the Achaean League. Many of his epigrams touch on the history of the period; several are directed against Philip III. of Macedonia. The earliest to which a date can be fixed is on the destruction of Macynus in Aetolia by Philip, B.C. 218 or 219 (Polyb. iv. 65), and the latest on the dead at the battle of Cynoscephalae, B.C. 197, written before their bones were collected and buried by order of Antiochus B.C. 191. This epigram is mentioned by Plutarch as having given offence to the Roman general Flaminius, on account of its giving the Aetolians an equal share with the Romans in the honour of the victory. Another is on the freedom of Flaminius, proclaimed at the Isthmia B.C. 196. An Alcaeus was one of the Epicurean philosophers expelled from Rome by decree of the Senate in B.C. 173, and may be the same. Others of his epigrams are on literary subjects. All are written in a hard style. There are twenty-two in all in the Anthology. Some of them are headed "Alcaeus of Mitylene," but there is no doubt as to the authorship; the confusion of this Alcaeus with the lyric poet of Mitylene could only be made by one very ignorant of Greek literature.

Of the same period is DAMAGETUS, the author of twelve epigrams in the Anthology, and included as "a dark violet" in the /Garland/ of
Meleager, l. 21. They are chiefly epitaphs, and are in the best style
of the period.

DIONYSIUS of Cyzicus must have flourished soon after 200 B.C. from his epitaph on Eratosthenes, who died B.C. 196. Eight other epigrams in the Palatine Anthology, and four more in Planudes, are attributed to a Dionysius. One is headed "Dionysius of Andros," one "Dionysius of Rhodes" (it is an epitaph on a Rhodian), one "Dionysius the Sophist," the others "Dionysius" simply. There were certainly several authors of the name, which was one of the commonest in Greece; but no distinction in style can be traced among these epigrams, and there is little against the theory that most if not all are by the same author, Dionysius of Cyzicus.

DIOSCORIDES, the author of forty-one epigrams in the Palatine Anthology, lived at Alexandria early in the second century B.C. An epitaph of his on the comedian Machon is quoted by Athenaeus, who says that Machon was master to Aristophanes of Byzantium, who flourished 200 B.C. His style shows imitation of Callimachus; the /Garland/ of Meleager, l. 23, speaks of him as "the cyclamen of Muses."

ARTEMIDORUS, a grammarian, pupil of Aristophanes of Byzantium and contemporary of Aristarchus, flourished about 180 B.C., and is the author of two epigrams in the Palatine Anthology, both mottoes, the one for a Theocritus, the other for a collection of the bucolic poets. The former is attributed in the Palatine MS. to Theocritus himself, but is assigned to Artemidorus on the authority of a MS. of Theocritus.

PAMPHILUS, also a grammarian, and pupil to Aristarchus, was one of the poets in the /Garland/ of Meleager (l. 17, "the spreading plane of the song of Pamphilus"). Only two epigrams of his are extant in the Anthology.

ANTIPATER OF SIDON is one of the most interesting figures of the close of this century, when Greek education began to permeate the Roman upper classes. Little is known about his life; part of it was spent at Rome in the society of the most cultured of the nobility. Cicero, /Or./ iii. 194, makes Crassus and Catulus speak of him as familiarly known to them, but then dead; the scene of the dialogue is laid in B.C. 91. Cicero and Pliny also mention the curious fact that he had an attack of fever on his birthday every winter. "The young Phoenician cypress of Antipater," in the /Garland/ of Meleager, l. 42, refers to him as one of the more modern poets in that collection.

There is much confusion in the Anthology between him and his equally prolific namesake of the next century, Antipater of Thessalonica. The matter would take long to disentangle completely. In brief the facts are these. In the Palatine Anthology there are one hundred and seventy-eight epigrams, of which forty-six are ascribed to Antipater of Sidon and thirty-six to Antipater of Thessalonica, the remaining ninety-six being headed "Antipater" merely. Twenty-eight other epigrams are given as by one or other in Planudes and Diogenes Laërtius. Jacobs assigns ninety epigrams in all to the Sidonian poet. Most of them are epideictic; a good many are on works of art and literature; there are some very beautiful epitaphs. There is in his work a tendency towards diffuseness which goes with his talent in improvisation mentioned by Cicero.

To this period seem to belong the following poets, of whom little or nothing is known: ARISTODICUS of Rhodes, author of two epigrams in the Palatine Anthology: ARISTON, author of three or four epigrams in the style of Leonidas of Tarentum: HERMOCREON, author of one dedication in the Palatine Anthology and another in Planudes: and TYMNES, author of seven epigrams in the Anthology, and included in the /Garland/ of Meleager, l. 19, with "the fair-foliaged white poplar" for his cognisance.

(5) MELEAGER son of Eucrates was born at the partially Hellenised town of Gadara in northern Palestine (the Ramoth-Gilead of the Old Testament), and educated at Tyre. His later life was spent in the island of Cos, where he died at an advanced age. The scholiast to the Palatine MS. says he flourished in the reign of the last Seleucus; this was Seleucus VI. Epiphanes, who reigned B.C. 95-93. The date of his celebrated Anthology cannot be much later, as it did not include the poems of his fellow-townsman Philodemus, who flourished about B.C. 60 or a little earlier. Like his contemporary Menippus, also a Gadarene, he wrote what were known as {spoudogeloia}, miscellaneous prose essays putting philosophy in popular form with humorous illustrations. These are completely lost, but we have fragments of the /Saturae Menippeae/ of Varro written in imitation of them, and they seem to have had a reputation like that of Addison and the English essayists of the eighteenth century. Meleager's fame however is securely founded on the one hundred and thirty-four epigrams of his own which he included in his Anthology. Some further account of the erotic epigrams, which are about four-fifths of the whole number, is given above. For all of these the MSS. of the Anthology are the sole source.

DIODORUS of Sardis, commonly called ZONAS, is spoken of by Strabo, who was a friend of his kinsman Diodorus the younger, as having flourished at the time of the invasion of Asia by Mithridates B.C. 88. He was a distinguished orator. Both of these poets were included in the Anthology of Philippus, and in the case of some of the epigrams it is not quite certain to which of the two they should be referred. Eight are usually ascribed to Zonas: they are chiefly dedicatory and pastoral, with great beauty of style and feeling for nature.

ERYCIUS of Cyzicus flourished about the middle of the first century B.C. One of his epigrams is on an Athenian woman who had in early life been captured at the sack of Athens by Sulla B.C. 80; another is against a grammarian Parthenius of Phocaea, possibly the same who was the master of Virgil. Of the fourteen epigrams in the Anthology under the name of Erycius one is headed "Erycius the Macedonian" and may be by a different author.

PHILODEMUS of Gadara was a distinguished Epicurean philosopher who lived at Rome in the best society of the Ciceronian age. He was an intimate friend of Piso, the Consul of B.C. 58, to whom two of his epigrams are addressed. Cicero, /in Pis./ § 68 foll., where he attacks Piso for consorting with /Graeculi/, almost goes out of his way to compliment Philodemus on his poetical genius and the unusual literary culture which he combined with the profession of philosophy: and again in the /de Finibus/ speaks of him as "a most worthy and learned man." He is also referred to by Horace, 1 /Sat./ ii. 121. Thirty-two of his epigrams, chiefly amatory, are in the Anthology, and five more are ascribed to him on doubtful authenticity.

IV. Roman period; from the establishment of the Empire to the decay of art and letters after the death of Marcus Aurelius, B.C. 30-A.D. 180.

This period falls into three subdivisions; (1) poets of the Augustan age; (2) those of what may roughly be called the Neronian age, about the middle of the first century; and (3) those of the brief and partial renascence of art and letters under Hadrian, which, before the accession of Commodus, had again sunk away, leaving a period of some centuries almost wholly without either, but for the beginnings of Christian art and the writings of the earlier Fathers of the Church. Even from the outset of this period the epigram begins to fall off. There is a tendency to choose trifling subjects, and treat them either sentimentally or cynically. The heaviness of Roman workmanship affects all but a few of the best epigrams, and there is a loss of simplicity and clearness of outline. Many of the poets of this period, if not most, lived as dependants in wealthy Roman families and wrote to order: and we see in their work the bad results of an excessive taste for rhetoric and the practice of fluent but empty improvisation.

(1) ANTIPATER OF THESSALONICA, the author of upwards of a hundred epigrams in the Anthology, is the most copious and perhaps the most interesting of the Augustan epigrammatists. There are many allusions in his work to contemporary history. He lived under the patronage of L. Calpurnius Piso, consul in B.C. 15, and afterwards proconsul of Macedonia for several years, and was appointed by him governor of Thessalonica. One of his epigrams celebrates the foundation of Nicopolis by Octavianus, after the battle of Actium; another anticipates his victory over the Parthians in the expedition of B.C. 20; another is addressed to Caius Caesar, who died in A.D. 4. None can be ascribed certainly to a later date than this.

ANTIPHANES the Macedonian is the author of ten epigrams in the Palatine Anthology; one of these, however, is headed "Antiphanes of Megalopolis" and may be by a different author. There is no precise indication of time in his poems.

BIANOR of Bithynia is the author of twenty-two epigrams in the Anthology. One of them is on the destruction of Sardis by an earthquake in A.D. 17. He is fond of sentimental treatment, which sometimes touches pathos but often becomes trifling.

CRINAGORAS of Mitylene lived at Rome as a sort of court poet during the latter part of the reign of Augustus. He is mentioned by Strabo as a contemporary of some distinction. In one of his epigrams he blames himself for hanging on to wealthy patrons; several others are complimentary verses sent with small presents to the children of his aristocratic friends: one is addressed to young Marcellus with a copy of the poems of Callimachus. Others are on the return of Marcellus from the Cantabrian war, B.C. 25; on the victories of Tiberius in Armenia and Germany; and on Antonia, daughter of the triumvir and wife of Drusus. Another, written in the spirit of that age of tourists, speaks of undertaking a voyage from Asia to Italy, visiting the Cyclades and Corcyra on the way. Fifty-one epigrams are attributed to him in the Anthology; one of these, however (/Anth. Pal./ ix. 235), is on the marriage of Berenice of Cyrene to Ptolemy III. Euergetes, and must be referred to Callimachus or one of his contemporaries.

DIODORUS, son of Diopeithes of Sardis, also called Diodorus the Younger, in distinction to Diodorus Zonas, is mentioned as a friend of his own by Strabo, and was a historian and melic poet besides being an epigrammatist. Seventeen of the epigrams in the Anthology under the name of Diodorus are usually ascribed to him, and include a few fine epitaphs.

EVENUS of Ascalon is probably the author of eight epigrams in the Anthology; but some of these may belong to other epigrammatists of the same name, Evenus of Athens, Evenus of Sicily, and Evenus Grammaticus, unless the last two of these are the same person. Evenus of Athens has been doubtfully identified with Evenus of Paros, and elegiac poet of some note contemporary with Socrates, mentioned in the /Phaedo/ and quoted by Aristotle: and it is just possible that some of the best of the epigrams, most of which are on works of art, may be his.

PARMENIO the Macedonian is the author of sixteen epigrams in the Anthology, most of which have little quality beyond commonplace rhetoric.

These seven poets were included in the Anthology of Philippus; of the same period, but not mentioned by name in the proem to that collection, are the following:—

APOLLONIDES, author of thirty-one epigrams in the Anthology, perhaps the same with an Apollonides of Nicaea mentioned by Diogenes Laërtius as having lived in the reign of Tiberius. One of his epigrams refers to the retirement of Tiberius at Rhodes from B.C. 6 to A.D. 2, and another mentions D. Laelius Balbus, who was consul in B.C. 6, as travelling in Greece.

GAETULICUS, the author of eight epigrams in the Palatine Anthology (vi. 154 and vii. 245 are wrongly ascribed to him), is usually identified with Gn. Lentulus Gaetulicus, legate of Upper Germany, executed on suspicion of conspiracy by Caligula, A.D. 39, and mentioned as a writer of amatory poetry by Martial and Pliny. But the identification is very doubtful, and perhaps he rather belongs to the second century A.D. No precise date is indicated in any of the epigrams.

POMPEIUS, author of two or three epigrams in the Palatine Anthology, also called Pompeius the Younger, is generally identified with M. Pompeius Theophanes, son of Theophanes of Mitylene, the friend of Pompey the Great, and himself a friend of Tiberius, according to Strabo.

To the same period probably belong QUINTUS MAECIUS or MACCIUS, author of twelve epigrams in the Anthology, and MARCUS ARGENTARIUS, perhaps the same with a rhetorician Argentarius mentioned by the elder Seneca, author of thirty-seven epigrams, chiefly amatory and convivial, some of which have much grace and fancy. Others place him in the age of Hadrian.

(2) PHILIPPUS of Thessalonica was the compiler of an Anthology of epigrammatists subsequent to Meleager and is himself the author of seventy-four extant epigrams in the Anthology besides six more dubiously ascribed to him. He wrote epigrams of all sorts, mainly imitated from older writers and showing but little original power or imagination. The latest certain historical allusion in his own work is one to Agrippa's mole at Puteoli, but Antiphilus, who was included in his collection, certainly wrote in the reign of Nero, and probably Philippus was of about the same date. Most of his epigrams being merely rhetorical exercises on stock themes give no clue to his precise period.

ANTIPHILUS of Byzantium, whose date is fixed by his epigram on the restoration of liberty to Rhodes by the emperor Nero, A.D. 53 (Tac. /Ann./ xii. 58), is the author of forty-nine epigrams in the Anthology, besides three doubtful. Among them are some graceful dedications, pastoral epigrams, and sea-pieces. The pretty epitaph on Agricola (/Anth. Pal./ ix. 549) gives no clue to his date, as it certainly is not on the father-in-law of Tacitus, and no other person of the name appears to be mentioned in history.

JULIUS POLYAENUS is the author of a group of three epigrams (/Anth. Pal./ ix. 7-9), which have a high seriousness rare in the work of this period. He has been probably identified with a C. Julius Polyaenus who is known from coins to have been a duumvir of Corinth (Colonia Julia) under Nero. He was a native of Corcyra, to which he retired after a life of much toil and travel, apparently as a merchant. The epigram by Polyaenus of Sardis (/Anth. Pal./ ix. 1), usually referred to the same author, is in a completely different manner.

LUCILIUS, the author of one hundred and twenty-three epigrams in the Palatine Anthology (twenty others are of doubtful authorship) was, as we learn from himself, a grammarian at Rome and a pensioner of Nero. He published two volumes of epigrams, somewhat like those of Martial, in a satiric and hyperbolical style.[1]

NICARCHUS is the author of forty-two epigrams of the same kind as those of Lucilius. Another given under his name (/Anth. Pal./ vii. 159) is of the early Alexandrian period, perhaps by Nicias of Miletus, as the converse mistake is made in the Palatine MS. with regard to xi. 398. A large proportion of his epigrams are directed against doctors. There is nothing to fix the precise part of the century in which he lived.

To some part of this century also belong SECUNDUS of Tarentum and MYRINUS, each the other of four epigrams in the Anthology. Nothing further is known of either.

(3) STRATO of Sardis, the collector of the Anthology called {Mousa Paidike Stratonos} and extant, apparently in an imperfect and mutilated form, as the twelfth section or first appendix of the Palatine Anthology may be placed with tolerable certainty in the reign of Hadrian. Besides his ninety-four epigrams preserved in his own Anthology, five others are attributed to him in the Palatine Anthology, and one more in Planudes.

AMMIANUS is the author of twenty-nine epigrams in the Anthology, all irrisory. One of them (/Anth. Pal./ xi. 226) is imitated from Martial, ix. 30. Another sneers at the neo-Atticism which had become the fashion in Greek prose writing. His date is fixed by an attack on Antonius Polemo, a well-known sophist of the age of Hadrian.

THYMOCLES is only known from his single epigram in Strato's Anthology. It is in the manner of Callimachus and may perhaps be of the Alexandrian period.

To this or an earlier date belongs ARCHIAS of Mitylene, the author of a number of miscellaneous epigrams, chiefly imitated from older writers such as Antipater and Leonidas. Forty-one epigrams in all are attributed on some authority to one Archias or another; most have the name simply; some are headed "Archias the Grammarian," "Archias the Younger," "Archias the Macedonian," "Archias of Byzantium." All are sufficiently like each other in style to be by the same hand. Some have been attributed to Cicero's client, Archias of Antioch, but they seem to be of a later period.

To the age of Hadrian also belongs the epigram inscribed on the Memnon statue at Thebes with the name of its author, ASCLEPIODOTUS, ix. 19 in this selection.

CLAUDIUS PTOLEMAEUS of Alexandria, mathematician, astronomer, and geographer, who gave his name to the Ptolemaïc system of the heavens, flourished in the latter half of the second century. His chief works are the {Megale Suntaxis tes Astronomias} in thirteen books, known to the Middle Ages in its Arabian translation under the title of the /Almagest/, and the {Geographike Uphegesis} in eight books. He also wrote on astrology, chronology, and music. A single epigram of his on his favourite science is preserved in the Anthology. Another commonplace couplet under the name of Ptolemaeus is probably by some different author.

LUCIAN of Samosata in Commagene, perhaps the most important figure in the literature of this period, was born about A.D. 120. He practised as an advocate at Antioch, and travelled very extensively throughout the empire. He was appointed procurator of a district of Egypt by the emperor Commodus (reigned A.D. 180-192) and probably died about A.D. 200. Besides his voluminous prose works he is the author of forty epigrams in the Anthology, and fourteen more are ascribed to him on doubtful or insufficient authority.

To some part of this period appear to belong ALPHEUS of Mitylene, author of twelve epigrams, some school-exercises, others on ancient towns, Mycenae, Argos, Tegea, and Troy, which he appears to have visited as a tourist; CARPYLLIDES or CARPHYLLIDES, author of one fine epitaph and another dull epigram in the moralising vein of this age: GLAUCUS of Nicopolis, author of six epigrams (one is headed "Glaucus of Athens," but is in the same late imperial style; and in this period the citizenship of Athens was sold for a trifle by the authorities to any one who cared for it: cf. the epigram of Automedon (/Anth. Pal./ xi. 319)); and SATYRUS (whose name is also given as Satyrius, Thyïlus, Thyïllus, and Satyrus Thyïllus), author of nine epigrams, chiefly dedications and pastoral pieces, some of them of great delicacy and beauty.

[1] The spelling /Lucillius/ is a mere barbarism, the /l/ being doubled to indicate the long vowel: so we find {Statullios}, etc.

V. Byzantine period; from the transference of the seat of empire to Constantinople, A.D. 330, to the formation of the Palatine Anthology in the reign of Constantine Porphyrogenitus, about the middle of the tenth century.

For the first two centuries of this period hardly any names have to be chronicled. Literature had almost ceased to exist except among lexicographers and grammarians; and though epigrams, Christian and pagan, continued to be written, they are for the most part of no literary account whatever. One name only of importance meets us before the reign of Justinian.

PALLADAS of Alexandria is the author of one hundred and fifty-one epigrams (besides twenty-three more doubtful) in the Anthology. His somber and melancholy figure is one of the last of the purely pagan world in its losing battle against Christianity. One of the epigrams attributed to him on the authority of Planudes is an eulogy on the celebrated Hypatia, daughter of Theon of Alexandria, whose tragic death took place A.D. 415 in the reign of Theodosius the Second. Another was, according to a scholium in the Palatine MS., written in the reign of Valentinian and Valens, joint-emperors, 364-375 A.D. The epigram on the destruction of Berytus, ix. 27 in this selection, gives no certain argument of date. Palladas was a grammarian by profession. An anonymous epigram (/Anth. Pal./ ix. 380) speaks of him as of high poetical reputation; and, indeed, in those dark ages the harsh and bitter force that underlies his crude thought and half-barbarous language is enough to give him a place of note. Casaubon dismisses him in two contemptuous words as "versificator insulsissimus"; this is true of a great part of his work, and would perhaps be true of it all but for the /saeva indignatio/ which kindles the verse, not into the flame of poetry, but as it were to a dull red heat. There is little direct allusion in his epigrams to the struggle against the new religion. One epigram speaks obscurely of the destruction of the idols of Alexandria by the Christian populace in the archiepiscopate of Theophilus, A.D. 389; another in even more enigmatic language (/Anth. Pal./ x. 90) seems to be a bitter attack on the doctrine of the Resurrection; and a scornful couplet against the swarms of Egyptian monks might have been written by a Reformer of the sixteenth century. For the most part his sympathy with the losing side is only betrayed in his despondency over all things. But it is in his criticism of life that the power of Palladas lies; with a remorselessness like that of Swift he tears the coverings from human frailty and holds it up in its meanness and misery. The lines on the Descent of Man (/Anth. Pal./ x. 45), which unfortunately cannot be included in this selection, fall as heavily on the Neo-Platonic martyr as on the Christian persecutor, and remain even now among the most mordant and crushing sarcasms ever passed upon mankind.

To the same period in thought—beyond this there is no clue to their date—belong AESOPUS and GLYCON, each the author of a single epigram in the Palatine Anthology. They belong to the age of the Byzantine metaphrasts, when infinite pains were taken to rewrite well-known poems or passages in different metres, by turning Homer into elegiacs or iambics, and recasting pieces of Euripides or Menander as epigrams.

A century later comes the Byzantine lawyer, MARIANUS, mentioned by Suidas as having flourished in the reign of Anastasius I., A.D. 491- 518. He turned Theocritus and Apollonius Rhodius into iambics. There are six epigrams of his in the Anthology, all descriptive, on places in the neighbourhood of Constantinople.

At the court of Justinian, A.D. 527-565, Greek poetry made its last serious effort; and together with the imposing victories of Belisarius and the final codification of Roman law carried out by the genius of Tribonian, his reign is signalised by a group of poets who still after three hundred years of barbarism handled the old language with remarkable grace and skill, and who, though much of their work is but clever imitation of the antique, and though the verbosity and vague conventionalism of all Byzantine writing keeps them out of the first rank of epigrammatists, are nevertheless not unworthy successors of the Alexandrians, and represent a culture which died hard. Eight considerable names come under this period, five of them officials of high place in the civil service or the imperial household, two more, and probably the third also, practising lawyers at Constantinople.

AGATHIAS son of Mamnonius, poet and historian, was born at Myrina in Mysia about the year 536 A.D. He received his early education in Alexandria, and at eighteen went to Constantinople to study law. Soon afterwards he published a volume of poems called /Daphniaca/ in nine books. The preface to it (/Anth. Pal./ vi. 80) is still extant, and many of his epigrams were no doubt included in it. His History, which breaks off abruptly in the fifth book, covers the years 553-558 A.D.; in the preface to it he speaks of his own early works, including his Anthology of recent and contemporary epigrams. One of the most pleasant of his poems is an epistle to his friend Paulus Silentiarius, written from a country house on the opposite coast of the Bosporus, where he had retired to pursue his legal studies away from the temptations of the city. He tells us himself that law was distasteful to him, and that his time was chiefly spent in the study of ancient poetry and history. In later life he seems to have returned to Myrina, where he carried out improvements in the town and was regarded as the most distinguished of the citizens (/Anth. Pal./ ix. 662). He is believed to have died about 582 A.D. Agathias is the author of ninety- seven epigrams in the Anthology, in a facile and diffuse style; often they are exorbitantly long, some running to twenty-four and even twenty-eight lines.

ARABIUS, author of seven epigrams in the Anthology, is called {skholastikos} or lawyer. Four of his epigrams are on works of art, one is a description of an imperial villa on the coast near Constantinople, and the other two are in praise of Longinus, prefect of Constantinople under Justinian. One of the last is referred to in an epigram by Macedonius (/Anth. Pal./ x. 380).

JOANNES BARBUCALLUS, also called JOANNES GRAMMATICUS, is the author of eleven epigrams in the Anthology. Three of them are on the destruction of Berytus by earthquake in A.D. 551: from these it may be conjectured that he had studied at the great school of civil law there. As to his name a scholiast in MS. Pal. says, {ethnikon estin enoma. Barboukale gar polis en tois [entos] Iberos tou potamou}. But this seems to be an incorrect reminiscence of the name {Arboukale}, a town in Hispania Tarraconensis, in the lexicon of Stephanus Byzantinus.

JULIANUS, commonly called JULIANUS AEGYPTIUS, is the author of seventy epigrams (and two more doubtful) in the Anthology. His full title is {apo uparkhon Aiguptou}, or ex-prefect of a division of Egypt, the same office which Lucian had held under Commodus. His date is fixed by two epitaphs on Hypatius, brother of the Emperor Anastasius, who was put to death by Justinian in A.D. 532.

LEONTIUS, called Scholasticus, author of twenty-four epigrams in the Anthology, is generally identified with a Leontius Referendarius, mentioned by Procopius under this reign. The Referendarii were a board of high officials, who, according to the commentator on the /Notitia imperii/, transmitted petitions and cases referred from the lower courts to the Emperor, and issued his decisions upon them. Under Justinian they were eighteen in number, and were /spectabiles/, their president being a /comes/. One of the epigrams of Leontius is on Gabriel, prefect of Constantinople under Justinian; another is on the famous charioteer Porphyrius. Most of them are on works of art.

MACEDONIUS of Thessalonica, mentioned by Suidas s.v. {Agathias} as consul in the reign of Justinian, is the author of forty-four epigrams in the Anthology, the best of which are some delicate and fanciful amatory pieces.

PAULUS, always spoken of with his official title of SILENTIARIUS, author of seventy-nine epigrams (and six others doubtful) in the Anthology, is the most distinguished poet of this period. Our knowledge of him is chiefly derived from Agathias, /Hist./ v. 9, who says he was of high birth and great wealth, and head of the thirty Silentiarii, or Gentlemen of the Bedchamber, who were among the highest functionaries of the Byzantine court. Two of his epigrams are replies to two others by Agathias (/Anth. Pal./ v. 292, 293; 299, 300); another is on the death of Damocharis of Cos, Agathias' favourite pupil, lamenting with almost literal truth that the harp of the Muses would thenceforth be silent. Besides the epigrams, we possess a long description of the church of Saint Sophia by him, partly in iambics and partly in hexameters, and a poem in dimeter iambics on the hot springs of Pythia. The "grace and genius beyond his age," which Jacobs justly attributes to him, reach their highest point in his amatory epigrams, forty in number, some of which are not inferior to those of Meleager.

RUFINUS, author of thirty-nine (and three more doubtful) amatory epigrams in the Palatine Anthology, is no doubt of the same period. In the heading of one of the epigrams he is called Rufinus Domesticus. The exact nature of his public office cannot be determined from this title. A Domestic was at the head of each of the chief departments of the imperial service, and was a high official. But the name was also given to the Emperor's Horse and Foot Guards, and to the bodyguards of the prefects in charge of provinces, cities, or armies.

ERATOSTHENES, called Scholasticus, is the author of five epigrams in the Palatine Anthology. Epigrams by Julianus, Macedonius, and Paulus Silentiarius, are ascribed to him in other MSS., and from this fact, as well as from the evidence of the style, he may be confidently placed under the same date. Nothing further is known of him. Probably to the same period belongs THEOPHANES, author of two epigrams in the miscellaneous appendix (xv.) to the Palatine Anthology, one of them in answer to an epigram by Constantinus Siculus, as to whose date there is the same uncertainty. Two epitaphs in the Anthology are also ascribed to Theophanes in Planudes.

With this brief latter summer the history of Greek poetry practically ends. The epigrams of Damocharis, the pupil of Agathias, seem already to show the decomposition of the art. The imposing fabric of empire reconstructed by the genius of Justinian and his ministers had no solidity, and was crumbling away even before the death of its founder: while the great plague, beginning in the fifteenth year of Justinian, continued for no less than fifty-two years to ravage every province of the empire and depopulate whole cities and provinces. In such a period as this the fragile and exotic poetry of the Byzantine Renaissance could not sustain itself. Political and theological epigrams continued to be written in profusion; but the collections may be searched through in vain for a single touch of imagination or beauty. Under Constantine VII. (reigned A.D. 911-959) comes the last shadowy name in the Anthology.

COMETAS, called Chartularius or Keeper of the Records, is the author of six epigrams in the Palatine Anthology, besides a poem in hexameters on the Raising of Lazarus. From some marginal notes in the MS. it appears that he was a contemporary of Constantinus Cephalas. Three of the epigrams are on a revised text of Homer which he edited. None are of any literary value, except one beautiful pastoral couplet, vi. 10 in this selection, which seems to be the very voice of ancient poetry bidding the world a lingering and reluctant farewell.